BIOTERROR
The Essential Threat

GLORIA CASALE

ARCHWAY
PUBLISHING

Archway Publishing books may be ordered through booksellers or by contacting:

Archway Publishing
1663 Liberty Drive
Bloomington, IN 47403
www.archwaypublishing.com
1 (888) 242-5904

Cover image by Eye of Science, Meckes & Ottawa Gbr

ISBN: 978-1-4808-2878-0 (sc)
ISBN: 978-1-4808-2879-7 (e)

Library of Congress Control Number: 2016903897

Print information available on the last page.

Archway Publishing rev. date: 4/13/2016

With a swift twist, Anne Damiano broke the seal on her bottle of water, set the plastic container on the speaker's podium, and glanced from face to face. She wore a well-cut business suit, with a simple gold lapel pin inlaid with diamonds, minimal makeup, and a few distinguished silver strands in her curly dark hair completed her professional appearance.

"Good afternoon, I'm Dr. Anne Damiano. Most of you know me. Many of you have worked with me. I've been active in bioterrorism preparation for the past fourteen years. Currently, I'm a member of the National Vaccine Advisory Committee as well as a member of the Secretary of Health's Vaccine Advisory Committee."

"Good afternoon," several of the attendees responded.

"For the past two days, we've concentrated on smallpox." A quick glance around the room let her know she had their full attention. "Our tabletop exercises gave us the opportunity to discuss how to prepare and carry out the necessary public health actions if an intentional introduction of smallpox should occur in the United States.

"These exercises have given us quite a bit to think about. But, we haven't discussed the populations who will choose not to seek treatment."

She removed the cap from the water bottle and took a sip before replacing it on the podium.

"The uninsured will wait until their symptoms are full-blown before they go to the hospital. Emergency departments will be filled with anxious and angry people. The homeless may never seek treatment."

She stood a little straighter and paused for effect. "Many will die before they're found."

Anne surveyed her audience. She watched several people nod in agreement. Some looked at neighbors to judge their reactions to Anne's words.

"Terrorists will use our gullibility to attack us. They might introduce pathogens to groups of schoolchildren in various cities on a specific date. Seven to ten days later the students would become infectious, but it would take much longer for health officials to comprehend the scope of the disease distribution. Once the disease is definitively diagnosed, widespread panic will ensue. The chaos will increase exponentially with every new report.

Terrorists could infect travelers, who would then carry the infection across the country before it could be diagnosed."

"Dr. Damiano," the meeting's moderator, Dr. Jeffery Delaney, interrupted, "be realistic. Stick to the program."

"I am being realistic, Dr. Delaney. You're being shortsighted. As I remember, you declared Ebola would never be transported to the United States." She noticed Delaney's face turn red. He put his head down and rummaged through his notes.

Anne continued, "Let me suggest another scenario. A terrorist could infect an auditorium full of public health physicians gathering for a conference." She looked across the room, again. This time she nodded at several acquaintances and smiled at several friends. I would guess there are about two hundred public health officials from Europe, Australia, Asia, and the Americas here today. Let's suppose a terrorist was able to introduce weaponized smallpox into the ventilation system of this room. Two weeks from now, about thirty percent of us would experience the initial flu-like symptoms of the infectious stage. Most of us would go to work, travel, and interact with others. We would ignore our low grade fever, aches, fatigue, and joint pain. Health care workers never seem to take off work until they're half dead. It's a bad habit, but it's what we do." She paused as quiet laughter rippled through the room. "We'd spread infection across our cities and countries. When the pox finally appeared on our faces, hands, and forearms, the problem would be obvious. But in the interim, we would have exposed millions of people to a deadly disease."

The audience sat silent, stunned. No whispers. No rustled papers. Some of the attendees glanced at the doors and air vents.

Anne leaned forward, her voice lowered. "By the time the CDC confirmed the diagnosis, there would be nationwide—if not worldwide—panic."

Jeffrey Delaney jumped to his feet and glared at her. "Dr. Damiano, you have a Machiavellian mind."

Anne sighed and shook her head. "No, I don't. I've considered how an attack could happen. Terrorists look for ways to cause mass disruption *as well as* mass destruction."

Delaney remained standing. "We've known for years how to control smallpox."

"Doctor Delaney we can't continue to spout words with no truth behind them. We're not prepared for a major bio attack. We weren't prepared for the measles outbreak, the whooping cough epidemic, and we're not prepared for a smallpox epidemic."

Delaney smirked, sat down, and pulled his microphone closer. "Okay, Dr. Damiano. Let's presume your hypothesis is correct. Please tell us where and when they'll attack."

"I can't tell you when they will attack, and I can't tell you where they would attack. I can, however, share some of the worst possible scenarios." She held up three fingers. "Black Friday at the Mall of America. A New Year's celebration at a famous hotel. Midnight Mass at the Vatican." She heard gasps. "As I said, terrorists take advantage of our gullibility, of our vulnerability."

Anne paused, smoothed her skirt, readjusted the cuffs of her jacket, and took a deep breath. "We are representatives of the public health community. It's our responsibility to prepare for the unthinkable. Americans have a hard time conceiving the fact that unbelievable evil exists in the world."

"We can't forget one beautiful September morning when thousands of people died, buildings were destroyed, airlines shut down, financial markets closed. And, all it took was four commercial airplanes and nineteen determined jihadists."

Anne Damiano tore through the hotel door and stormed across the polished gold and white tile floor toward the elevator. Intent on a hot shower and a few hours of rest, she clutched the shoulder strap of her leather briefcase and blew past the reception desk.

This is getting monotonous, she thought. Thirty years of butting heads with narrow-minded thinkers is getting to me.

Cordovan loafers beneath glacier-sharp creased khakis blocked her path. "Hello, Wiggles."

Her head snapped up. Black Irish good looks and a gotcha grin. "Connor Quinlan, what are you doing here?"

"I heard you were in town for the CDC meeting."

"Meeting? Open warfare would be a better definition."

"Another fight with Jeffrey Delaney?"

"Yes. And I'll continue to push back until he realizes how wrong he is." The stubborn tilt of her chin warned against any argument.

"His animosity toward you is so profound, he may never change his opinion."

"He wouldn't reconsider his position, even after the anthrax attack in 2001." Contempt pierced her words. "He's insisted on the same damn scenarios year after year after year. One terrorist brings smallpox into a city. Two terrorists bring smallpox into the same hospital. Two terrorists, one city, and two hospitals in . . ." She made a sweeping gesture with her right arm. Her briefcase missed Connor by inches. "Damn it, Connor, they *will* attack again. They *will* use our gullibility to infect massive numbers of people. They *will* cause chaos. And, they *will* kill."

He dodged a second gesture, grabbed her hands, and gently pulled her toward him.

"Whoa, Anne. Your Italian is showing."

"I know, I know." Her heart skittered in random circles at the long remembered touch of his strong hands.

She met his gaze. "How come you're in DC? I thought Donovan only let you out of Langley to give the President his morning briefing."

"Hey, when my best friend is in town, this poor country lawyer gets to take an evening off."

"Poor country lawyer? Half the world knows you're the President's National Security Advisor. Your years of lawyerin' are long gone."

He pointed his chin toward the lounge. "Buy you a drink? How 'bout a glass of Sambuca?"

"Sambuca would be good. We shouldn't let tradition die." Or vaporize into sticky residue like my dream of our life together. "Why didn't you call?"

"I didn't know if I could get here until the last minute." Connor helped her out of her coat and carried it into the lounge.

She tilted her head and gave him a smile. "The good manners the Benedictine monks ground into you still haven't worn off."

"Always a gentleman." He bowed and made a sweeping gesture with his right arm.

"I'm surprised to see you. Does Donovan know you're in Georgetown this evening?"

"Of course. He even approves." A hint of laughter lightened his mellow baritone voice. "My sources tell me that your Jersey-girl, you-can't-feed-me-that-crap attitude, created quite a sensation today. Sounds like you won a major battle in your fight with Delaney."

She lowered her voice. "Are your spies everywhere? Surely the CIA could spend its resources and time more productively."

Her hands curled into tight fists. "You know how straightforward women from New Jersey are; you've had to put up with them all your life. Your sister, your cousins, your aunts, your mother, your ex-girlfriend. We all speak our minds."

Connor gave a wry smile and a nod. "You're right about that."

"I've listened to so many of Delaney's vacuous speeches. *Way* too many. He's been a carbuncle on the backside of public health for as long as I can remember."

She let Connor guide her through the seating area to the far corner of the room. He gestured to the corner table and pulled out a velvet upholstered chair for her, placed a second chair next to hers, then draped her coat over a chair at an adjoining table. They each had their backs against the wall and a view of the lobby. Long years of training ensured they always had an escape route in sight.

The Sambuca was served en flambé. She waited for the last flicker to subside and swirled the dark coffee beans in the sticky liqueur. "Remember way back, when no one thought either of us would accomplish anything?"

"Of course I do. A lot of the guys in New Jersey would've made book on it."

Anne laughed and nodded. "Why not? They made book on anything and everything else. Even raindrops sliding down the window pane, or ants scurrying toward a crack in the sidewalk."

"As it worked out there's no way that they'll ever figure out half of what we've done, let alone how much we've accomplished."

"It's time to toast our hometowns. Are you ready?" She raised her glass. "To Garwood."

"To Belleville." Connor clicked his glass against hers.

"And long lazy days on the Jersey Shore," they exclaimed in unison.

He leaned across the table. "Lots of nice, warm memories in this hotel."

She straightened. "Those memories faded a long time ago." Her gaze did not go to his eyes but to his lips. "Days gone by, Connor. Too many days gone by."

"I miss you, Wiggles."

She swallowed the bowling-ball sized lump in her throat. She missed him, too, but she wasn't about to admit it. He was decades late.

She sipped the anise flavored liquor. "Do you realize how tacky it is for you to continue calling me Wiggles?"

"I'll always call you Wiggles." He raised his glass. "It's your own fault. You were the one who tried to fool me with that silly blond wig and tight red dress."

"For heaven's sake. I was seventeen. It was a silly bet. You were the one who said you'd I'd never be able to fool you. I did my damnedest to hide my identity from you."

"It was a nice try." He chuckled. "But the wiggle in your walk gave you away."

"Well, thanks to the Company, I've had forty years to learn about disguise and covert operations."

"We both have." His smile was rueful. "By the way, you still have the wiggle in your walk."

Anne wadded up a cocktail napkin and threw it at him. "I guess I shouldn't ask how you knew I'd be here."

"Coincidence?"

"Connor Quinlan, no CIA operative believes in coincidence."

RUSSIA

"All men are tempted. There is no man that lives that can't be broken down, provided it is the right temptation, put in the right spot."—Henry Ward Beecher, Proverbs from Plymouth Pulpit

December 30
Zakhody, Russia

A few more steps and they would be at her mother's house. Sudden tears blurred Iveta's vision, froze her eyelashes, burned her chapped cheeks. Warmth, love, and safety waited inside.

Josef, age three, and Ondrek, age five, were hunched deep in their snowsuits. Baby Maruska slept in a sling under Iveta's thick wool coat. Iveta used her last burst of energy to climb the three ancient steps.

Olga Chazova pulled the heavy door open. A wool shawl covered the older woman's thick hair. "Come in! Come in!"

A blast of frigid wind howled around the corner of the house and pushed Iveta and the children across the threshold. She nudged the boys toward the huge kitchen then closed the door, leaned against it, and breathed in the warm, welcoming aroma of her mother's chicken soup.

"Mama." The word echoed the sweet voice of her childhood, not the anxious tone of the past year. She shrugged out of her heavy coat, hung it on a peg and swiped at her tears with the back of her hand.

The boys struggled to take off their snowsuits. Iveta knelt, pulled off their mittens and helped them unbutton and unzip the heavy clothing.

Olga closed the heavy winter drape that insulated the vestibule from the kitchen. She reached for the sling strapped to Iveta's body and gentled the baby out of the canvas hammock.

"My Maruska." She rocked from foot to foot. "I was worried. I expected you hours ago." Olga patted the infant and received happy gurgles in return. "Now you are here, and you are safe."

Olga's gentle voice, the familiar odor of hearty soup, and the warmth radiating from the blue-tiled stove raised Iveta's spirits.

The furniture was polished to a mirror finish. Embroidered cloths with crocheted edging covered the arm rests. Iveta knew that hand-made lace curtains hung beneath the thick winter drapes.

Olga put Maruska in a cradle close to the stove, covered her with the shawl, and stooped to give Ondrek and Josef crushing hugs.

"Such good boys!" She straightened and walked to the cupboard to gather bowls and cups. "Did you see anyone in Zakhody, on your way from the train station?"

"No, Mama. We got off when the locomotive stopped for water and supplies outside town. We walked across the field. The walk through town takes twice as long."

"No one saw you? Did you get your papers stamped?"

"All the passengers were asleep and the workers were busy with their chores." Iveta laughed. "And, the train officials stayed in their warm coach." She stared at the worn floorboards, and ran the toe of her boot along the edge of a hand-knotted rug. Her shoulders slumped. "I know the officials will be angry when we're ready to go home. But we were so tired. And, it was so cold."

Olga smiled. "So, no one has proof you came here?" Olga stood a little straighter, shoulder's back, her ample breasts prominent. "I'm happy you walked across the field." Her smile broadened. "The authorities can't prove you were here. If you were never here and you do not return to Zagorsk they will not be able to trace your steps."

"What do you mean? Of course we will go back to Zagorsk. Yuri wants us to stay here until spring. But after that, where else would we go?"

"West. We will go west. But, we will not wait for spring. Tomorrow night we will be at your Uncle Grigori's house. Anya will fill our plates with her vegetable stew."

"Grigori and Anya live in Latvia. We have no papers, the guards will not let us cross." Iveta put her hands on her hips and shook her head. "We don't have permission."

"Permission. Papers." Olga spat out the words as if they were poison. "Uncle Grigori's house is five kilometers from here. I visit them often. I don't ask permission." Olga mirrored Iveta's stance. Hands on hips, head thrust forward. "Tomorrow is New Year's Eve. No one will know we left Russia." Olga laughed. "By the time we get to the border the guards will be half-drunk."

"How could we get back?"

"We won't come back. We will continue our journey to the west."

"But, what will Yuri do? He said he would be here for Epiphany."

"Yes. He will be here on the fifth of January and he will cross to Latvia that night—the Eve of Epiphany."

"Mama, what are you saying? I don't understand." She raised her hands in a gesture of helplessness. "Yuri hasn't talked about going west. How long would we be gone? Where are we going?"

Olga nodded toward the children. "We'll talk about it later, once the little ones are fed and settled."

Two hours later, the children were fast asleep under down-filled quilts. Olga pulled out a heavy chair and patted the backrest. "Sit. I will get you some tea and explain. Yuri plans to leave Russia. He wants us to be well away from the motherland before he tries to cross."

"He didn't discuss this with me." Iveta's fingers began to tingle. Her hands shook. "Where would we go? How could he make this decision without me?"

"Yuri felt it was safer. He didn't want anyone in Zagorsk to know. He didn't want you to have to lie to anyone. And, it was safer not to let the boys overhear." Olga removed a few bricks from the wall behind the stove. "Yuri does not want to remain in Russia. He wants a better life for you and the children."

"We could apply for an exit..."

Olga cut her off. "And you think the government would let you leave the country? The government would not allow an important scientist and his entire family to go to the West." Olga removed two more bricks from the side of the stove and pulled out a package. She pursed her lips and shook her head. "Besides, where would you have gotten the money for the fees, even if it was approved?"

Iveta bowed her head and covered her eyes with both hands. "You're right. They wouldn't let him leave, and we have no money."

"Putin is returning to the old ways. Invading countries, all the money is spent on the military." Olga choked. "Just to restore Mother Russia." She shoved the package into Iveta's hands.

Iveta stared at the bundle. "What is this?"

"Open it."

Iveta examined the looped twine. She shivered. *When I open this, my life will be changed forever.* She closed her eyes and said a short prayer. *Help me. Help me do what is right. Give me strength.*

When she opened her eyes, Olga was standing over her with her arms crossed, eyes half closed, lips set in a thin line. Iveta knew the look. It carried one meaning: absolute, unshakable resolve.

Iveta's shoulders slumped. She took a deep breath, untied the twine, and opened the package.

Passports, False IDs, and thousands of Euros tumbled onto the table. "Where did this come from?"

"I don't know. The country that wants Yuri gave it to him." Olga threw up her hands, walked a few paces, stopped, and retraced her steps.

"But who? Who would give him all this money? Who would *have* this much money?"

"He wouldn't tell me. Yuri said they gave him the money and the papers to make it possible for us to leave. He said we should go to London. His cousin, Stefan Golovin knows we are coming. Stefan will find a place for us to live. When Yuri is established in his new position, he will send for us."

December 31
The next day

Olga slid her finger along the heavy window drape and opened a slit. Once again, the ache in her joints accurately predicted the weather.

Snow fell.

Heavy.

Thick.

Silent.

"We'll leave in a few hours. The snow will cover our tracks." She returned to her chair and leaned back. "Make sure the boys are wearing several pairs of pants and sweaters and socks. You and I will wear several changes of clothing as well. We can't allow heavy rucksacks to slow us down, we can't struggle under bulky weight, we can only carry essentials."

"How can we travel to London without supplies?"

"We have money. We will buy what we need as we travel."

Iveta nodded, drained her teacup and stood. "Ondrek, Josef, it's time for you to take a nap."

"I am too old to take a nap," Ondrek declared.

"Me too," Josef echoed. "Maruska takes a naps. She's a baby."

"You will stay up late tonight. Far past your bed-time. How can you stay awake if you don't take a nap?" Iveta took their hands and walked with them to the bed.

"We will be allowed to stay up late tonight?" Ondrek's face lit with excitement, and he jumped into the bed and pulled up the covers.

"Yes. And, when you wake up, we will go for a hike. A long hike through the forest." She used the index and middle fingers of both hands to imitate little legs scampering across the quilt.

The boys were enthralled. Their mother's smile, love, and energy made everything sound like an adventure.

Olga had their coats draped on a wood frame, warmed and ready for the trip. Four packs were in a line near the vestibule. There were two large packs for Iveta and Olga. The smaller ones for Ondrek and Josef.

They started their trek at four in the afternoon. The winter sun had set, and the rising moon was obscured by thick clouds. The storm receded, but they would still have to deal with blowing snow and bitter cold.

Each woman carried a packet with a portion of the cash and IDs in her rucksack, along with diapers, sweaters, undergarments, and multiple pairs of socks.

For the first half-kilometer they struggled through fresh snow. Olga aimed for the forest path. The route through the wood would add half a kilometer to their trek, but the massive trees would block the wind and help to keep their path clear.

Two hours later the snow began to fall thick and heavy. Olga could barely make out the dim light that shined through the windows in the guard shack. She blinked several times to make sure the light was not a figment of her imagination. She knew exhaustion and hours of limited visibility could trick her mind into thinking there were lights ahead. A shadow moved across the window. Now she was sure.

Olga signaled a stop. The Russian/Latvian border was fifteen meters away.

"Remember," she whispered, "we must be silent like little mice."

The boys giggled.

Olga shook her head and placed her finger against her lips, her words soft as the falling snow. "If the mice are quiet the cat cannot hear them. Then the mice can steal the cheese." Her words were playful, but the laughter was gone from her voice.

Silent prayers tamped down her fear.

Iveta made the sign of the cross and shifted the sling that held Maruska, under her coat.

When Olga squatted down against a tree, Iveta and the boys did the same.

Seconds later, a sentry appeared a few feet from them. He struggled through the storm, plodding along his route. Olga turned toward the boys again with her gloved index finger over her lips.

The guard, a rifle on his right shoulder, walked with measured steps, head down, as if to protect his face from the wind. He turned a corner and vanished into the thick curtain of heavy snow. Grabbing the boys' hands—Josef on her left and Ondrek on her right—Olga crossed the guard path and moved into the field beyond.

Iveta followed in her mother's path.

When she was sure they were in Latvia, Olga lengthened her stride and aimed for a grove of trees. Iveta kept up with her mother and the two boys. The vapor from her labored breaths coated her lips with a layer of frost.

Maruska whimpered. Iveta pulled the child tight against her chest and ran. The baby's whimper swelled to a cry. Iveta patted her coat. Maruska wailed. Despite the thick wool of her coat, the child's protest seemed to echo across the flat land.

"Who's there?" the guard's voice thundered. "Stop!"

Olga swept both boys into her arms, put her head down and hurtled with them into the shrubbery. Iveta tumbled with Maruska into the bushes behind them.

"We are in Latvia, we are in Latvia, we are in Latvia." Olga whispered the mantra like a prayer.

Latvia is escape.

Latvia is safety.

Latvia is freedom.

The wind changed direction and increased in intensity.

She heard a man shout, "Vlad, get the dogs."

"The dogs?" a voice answered. "Why do you want the dogs? What do you see?"

"Someone ran across the field."

"I can't see anything."

"Someone hid in those trees. Send the dogs."

Olga's jaws were clenched so tight her teeth ached.

"Who would be out in this storm?"

Maruska howled.

The men's voices carried across the field. Olga held tight to the boys. Iveta patted Maruska.

"Sounds like a wolf to me."

"How can we be sure it wasn't someone escaping?"

"Your eyes are playing tricks on you. Come inside."

"We should send the dogs."

"What would the dogs be able to do if it *is* a wolf looking for his mate? What else would be out in this storm?" Their voices rang clear across the open land. "We don't need to have the dogs injured or killed by an angry pack of wolves."

"It wasn't a wolf."

"I don't care what it was. I'm not sending the dogs. Those trees are in Latvia. I doubt that any Latvian peasant would be stupid enough to be out in this weather."

"Come inside. It's New Year's Eve, time to celebrate."

January 3
Zagorsk, Russia

Far to the east, Yuri yanked the heavy winter drape aside. A beautiful bleak landscape spread out before him. Four days of snowfall had left a thick white blanket over the land. Evergreen trees heavy with snow contrasted with leafless trees that stood bare, black, and unmoving. The few brief hours of weak winter daylight had begun. A faint pink of early dawn underlined low, dark clouds across the eastern horizon and accentuated the golden domes of the cathedral and the spire atop the bell tower.

Cold seeped through a cracked window frame. He closed the drape and returned to the table.

"Potatoes . . ." Yuri Bushinikov pushed his plate away in disgust and poured another glass of tea. "Potatoes and turnips... potatoes and cabbage... boiled beets and onions." He ground his teeth. "And *potatoes.*"

Yuri plunked back in his chair, pulled his plate back, took another bite, and swilled a mouthful of tea to wash it down. He slammed the table with the flat of his hand. The glass jumped and tea sloshed across the smooth boards. He sprang up. The back of his legs hit the edge of the chair and sent it crashing to the floor.

"*Blya.*"

Tea dripped from the table to the carpet.

He stalked across the room, grabbed the vodka bottle from the shelf above the refrigerator, clumped back to the table, and shoveled more potatoes into his mouth. He chewed for a moment, unscrewed the bottle cap and gulped. The raw liquor burned its way to his stomach.

He gazed around the room. The shawl Iveta embroidered while she was pregnant with Ondrek was draped over a chair. His eyes traced a line of stitches on the cloth.

So many memories.

"We have no cheese or butter, no milk, no meat," he mumbled to the silent room. "Iveta goes without food. The children are hungry. Day in and day out, it is the same. The State gives us potatoes to fill our stomachs. And cheap vodka to dull our minds."

He silently cursed Russia, he cursed the government and the institute. Vektor! No pay for six months. Every day he heard an unending diatribe against America. America is evil. America hates Russia. We must stay ahead of America.

Yuri kicked the chair. What did it all come to? Nothing but cold and starvation.

He shook his fist at the crucifix nailed to the door lintel. "Why don't You intercede when we need You? My family deserves better!" he shouted at the icon.

"The Motherland." He spat the word. "Misery, poverty, and disappointment" Turning back to the table, he rubbed the nape of his neck.

"Have I made the wrong decision?" He took several steps.

"Nyet." The downward slash of his hand finalized his decision. "I took the Syrian's money. I accepted their offer. I cannot turn back now."

Tears filled his eyes. He moaned, turned back, and raised his hands in prayer to the crucifix. "I've sent them to the West. I had no choice. I couldn't let them starve. Watch over them. Keep them safe." Yuri bowed his head and made the sign of the cross. "Please, please, help them reach London."

Icy snow spattered against the windows. Wind moaned down the chimney.

Yuri walked to the vestibule, struggled into a wool jacket, pulled open the door, and slogged across the small yard to the stone wall behind the house. Needle-sharp sleet lashed his face.

A corner of a thick, insulated envelope was visible between the foundation stones. He slid the package free, eased open the flap. The delicate, frosted vials inside looked innocent, like small bottles of frozen milk.

"God help me."

He closed the envelope with care, carried the precious package into the house, and shouldered the door shut.

He would not return to the institute after the holiday. The institute would send someone to the house to check on him. It would not take long for them to know he was not coming back. The government would search the house. They would send out search parties and check the railroad rosters. They would check Olga's house. They would interview everyone at the lab and question everyone in Zagorsk. He and his family would be hunted. If he was caught, there would be no mercy. He would face imprisonment. He would be tortured. And, he would never be heard from again.

Yuri reviewed each step he took to delay detection. Lab security would count the vials in the refrigerators. At first, they wouldn't see any reason to be concerned. After counting the correct number of vials, each vial labeled to match the template. The first time the authorities checked the refrigeration units, nothing would look like the vials had been disturbed. In time they would test the contents of the vials, and would realize some of the labels were incorrect. Two of the vials would not contain smallpox but rather harmless, frozen whey.

I hope it gives me enough time to travel far to the west.

Yuri kissed the outside of the stuffed envelope and raised the package toward the crucifix. "For Iveta and our children!"

He lifted his bulging backpack from its peg and shoved the envelope deep inside. After wrapping the last chunk of bread in a piece of oilcloth, he stuffed the small bundle into a pocket, pulled on his wolverine-fur-lined coat, zipped up the front, shouldered the pack, and pulled the door open.

Taking a last look around the kitchen, he walked back across the room, pulled Iveta's embroidered piece from the table, and yanked the crucifix from the lintel.

He wrapped the cross in the cloth and shoved the parcel into a deep coat pocket, went back to the open door, and stepped out into the storm.

January 5
Zakhody

The trip to Zakhody took almost two days. A failing railway system was one more consequence of the Russian government's concentration on military spending.

Yuri, along with the other able-bodied men on the train, were called on several times to help clear the snow drifts from the tracks. Each time he struggled back to his seat, grateful for a few hours of sleep and the meager amount of food in his backpack. The guards checked his papers every time he got off the train and again when he returned to his seat. Everyone had to be accounted for. No one could be left behind.

The train chugged into another snow drift. Zakhody was five miles to the west.

Yuri shouldered his pack, grabbed a shovel, and climbed from the train. He joined the line of men and worked with them to clear the track.

The whistle blast was a warning for the men to return to the train. Yuri handed one of the men his shovel and mumbled an excuse about having to relieve himself. He ducked behind the highest mound, stretched his body along the base of the embankment, and burrowed into the snow. Another sharp whistle blast, and the wheels of the train began to turn.

When he could no longer hear the train, he slid out of his hiding place, staggered to his feet, rubbed his hands and arms, then jumped up and down. He crossed the fields and walked to Olga's house.

The house was cold and dark, but offered a temporary safe haven for rest and food. Yuri lit a lantern but kept the flame low.

He struck a match to the bit of kindling and paper Olga left in the stove, and gradually added small pieces of wood. When the fire caught, he went outside to hide the envelope behind the garden tools in the barn.

A ham hung from a chain in the smoke house. Yuri cut a thick slice from the meat and carried it into the house.

Olga left one of her porcelain pots on the counter. A jar of preserved carrots sat next to it. Yuri crept down the ladder and took an onion and a potato from the root cellar. He cut up the meat, onion, and potato, topped it all with the canned carrots and several cups of fresh snow.

He covered the pot, slid it to the back of the stove, and added one last piece of wood to the fire.

Yuri removed his boots and coat. He fell into one of the beds and pulled a thick feather blanket up to his chin, then fell into and exhausted sleep.

Several hours later Yuri woke, crawled out of bed and slipped on his boots. He ate the soup with a heel of stale bread from the pantry. When he was finished, he cleaned the pot with fresh snow, then checked the fire. Only glowing embers remained.

He walked the few steps to the window, opened the thick curtain and stared outside. A crescent moon hung low on the eastern horizon in a sky so clear and bright the North Star was clearly visible.

A sign, he thought. A good sign.

He pulled on his coat, locked the house, and carried his backpack to the barn. Once the envelope was tucked into his pack, he took snowshoes down from the wall and fastened them to his boots.

Finally, he crossed himself and started out.

The two-kilometer trek through the deep woods left his nose numb and burned the skin of his cheeks. Inside the thick gloves his fingers felt brittle, as though each one might shatter if he tried to clench his fist.

When he caught a whiff of cheap tobacco, he slowed, watched for guards, listened for dogs, and waited for his pounding heart to settle.

One tree. Wait.

Catch his breath.

Slide to another tree.

Wait.

After twenty minutes, he heard the guards call to one another. A match flared.

Yuri slid to another tree. A twig snapped under his boot.

Dogs bayed. The sound echoed through the forest.

Yuri froze. His heart jackhammered. He leaned into a tree and slid inch by inch to one knee.

The voices grew louder, closer.

Yuri closed his eyes and prayed.

A gunshot.

The dogs fell silent.

"Good work, Stavros," a man shouted.

"Hang him from a tree," another ordered.

"Skin the fox in the morning. It's time to eat dinner and open our gifts."

A door creaked, then slammed shut.

Stars and flashing lights danced in his eyes. Yuri gasped.

He'd been holding his breath.

Latvia
Two hours later

Yuri paused near the rock wall alongside Grigori's house and searched for a niche to hide the envelope. The bitter cold would keep the virus frozen. He knelt and tucked the envelope into a narrow space between the stones. Seconds later, he knocked on the heavy wooden door and heard footsteps. The door swung open.

"Come in, come in." Grigori welcomed Yuri with hugs and hearty back slaps. "Anya, Yuri is here."

She ran to the men, her face red and her hair mussed. "I'm happy you are here." She wiped her hands on her apron. "I was so worried."

Yuri placed his pack on a bench near the door, his coat on a hook, sat on the bench and pulled off his heavy boots.

"I am glad to be here. Was my family here? Did they cross safely?"

Anya handed him a pair of felt slippers. "Yes. Yes. They were able to get across the border. We all celebrated New Year's Eve. They stayed for a few days. I wish the visit could have been longer. We put them on the train two days ago. They should be at Pauline's house in Krakow."

"Are they well? How was their crossing?"

"We'll tell you their story when we eat. Sit by the fire and get warm."

"Did you have any trouble at the border?" Grigori asked.

Yuri told them about the fox hunt, and listened to Anya and Grigori chuckle.

"It is a humorous story now . . ." Yuri said. "It wasn't funny at the time."

"Slivovitz?" Grigori held up a bottle and pointed at two glasses on the table. "It will help warm you."

"Yes. Of course." Yuri smiled.

Tradition.

Family.

He heaved a sigh of relief.

Grigori poured two glasses of the plum brandy, handed one to Yuri, and held the other high. "To successful fox hunts."

Iveta, Olga, and the children arrived at the Glowny railroad station. Olga's cousin, Pauline, and Pauline's daughter, Elzbieta met them. Pauline hugged Olga for several long moments. They hadn't seen one another since childhood. Once they were all settled into her vehicle, Elzbieta drove them to Pauline's apartment.

Enthusiastic cries of welcome from a crowd of relatives greeted Olga, Iveta, and the children. Iveta had never met any of these relatives. And, except for Pauline, Olga only knew them from letters exchanged over the past few years.

After the adults made a great fuss over Maruska, a seventeen-year-old girl whisked her into the adjoining room so the adults could visit.

Cousins with children the same age as Josef and Ondrek pulled the boys into an adjoining room. They shared their toy cars and trucks with the boys. The barrier between Polish and Russian fell away. The children seemed to understand each other. No translation was necessary.

Elzbieta and Iveta worked together in the kitchen. They stumbled on the pronunciation of some words but were eager to prepare a large meal. The women laughed as they taught each other the names of the food. Iveta offered the Russian word and Elzbieta would reply with the Polish pronunciation. Roasted pork. Dumplings filled with cheesy mashed potatoes, fried cabbage, or prune butter. Loaves of Three King's Bread. Steamed asparagus. Boiled beets. A feast.

During the meal each adult shared their stories of the intervening years. Joys, sorrows, and struggles. Most of the stories included times of constant hunger and fear. Olga's husband died of hard work, heavy smoking and, like so many men, the ravages of excessive vodka during the long years of the Soviet regime. Pauline's husband died of a lung disease contracted in prison after the revolution.

Olga and Pauline bragged about their children, their children's spouses, their grandchildren.

Despite the festive atmosphere, a quiet sadness laced Iveta's heart.

Where was Yuri?

Was he safe?

Was he alive?

Dr. Maria De Costa and Mary-Katherine Fitzgerald, the junior sena-
tor from Massachusetts, met for lunch once a week at Bistro Bis. The
restaurant was nestled in the Hotel George, two blocks from Capitol
Hill and Union Station. A short-walk compromise from both Mary-
Katherine's office in the Senate office building and Maria's Union
Station Metro stop.

Maria, a preventive medicine physician, taught at the F. Edward
Hébert School of Medicine, better known as the Uniformed Services
University of the Health Sciences in Bethesda, Maryland. She and
Mary-Katherine were in the middle of a long standing disagreement.

Maria took a deep breath and tried again, even though, down
deep, she knew her friend would never change her mind. "Mary-
Katherine," Maria's tone was soft but firm, authoritative. "We've been
friends forever. Please believe me, bioterrorism isn't a fantasy."

Senator Fitzgerald faked a yawn and studied the two-story teak
columns and the green and white marble floor tiles. "So my Republican
colleagues remind me, almost daily, might I add."

"Come on, this goes beyond political views. When any contagious
disease spreads, it affects constituents from both political parties."

"I don't know why you're so sure our enemies would use smallpox. Aren't there other virulent diseases they could use?"

"Of course. And, we have to watch for all of them. It hasn't been
long since there was concern about Ebola spreading across the US.
Around the same time, we had the measles epidemic. Now, in addition
to a whooping cough epidemic, we're worried about the Zika virus."

"Exactly, you just made my point. Thank you very much. Ebola
didn't spread."

"No, it didn't. But, all the other diseases did." Maria closed
her eyes and tried to think of a way to convince Mary-Katherine.

"Multiple organisms could be used by a terrorist. Smallpox is just one of them. Terrorists can and will release any bioweapon they can get their hands on. We *need* to put an immunization program in place."

"You know I can't take a stance in support of vaccination."

"Really? California has."

"Yeah, and look at the blowback they got." She handed the dessert menu to Maria. "Even if I believed your stance was correct, the majority of my constituency is opposed to vaccination."

"They," Maria drew out the word, "have been brainwashed by foolish, high-profile personalities promoting junk science. One actress had a child who developed autism. She seized on an unsubstantiated article by a British physician and became a one woman anti-vaccination publicity machine. The doctor who spread the myth has been disproven time and again. Vaccinations *do not* cause autism."

"Even so, because of your harping in the subject, I've contacted specialists to get some perspective. The infectious disease specialists at Mass General tell me there is NO bioterrorism threat."

Maria lowered her voice and leaned across the table. "I don't care what the eggheads in Boston think. You're on the Intelligence Committee. You've been briefed on weaponized infectious particles. Smallpox, anthrax, botulinum, Q-fever, VEE, EEE. Should I go on?"

"No," Mary-Katherine crossed her arms, "Dr. Delaney is opposed to a universal smallpox vaccination program. He says no government in the world would be willing to set off a bioweapon like smallpox. Their own population might be decimated."

"Jeffrey Delaney." Maria's voice dripped with disdain. "Using Delaney's reasoning kills your argument."

"Dr. Delaney is respected. He's a world-acclaimed expert."

"Try self-acclaimed. His arguments are easy to refute. The biggest error he makes is thinking that terrorists are state sponsored. Terrorists are not state sponsored. Terrorists are driven by devotion to a cause. They have no national affiliation." Maria made a conscious effort to keep her voice low. "Their cause is to destroy the infidel. And, they'll kill anyone who falls into their loose interpretation of *infidel*.

They're consumed by their belief. Self-preservation is not a part of their nature. They sacrifice their lives to eliminate the individual, group, social construct..."

Mary-Katherine put up her right hand. "I've heard your arguments time and time again." She gave a frustrated sigh. "We were talking about immunization. And the bottom line, the *only* bottom line I'm going to consider, is the number of children who have died from smallpox vaccination."

She held up both hands as if to push Maria's argument away. "Many adults have had serious complications from the vaccine. We don't have enough immune globulin ready for people who are immunosuppressed." She held up all three fingers. "What are we going to tell the parents of dead children? Or those we can't protect? What will we tell the adults who are horribly scarred from the vaccination?"

Maria closed her eyes. "Your argument is becoming extremely abstract. You're quoting information from decades ago. It's not 1940. If we have an attack, thousands upon thousands will die. And, you wouldn't worry about the few people who have an adverse reaction to the vaccine. That concern would be pretty low on your list."

Mary-Katherine straightened the lapel of her suit and patted her auburn curls. "Arguing is pointless! We've been through this before."

Maria reached for Mary-Katherine's hand. "The odds are stacked against you." Her voice softened. "With the Middle East the way it is now . . ." She gave her friend a profound, exaggerated shrug. "I don't know how safe we are. But you're right. Arguing is getting us nowhere."

"Neither of us is ever going to relent."

Maria was tempted to come back with an acid remark, but changed her mind.

The women remained silent for a few minutes.

Maria pushed back her plate, sipped her coffee, and watched Mary-Katherine pop the last bite of her steak into her mouth.

Unable to stand the tension, Maria changed the subject, "So, how are Todd and my favorite redheaded godchild?"

"Todd's fine. He has his hands full being the husband of the junior senator from Massachusetts and handling his law practice. And as far as Miss Brittany is concerned, she's your *only* redheaded godchild." Mary-Katherine shook her head. "She's reduced her timeouts at school down to three a week. Sister Mary Joseph calls me on a regular basis. I have no idea how often she has to call Todd. I'm told the entire staff gets apprehensive when they see Brittany's green eyes start to sparkle and she tosses her strawberry curls. Sister says she's far too smart for her own good."

January 10
Berlin, Germany
Five days later

Yuri breathed a sigh of relief as he closed the door. The simple hotel room was warm and clean. It held a bed, telephone, table, and chair. White walls, white curtains, and white linens. Pure, clean luxury after days of rocking in a crowded train.

Four drunk and noisy university students had piled into his compartment. They were happy to share their cheap wine and food. Yuri added tinned biscuits and sausages to the provisions, making the best of the trip across Germany.

He lowered his pack to the floor, and peeled off his heavy jacket and boots. He pulled the envelope out of his rucksack, opened it, and peeked at the contents.

Still frozen.

Yuri opened the window, and hand-scooped snow from the broad sill into a small plastic wastebasket from the bathroom. When the container was half full, he tucked in the envelope, then scooped more snow and ice on top.

With a thankful sigh, he took in the spectacular evening sky stretched out before him. Scattered clouds reflected a rosy blush from the setting sun's last rays.

Yuri closed his eyes and said a short, silent prayer. I am grateful for Your protection. Please, watch over my family. Keep them safe.

The soft glow of twilight faded, the sky darkened, and lights winked on across the city. A bus weaved in and out of traffic. Horns blared. Music floated through the air.

He placed the wastebasket into a pillowcase and closed the window on a corner of the fabric.

Weary from his days of travel, he sank into a chair and absentmindedly studied his fingernails.

Did I make the right decision?

Can I trust the Syrian?

He slumped further into the chair and stared at the phone, shaking off an unexpected shiver of dread.

The Syrian had given him a number to call. It would be madness to wait any longer. He picked up the receiver, and felt icy threads of doubt with each click of the dial. After a stomach-burning wait, the call was answered.

"Yes."

"For the jihad."

"Berlin?"

"Yes."

"The gift?"

"In my possession."

"A plane ticket will be delivered to your hotel in the next few hours. You will leave for Jakarta in the morning."

The bed, piled high with down quilts and feather pillows, tempted Yuri to sink into oblivion. Yuri looked in the bathroom mirror. A man with unkempt too-long hair and whiskers grown well beyond a five-o'clock-shadow looked back at him. He laughed at the reflection. *Even Iveta would not recognize this unkempt person staring back at me.* The thought brought a pang of loneliness. Iveta, my Iveta. *How I wish you were here.*

Hours later he woke, dressed, and went to the hotel lobby, where he used the hotel's computer to make sure the promised money had been deposited in the pre-arranged Swiss bank account. So . . . They've kept their part of the bargain. He transferred the funds to another Swiss account. An account only Iveta or Olga could access.

He returned to his room and put a call through to his cousin in London.

"Hello, Stefan. Has Iveta reached Great Britain? Have you heard from my family?"

"No, Yuri, they are not here yet. They have not called me. But, I've found a cottage for them, in the countryside, a few kilometers from London."

Yuri put the receiver back in the stand and stared at the telephone for several long minutes. Finally, he sat on the edge of the bed and pulled off his shoes and socks. He peeled off his pants and shirt, folded the garments, and laid them over the back of the chair, then climbed back into bed in his underwear and drew the covers to his chin.

"My Iveta, please be safe," he whispered before sleep pulled him under.

January 11
NSA Offices
Ft. Meade, Maryland

National Security Agency analyst Josh Hollingsworth stepped out of his car and stretched. His back ached. The damp cold air of Maryland didn't help. He really wanted to stay in bed this morning.

With a job that was demanding, challenging, and fascinating, he looked forward to coming to work on most days. But today he wanted boring. He wasn't up to dealing with demands, challenges, or, God knew, anything *fascinating*.

One hand held a travel cup half full of coffee. A sticky bun wrapped in waxed paper was balanced on top. With the other hand, he swiped his ID card and punched in his security code at door, after door, after door.

Saggy jeans, scuffed sneakers, stretched sweater, and a backpack with frayed corners left no doubt as to his geek status.

Snow was predicted for later in the afternoon. The heavy gray clouds and piercing damp cold was only going to get worse.

Shouldn't have stayed out until one a.m.

Too many hours at an Ellicott City tavern with college friends, loud music, bawdy jokes, and too many mugs of beer, left him with a sour taste in his mouth and a pounding headache. Maybe a couple of aspirin and the sugar and caffeine would help.

His office walls were painted standard institutional green. Brown carpet covered the floor. Blotches from spilled coffee and cola bore testimony to long hours of drudgery. Two desks and a table, shelves, and file cabinets crowded the room. Each desk and the table held double computer screens. Josh put his coffee cup and sticky bun on the table, sat in his office chair and rolled down the line to switch on the bank of computers. His bad mood began to lighten as he munched on the sticky bun and took another sip of the sweet, strong coffee he'd picked up on the drive to work. He pulled open a desk drawer, took out a bottle of aspirin, shook out two tablets, and inhaled them with a gulp of coffee.

While the machines warmed up, he ate the last bite of the sticky bun and licked the icing off his fingers.

The NSA's enormous phalanx of central computers were programmed to filter and send messages "of interest" to each appropriate analyst. Only communications with certain phrases or key words the government had identified as parameters of interest would sift down through the system. Josh was the final filter for the Berlin desk.

A few minutes before noon he swallowed two more aspirin and chased them with a bottle of water. Maybe a couple of laps around the building would clear his head. He pushed away from his desk, locked the computers, locked his office door, and locked the door to his suite.

Back in his office half an hour later his headache was gone. The aspirin and a brief walk had relaxed his lower-back muscles. As soon as the computers booted up again he saw a call from Berlin to Damascus. The phone call was made yesterday. His fingers flew over the keyboard. Another call from the number in Berlin to a bank in Switzerland followed. All complaints of back pain were now gone.

A call to London from the same number, two more calls to Jakarta. The callers did not speak German. Josh thought it sounded like Russian. Now he was wide awake and alert, the revelry from last night forgotten. An adrenalin surge erased his muscle pain and headache. He sent the messages for immediate translation.

He let out a strangled whisper when the interpretation came back. "Oh my God, this is important." Maybe one of the other desks has picked up related noise. *I better check.* He shut down and locked the computers and the doors, and double-checked to be certain they were secured. His clearance allowed access to the adjoining suite, but not to the individual offices. He knocked Arlene Post's door. She worked the Moscow desk.

Carl Anderson opened the door. Arlene sat at her desk.

Josh stepped in the room and nodded. "Hi, glad you're both here. Have you picked up any unusual noise today?"

"Funny you should ask." Arlene stood and hitched up her jeans. "We were about to come to your office with a similar question. I've picked up a lot of chatter between Kosovo and Moscow, followed by an unusual flurry of calls to the central office in Moscow."

Arlene paused and picked up the papers, her face flushed. "The translations came in a few minutes ago." She handed the translation to Josh and summarized the contents. "A scientist has gone missing from a lab in Novosibirsk. Their director of biologicals."

Carl waved several sheets of paper he held in his hand. "And, that's not all. I had a flurry of strange calls, too. They were back and forth between Dumayr and Jakarta. The calls were to and from the Syrian Institute for Science and International Security."

He handed the papers to Josh. "Read these."

Josh grabbed the papers. His stomach flipped. Something was going down. *Something important.*

Carl sat down for a few seconds, then jumped back on to his feet. "The last message went from Jakarta to Dumayr. The translation hasn't come in yet."

"This is big," Arlene said, rubbing the tips of her fingers together.

Josh nodded and picked up the phone.

"It's time to call our section leader."

'Considering the extraordinary character of the times in which we live, our attention should unremittingly be fixed on the safety of our country,'
Thomas Jefferson, in his final message to Congress

Situation Room
White House
Several hours later

The President's National Security Council members waited.

Hugh Donovan, the director of Central Intelligence, glanced at the clock every few seconds. He felt the room's tension increase. The anxiety in the room seemed to coalesce into a malignant force real enough and strong enough to smother them.

President Julian stood. Silver-gray hair, six-foot-four, marathon-runner slender. If Hollywood wanted someone to play the role of chief executive, they would have chosen Ed Julian. Tonight his campaign smile and crinkled, laughing eyes were absent. His casual, good-old-boy stance had been replaced with a military posture. His ruddy complexion had turned ashen; a gray-green tinge underlined his eyes.

"Good evening. Thank you for coming." The President cleared his throat. "We're waiting for Doctor Ann Damiano. The helicopter picked her up thirty minutes ago, so she should be here any…"

A single knock sounded, the conference-room door opened, and Anne Damiano entered. Minimal makeup, black pantsuit, high heels.

President Julian gestured to an empty seat near the head of the polished table. "Welcome, Anne. Sorry to have pulled you from Fort Dietrich with no explanation."

He scanned the room and nodded at Donovan. "Hugh, please bring us up to date."

Donovan held a slim file. His poise and rich, deep voice took instant command of the room. "Vektor's director of bioengineering went missing several days ago." He flipped open the documents.

The leader of the Senate Intelligence Committee jerked back in her chair, eyes wide.

Donovan continued. "Yuri Bushinikov is a well published and well regarded scientist in his field. His research interest is the genetic manipulation of smallpox. Our sources tell us he left his home in..." Donovan paused, consulted his notes, "Zagorsk on January fifth. He was supposed to join his family at his mother-in-law's home in . . ." another glance at the notes, "Zahkody, a small village close to the Latvian border. However, no official record shows that Bushinikov ever arrived there."

Donovan was silent for a few seconds, a frown creased his forehead. "His wife and children were on a train to Zahkody a week before Bushinikov went missing. There's no official record that they ever reached Zahkody, either."

Donovan scanned the faces of each person in the room. "Russia House reports they found no sign of his wife, their children, or his mother-in-law. The Russians are mystified. It's as if Bushinikov, his wife, children, and mother-in-law disappeared into thin air. The Russians are using their formidable assets to find them."

President Julian nodded toward Anne. "Dr. Damiano, please give us a refresher course on the possible dangers this situation presents."

Anne took a deep breath and turned to the President. "Thank you, Sir, for including me in this discussion." She bowed her head and rubbed the nape of her neck. "I think we have to assume Bushinikov left Russia."

Donovan bobbed his head. "Our information is scant at this point. What we know is the scientist, his family, and his mother-in-law are missing. And the Russians can't find them."

Anne exhaled. "Okay, I'm going to assume the worst case scenario."

She closed her eyes and dropped her head and allowed seconds to tick by. She raised her head, "Vektor is the creative center for the production of bioterror weapons. We knew it as *Biopreparat* during the Soviet era." Anne drew in a deep breath to stop the slow roll of her stomach.

"The maintenance on Vektor's labs has never been adequate.

Upkeep wasn't good during the Soviet era and hasn't improved under the current regime. The labs have unreliable refrigeration units, deteriorating storage tanks, and failing equipment."

She turned to President Julian, with her hands raised palms up. "We know that their economy is a disaster."

The President nodded.

"Their scientists are ripe for being bribed. They haven't been paid for months." She uncapped a bottle of water and took a sip. "If we assume Bushinikov's disappearance is related to his expertise and his access to biologicals . . ." She nibbled at her lower lip for a moment. "We'll also have to assume a foreign government or hostile organization facilitated his exodus from Russia. He couldn't have had the money or the means to leave Russia on his own."

The President shifted in his chair. "Worst-case scenario?"

"It could be serious. Might even be disastrous. Considering Bushinikov's research and expertise, I would have to assume he acquired several vials filled with Variola virus." She paused, "smallpox."

The President coughed. "Why do you think he would have taken smallpox?"

"The cost to get Bushinikov and his entire family out of Russia had to be enormous. I'm sure whoever engineered his escape will be glad to get his expertise. But, the real value, what they paid for, was the virus."

The Secretary of Health and Human Services, a small woman with a distinct white streak in her hair and Asian features raised her hand. "The United States has stores of smallpox."

"Yes, Secretary Lee, we do. But we're talking about a missing Russian scientist, not a turned American scientist."

"Why would they want smallpox?" This question came from the Secretary of State.

"Several reasons, Secretary Daley." Anne held up one finger. "The last case of smallpox in the United States occurred in 1949." She held up a second finger, "The Western Hemisphere was declared smallpox-free in April of 1971." She held up a third finger. "We stopped childhood immunization for smallpox in 1972."

When Connor Quinlan stifled a yawn and raised two fingers, she responded, "Yes, Connor?"

"Why does any country have stores of the virus? Why weren't all the stores destroyed?"

"Good question. As far as we know, only the U.S. and Russia have stores of variola. The U.S. doesn't trust the Russians to destroy all their stores, and Russia doesn't trust the U.S. It's a problem that goes back to the Cold War and the balance of power."

"What should we be concerned about at the present time?" President Julian asked.

"We have to assume he and his family are on their way to a hostile country or organization with enormous amounts of money at their disposal. If smallpox is used as a bioweapon, our population is at risk. The world is at risk. An outbreak of smallpox in the United States would have a fifty-four percent morbidity rate."

Anne noticed expressions of confusion on several faces. "The morbidity rate refers to the number of people who contract the disease. For those immunized more than fifteen to twenty years ago, we expect an eleven to fifteen percent morbidity rate. The mortality rate, the percentage of people who will *die* from the disease, is expected to be about thirty–five percent overall."

The Treasury Secretary raised his hand. "Excuse me, Dr. Damiano."

"Yes, Mr. Creighton?"

"We have a tremendous amount of vaccine available. Why haven't we started an immunization program?"

"Another excellent question." She tented her hands. "You're right. We have a tremendous store of vaccine. Almost enough to immunize each man, woman, and child in the United States. After 9/11 we immunized many first responders, lab workers, government officials, and most of our military personnel. But the decision was made at that time to not offer smallpox vaccination to the general public."

Connor Quinlan raised his hand again. "That doesn't make much sense. Why not immunize everyone?"

"The anti-immunization sentiment in this country, for one. We don't have enough Vaccine Immune Globulin to protect the immuno-suppressed population is another. And, rare but serious complications can occur from the vaccine."

The President stood. "Thank you for your candor, Dr. Damiano."

Anne eased into her chair, giving him the floor.

The President addressed the Security Council. "I want each of you to meet with your most trusted team members. I need to know how long it would take to produce enough vaccine and immune globulin, and to find enough health care workers to distribute the vaccine. I need estimates for the cost to implement the program. You need to gather as much information as possible. We need to know what effective steps we can take to control the accompanying panic the rumors of a smallpox epidemic would engender." The President looked at each member of the Security Council, then spoke again, his voice a whisper.

"There. Are. To. Be. No. Leaks."

Donovan gestured toward a full coffee carafe centered on the table and waited while both Anne and Connor filled their cups.

Donovan picked up a file. "Okay – there's a bunch of information the President didn't share with the Security Council." He leafed through the file. "A credible source has reported the director of the Syrian Institute for Science and Information had been in direct contact with Bushinikov."

Anne looked up. "The Institute is in Dumayr. That's not a place most Russians visit."

"How did the Syrians contact Bushinikov?" Connor asked. He already had his page half filled with doodles.

"Al Halbi, the director, met with Bushinikov at a scientific meeting in Damascus last September." Donovan closed his file. "We've known for quite some time Al Halbi's focus has been to develop a powerful bioweapon."

Anne rubbed her right temple with the heel of her hand. "I'm willing to bet he knew about Bushinikov and the work being done at Vektor."

"Word is," Donovan continued, "Al Halbi's working on a bio weapon that will be used against the Kurds, Israel, and the United States. And, he wants his scientists to have it completed by year's end. There's been some evidence his team has been experimenting with anthrax and botulinum."

Anne rolled her head from right to left. The crackles and pops of the muscles and tendons relieved some of the tension in her neck. "Al Halbi's ambitions sound like they fit in with the overall objectives of the Muslim Brotherhood."

Donovan nodded. "Intelligence reports that Al Halbi is a member of the Muslim Brotherhood."

Connor straightened. "We know Bushinikov made his way out of Russia and was able to reach Berlin."

Anne paused mid-pour. Several drops of coffee hit the conference table. "How do we know he was in Berlin?" She grabbed a napkin and wiped up the mess she'd made.

"Bushinikov made phone calls from a hotel in Berlin." Those phone calls alerted the analyst at the NSA to the situation. And, there have been two huge money transfers in the past few days. A total of over two million dollars has been transferred from Syria to a Swiss bank account."

Connor whistled through his teeth and added a line of circles to the page of doodles. "Where's Bushinikov now?"

Anne twisted and stretched the muscles in her back and shoulders and watched Donovan pick up a stack of papers and bounce them on edge.

"Jakarta." His tone was casual, a matter-of-fact statement.

"Jakarta?" Anne and Connor chorused.

Anne swiveled her head and heard a pop. A flash of pain faded into the relief of muscle relaxation.

"When we got word of the phone calls, we contacted our most trusted agent in the area. Unfortunately, Bushinikov had already checked out of his hotel. By the time the agent got to the airport the plane had been in the air for thirty minutes."

Anne continued to massage the muscles in her neck. "Sending Bushinikov to Jakarta doesn't make sense. If the Syrian's paid him huge sums of money and provided him with fake IDs. Why would they send him to Indonesia? Why not Turkey? The Syrians could have flown him to Dumayr from Istanbul."

"I don't know." Donovan spread his hands in a gesture of helplessness. "We have surveillance set up in Jakarta. With any luck they'll be able to pick up his trail at the airport and follow him." Donovan fussed with the pile of papers. He picked them up for the second time and tried to align the edges.

"You have more?" Connor ripped off a page of doodles, mashed the paper into a ball, and poised his pencil over a fresh sheet.

"I do. The wife, mother-in-law, and children left Russia before Bushinikov. We have credible information confirming they were in Latvia on New Year's Eve."

Anne looked up. "Where's his family now?"

Donovan blew his frustration through pursed lips. "Don't know. There was an unconfirmed report indicating they may have stayed with another relative in Poland. We're guessing the Syrians not only supplied Bushinikov with alternate IDs. They must have supplied fake IDs for each member of his family. Passports and cash, as well."

"How would they have delivered all the money and papers to Bushinikov?"

"My guess? Al Halbi must have had those items with him in Damascus. It would have been a powerful pull to get Bushinikov. I doubt promises would have worked so well or so quickly. We don't have a clue as to where the family is right now, because we don't know what names they're using. But we know where they're going."

Connor's pen stopped mid-doodle. "How do we know that?"

"Bushinikov told us. One of the calls he made from Berlin was to his cousin, Stefan Golovin. Golovin is a student in Great Britain on a Soviet state-approved fellowship."

"Do we have eyes on him?"

"Better. Stefan wants to stay in the West. He does *not* want to go back to Russia. He made a deal with the Brits. MI6 agreed."

"What did they agree to?"

"The British Intelligence Service will intercept the Bushinikovs and get them to a safe house."

"In exchange for?"

"Political asylum for Golovin and the Bushinikovs." Donovan paused. "At this point the Russians are scrambling like mad to find Bushinikov and his family."

Anne's brow furrowed. "I'm sure they are. I hope *we're* scrambling like mad to find Bushinikov. But there's another concern that's equally important. It might be more important"

"What?" Donovan and Connor said.

"If Syria's made a deal to acquire live virus, they must have a lab ready to receive it."

"You mean one of those labs with all the special showers and ventilation systems?"

"Yes, they'd need a Level Four Bio-Safety Lab ready and waiting to process the virus."

January 12
Jakarta, Indonesia

Yuri deplaned in Jakarta and stepped into exotic heat, crushing humidity, and lung-killing vehicle exhaust fumes. An unsmiling man met him at the airport and handed him an envelope. He guided Bushinikov to a black Mercedes, held the door open, and waited for Bushinikov to slide into the back seat.

Yuri opened the envelope. It contained a room key, a passport with his picture, and the name 'Vladmir Yohzin'. There was also a short note: "Wait for my call." A burn began in Yuri's gut and smoldered during the drive to the Mercure Convention Center Hotel.

His room was simple. Polished teak floors, ultra-modern furniture, grass cloth wallpaper. Yuri pulled the silver-gray draperies aside and looked out at a spectacular view of the Java Sea.

The telephone rang.

Yuri stared at the receiver. A cramp tightened his stomach. He swallowed back a wave of nausea.

The phone rang again. Yuri gagged.

A third ring. Yuri's hand shook as he picked up the receiver. "Yes?"

"You have the gift?" The voice was hollow, guttural, mechanically altered.

"It is in my possession," Yuri responded.

"A driver will come for you at six o'clock tomorrow evening. He'll take you to an office in the warehouse district. Bring the gift."

The connection went dead.

About midnight, Yuri fell into a restless sleep. He woke up before daylight soaked in a cold sweat. The bed covers tangled and twisted around his legs and feet.

Unsettled dreams.

Unidentified figures.

Unsmiling men.

And overwhelming terror.

London, England
Later the same day

Iveta, Olga, and the children huddled together in the hallway outside Stefan's flat. Iveta knocked. The door cracked open, and Stefan peered through the narrow slit. He pulled the door open and hurried the group in. "Come in, come in. You must be exhausted. Take off your coats." The words tumbled from his lips in an almost unintelligible jumble. "I'm sorry this room is so cold. I will turn up the heat. Let me make you tea."

Stefan was thin and pale. His drab clothes hung on what was left of a once robust frame. A gray wool scarf thrown around his neck and over his shoulder seemed a pitiful attempt at nonchalance.

Iveta couldn't help but wonder if Stefan was ill.

The flat had fourth-hand furniture and mustard colored walls. His computer table was littered with manuscripts. Bricks held boards fashioned into shelves that sagged in the middle, heavy with books, journals, and papers. A threadbare brown carpet covered the floor. The electric heater huddled in a corner, did little to warm the room. His couch had seen better days, and three scarred chairs surrounded a small table. The fourth chair was placed in front of his computer.

Stefan lifted the tea canister. He struggled to open the metal container. His hands shook so badly the lid flew across the room, and tea leaves scattered across the counter. In his attempt to rescue the tea leaves, cups rattled, water sloshed.

Olga pushed him aside. "Here, I will make the tea."

Stefan nodded, wrung his hands and retreated to the window.

Iveta rubbed her arms to relieve the goose bumps. She shivered. As much from fear, as from the chill in the room.

Stefan had been a serious but affable gymnasium student. Today he was nervous, unsmiling. He looked at his watch, then peered out of the window, looked up and down the street, and checked his watch again.

Iveta felt a deeper chill, unsettled by Stefan's behavior. "What's wrong, Stefan?" She crossed her arms to ward off a shiver.

"Wrong? Nothing's wrong. What could be the matter?" He shook his head and did not meet her gaze. "I'm happy you're here."

Iveta shivered again.

He pulled off his scarf and wrapped it around Iveta's shoulders. "I'm sorry it is so cold in my flat." Stefan looked out the window again.

"What are you looking for?" Iveta walked to the window and looked down. The street was empty of traffic.

"I am not looking for anything." Stefan glanced down to the street. "Did anyone see you come into the building?"

"No one was in the hallway when we came in. I don't think we were seen." Iveta frowned, "What difference would it make? Aren't you allowed to have visitors?"

"Of course I'm allowed to have visitors." Stefan shoved his hands back into his pockets. "Yuri has called me several times. He will be happy to know you're here. He has been worried." Stefan scanned the street again.

"The tea is ready." Olga carried the teapot to the table. "Come. Sit."

Iveta began to move away from the window, when she caught a movement in her peripheral vision. She stopped and looked down at the street.

Three black cars came to a stop in front of the apartment building. Several people jumped out of the first car and hurried to the entrance.

Iveta felt her throat constrict. She pointed out the window. "Are those the people you've been waiting for?"

Stefan didn't answer. He lowered his head, fisted his hands, cleared his throat, and spun away from the window.

"Police." Iveta's voice was flat.

"No, not police." Beads of sweat peppered Stefan's forehead, and his entire body trembled. He tried to clear his throat, but couldn't erase the shrill from his voice. "They are government officials."

"Officials. Why would you do this? Why would you report us?"

Stefan jumped back. "No, no, I told you. They are not police. They are government officials."

"Officials – police – no difference. – they have come to arrest us."

"This is not Russia. It is not the same. You don't understand."

"Stevko, Josef, get your coats. Mother, wrap Maruska in her blanket." Iveta's shoulders slumped.

Stefan raised his hands, "No, no," he pleaded. "It is different here."

"You have reported us. The police are in the building. What will they do to us?"

"They have come to help you. They will keep you safe."

She glared at Stefan. "They will take us to jail."

Three measured taps on the front door echoed throughout the small apartment.

Iveta turned to face the door, feet apart, shoulders squared. Olga moved to her side. The boys huddled behind them.

Stefan opened the door.

Two men and a woman entered the apartment. The tallest man had thick brown hair, ruddy skin, and a deep soft voice. "Iveta Bushinikova," he said with a pronounced British accent. "My name is William Sellers. I'm with the British Intelligence Service."

Iveta didn't answer. She felt the rapid beat of her heart and could hear the pulse resound in her head.

"Please, sit." He gestured to the chairs.

Iveta stood a little straighter, her chin lifted a little higher.

"We've come to help you."

"I don't believe you."

William Sellers said it again, strong and clear: "We've come to help you."

"How will you help us?" Iveta crossed her arms. "By putting us in prison?"

"The United States intelligence service told us you'd come here. They've asked us to ensure your safety."

Iveta understood the words but could not grasp their meaning. "Americans sent you here? Why would the Americans care about us? Two women and three little children..." She stood a little straighter. "How did they know we'd come here?"

Sellers pulled out a chair and sat at the table. "Let me explain." His voice was soft, gentle. There was no hint of anger. He gestured for Iveta to sit.

Iveta stood firm.

"The American government knew you would come to London. We've been waiting for you."

"How could the Americans know anything about us?"

"Your husband let them know."

"My husband told the Americans that we were coming here?"

"Not directly. If you will sit, please, I will explain."

Iveta slid into the chair, but kept her hands clasped, her eyes on Sellers, and her back straight.

Sellers didn't smile, but his eyes held no malice.

"Explain."

"Your husband called Stefan from Berlin. The Americans intercepted the phone call."

She tried to tamp down a seed of fear that grew with each word he spoke. Her chin came up. "The Americans want to send us back to Russia."

"No. They want us to keep you safe."

Iveta's eyes narrowed slightly. "Safe? We have no one to fear," she scoffed.

"Iveta, the Russians are very angry. They are angry that your husband left Vector. They are angry that you and your mother and your children left Russia. They are looking for you, but they don't know you are in London. The people who gave your husband the money and passports you used to escape Russia are looking for you. If they capture you..." He looked at the children and shook his head.

"How can you keep us safe?"

"We've made arrangements for you and your family to stay at a cottage in the English countryside. It's quite pleasant and well-guarded."

"What choice do I have?"

Sellers shook his head. "You have no real choice. You will have to trust us. Returning to Russia would be a very poor choice. Allowing your husband's benefactors to capture you would be worse."

Iveta remained silent.

"We will protect you. You are free to decide if you want to go back to Russia. If you decide to stay, you will have the choice to remain in Great Britain or live in the United States."

Iveta's eyes slid to Stefan.

Sellers shook his head. "For now, Stefan must remain in London."

"Why is that? If we are in danger, Stefan must be in danger as well."

"The Russians will be watching Stefan. For his safety, he must continue his usual routine. No one can know he helped you. He won't know where you are, and it will be too dangerous for you to contact him." He paused. "We would like you to be our guests."

"This doesn't sound like guest to me. It sounds like prisoner."

Maria De Costa's kitchen
Columbia, Maryland
Later the same evening

Anne leaned back in her chair. She looked out the window. Rain. The drive to Swan Cove was going to be very wet and very cold. Maria's kitchen was warm and inviting. "You're as good a cook as your mother, Maria."

"Thanks, Aunt Anne. That's quite a compliment coming from you." Maria placed the last of the dinner dishes in the dishwasher. "I made wedding cookies to go along with our coffee." She carried the tray of cookies and cups to the table. "Do you still take your coffee black?"

Anne nodded and nibbled one of the sweets. "Can't improve on perfection. The De Costa recipe is the best."

"I'm glad you told me you would be in town today. It's great to have some time with you. Did you have a meeting at Health and Human Services?"

"No, just a short visit with some old friends."

"Anybody I know?" Maria poured Anne's coffee.

Anne nodded. "Yes, Connor Quinlan and another old friend."

Maria's hand stopped in mid-air. She almost dropped the cup of coffee she was handing to Anne. "Mr. C-I-A Quinlan?"

"The one and only," Anne responded with a chuckle.

"How would I know Mr. Quinlan?"

"You've known him since you were a little girl."

"What do you mean?" Maria looked genuinely confused.

"He often came to the beach house in Lavallette when you were growing up. He was at Mary-Katherine's college graduation and her graduation from law school. He's gone to all the major Quinlan and Fitzgerald family functions for as long as I can remember. He was at M-K's wedding. And, he was at Brittany's baptism."

"Connor Quinlan's part of M-K's family?"

"He's Mary-Katherine's uncle and godfather. Mary-Katherine's mother was a Quinlan."

Maria hit the heel of her hand against her head. "Mary-Katherine's Uncle Connor is Connor Quinlan?"

"'Fraid so."

"Did you get to be friends with him when you were an agent?"

Anne's smile was wistful. "No, I've known him a long time."

"How did you meet him?"

Anne visualized the pristine sand beach, the hollow between the dunes the gang made their own, the friends, the cousins, and the long, lazy summer days. "Connor and I have been friends since sandbox days."

"Sandbox? You mean when you were a little kid?"

Anne's smile turned into a grin. She nodded. "Yes. And our 'sandbox' was the beach in Lavallette. The Damianos and the Quinlans had summer homes there. They were about a block away from the De Costa and O'Reilly beach houses. We were in and out of one another's houses all summer."

"I'm sorry my folks sold the shore house. I miss August in Lavallette. I miss the Jersey shore."

"I do too." Anne sighed.

"By all accounts, Connor Quinlan is quite a guy." Maria bit into her cookie. Crumbs sprinkled the front of her sweater.

"Quite a guy. A good way to describe Connor. And, to answer your question, we did work together when I was in the CIA. He was a part of the reason I was recruited."

"Really?" Maria looked both surprised and doubtful. "Tell me about it."

"About two years after I finished my psychiatry residency I was working at a clinic in Georgetown..."

"Psych residency? But you're a Public Health doc." Maria tried to brush the off crumbs.

"You were just a little girl. The story is a bit complicated. Tonight you'll get the short form. I was working in Georgetown. Connor was a CIA operative. He was in Washington for a few days before he left on assignment. Some very bad people saw us together at dinner one night and decided to kidnap me so they could get to Connor."

"You were kidnapped?" Maria's eyes went wide and unblinking.

Anne gave Maria a 'you-don't-want-to-go-there' look. "No, but it wasn't because they didn't try. I outsmarted them. Connor's boss was impressed. He offered me a job. That was when I did my second residency."

"Connor Quinlan's a handsome man, Aunt Anne. I'm surprised you didn't take him home and keep him for your own."

Anne winced.

"Oops… Didn't mean to hit a sore spot."

"Doesn't matter. Connor and I dated all through high school and part of the way through college."

"So, what happened?"

Anne spread her hands. "We drifted further and further apart during college. He went to law school and into the military. I went to medical school and into my residency." Anne paused to sip a little more coffee.

"That's it?"

"No, of course not. He'd been at Fort Benning for Special Forces training and was home on leave. We went out for dinner. When we got back to my apartment he told me he was going away. He said he probably wouldn't be back and said I shouldn't wait for him."

"But he did come back."

"Yes."

"And?"

"And," Anne leaned back in her chair. Her voice was low, sad, "We never were a couple again." Anne looked down and smoothed her napkin.

Maria pointed her index finger up. "But…"

Anne waved her off. "I'd rather not talk about it. Connor and I have stayed friends."

"More coffee, Aunt Anne?"

"Yes, and another cookie. I have to admit there was another reason I wanted to have dinner with you tonight."

Marie stopped brushing the powdered sugar from her sweater.

"I have a proposal for you."

"A proposal?"

"Do you know about the US AMRIID bio and chem warfare preparedness course?"

"I've heard about it."

"Would you like to take the course?"

"Would I? I'd love to." Maria perked up. "Is there a chance?"

"Yes, but I have to warn you. There's lots of statistics. As I remember, stats wasn't your favorite subject."

Maria's face clouded. "No, but I aced it."

"You aced all your courses in grad school."

Maria brushed off the compliment. "Getting a master's degree from the School of Public Health was a breeze after going through medical school and an Internal Medicine residency."

"There's lots of strenuous drills in the US AMRIID program."

Maria wrinkled her nose. "What kind of drills?"

"The course centers on in-depth preparation for a terrorist attack—bio and chem."

Maria straightened. "Tell me more."

"The class is comprised of people from all the government departments considered essential to the first response team. Military, of course, Health and Human Services, Intelligence."

"Okay, with or without statistics, I'm hooked." She reached for a pencil and paper. "What do I have to do?"

January 13
Jakarta

Perspiration dripped from Yuri's brow, stung his eyes, and glued his shirt to his back. Tossed side to side on the seat of the three-wheeled Bajaj, he clutched the rickety frame to stay upright in the vehicle as it careened through the streets. Yuri was barely able to keep the packet of frozen vials from being crushed.

Tonight I'll give them the envelope, he told himself. Tomorrow I'm not going to fly to Dumayr."

Icy cold settled in his gut and turned the heat and humidity cold and damp. What would they do when they find out he didn't use their ticket and get on the plane to Dumayr. How long would it take them to figure out he flew to London instead.

Seconds later all the minarets in the city erupted with the call to evening prayer.

The driver whipped the Bajaj around and screeched to a halt. Yuri's sweat-slicked hands slipped. He flew forward and slammed his forehead against a metal bar. The driver grabbed his prayer rug, jumped from the vehicle and ran into a mosque.

Yuri pulled a handkerchief from his pocket to mop the perspiration from his forehead. The cloth was soaked with sweat and smeared with blood. Dust and grit coated his teeth. He wiped his mouth with the back of his hand but only succeeded in rubbing more grit onto his lips and into his mouth.

He tried to figure out everything that could go wrong. Will there be someone at the airport to make sure I get on the plane to Dumayr? Will Great Britain grant me political asylum? Will they send me back to Russia? Yuri spent the next half hour trying to consider of all the possibilities." He crossed himself. *Please God, make it work.*

Yuri's driver didn't return when the mosque emptied. Yuri waited. Fog snaked through the filthy streets. Finally, he climbed out of the vehicle and took several tentative steps toward the warehouses.

The vials will not remain frozen for much longer, he thought. Dead virus would be useless.

Huge rats dragged chunks of garbage along the cobblestones. Yuri shrank from them. He tripped on rubbish scattered along the dark street. The smell of rotted fish, mold, urine, and night soil carried by the swirling fog filled his lungs and soaked into his clothes.

Unidentifiable filth sucked at the soles of his shoes.

"Blaya." Yuri cursed. "Whore." He cursed the driver. He cursed the foul smelling fog. And, he cursed Al Halbi.

Full dark descended, the fog thickened and his resolve weakened.

Yuri tried breathing through his mouth so he didn't have to smell the putrid air. But when he opened his mouth, the stench coated his tongue. The disgusting taste seemed to infuse his blood and sweat.

The heart of Jakarta is rotten. This city is the gateway to hell. Yuri thought of snow, of clean fresh air.

There are no people. No lights. No traffic. No landmarks.

Fog rolled over the bulwark of the canal and slinked serpent-like through the warehouse district.

Lazy blankets of thick greasy mist crept along the walls.

Prickles of fear crawled along Yuri's spine, like scorpions hoping to find a target for their lethal poison.

A low whistle. Yuri snapped his head toward the sound.

"Alms, alms for Allah," a young beggar cried.

Yuri collapsed against the wall, cursed, and threw a few coins toward the voice. "Allah Akbar."

A swirl of mist, a break in the thick fog. A man stepped in front of Yuri. "Your gift from Russia?"

Yuri clutched his chest, raised his head, and looked into the blackest eyes he'd ever seen. "Oh, thank God." He could hear his heart pounding. "For the Jihad."

The hood of the man's gray bisht was pulled over his head. Yuri could only see the coal-black eyes. The man snatched the package, shoved an envelope against Yuri's chest, took a few steps to the left, and vanished, enveloped by the fog.

"Foreigners should not walk the Jakarta waterfront at night." A husky whisper floated through the dark. Yuri couldn't tell if the words were in his head or spoken by the man with the ink-black eyes.

Again the young beggar cried, "Alms, alms for Allah."

"Wait!" Yuri's hoarse cry was consumed by the mist. He reached out for the warehouse wall. Empty space. An alley? Yuri cupped his hands beside his mouth. "How will I get to my hotel?" He listened to the hollow words bounce off the alley walls. Yuri took a hesitant step into the alley, then turned to retrace his steps.

"I can't see any lights. Someone, please, help me."

Yuri muttered a prayer from his childhood. "Baby Boja hear me . . ." He wiped away tears. "Boja . . . Boja . . . help me," he moaned. "I'm afraid." He crossed himself. "Help me," he cried. "Please, God, help me. Keep me safe. Please, God. Get me to my hotel."

The fog lifted.

"I see the lights! It is not far. Thank God." Yuri took a deep breath and stepped forward.

Another low whistle.

Then, a grunt, a gurgle, and a thud.

Ibrihim's yacht
Jakarta Waterfront
The same evening

Ibrihim waited on the deck of his yacht and peered into the thick fog. He watched the mist rise from the water and curl toward the dock. His yacht was luxurious and comfortable. The crew was well trained and loyal. They made sure whatever he needed or wanted was at his side or in his hands before he asked.

Tonight was different. The crew had no magic potion to settle his discomfort.

Ibrihim shook his head, and again squinted into the thick fog. Jamul and the boy should have returned by now. "They've been gone too long," he muttered. He paced, stopping after a few steps to stare into the mist.

Finally, two shapes emerged, changing from vaporous gray shadows into solid forms. The boy jumped onto the deck and ran down the steps. Jamul stopped at the top of the gangplank and presented an envelope to Ibrihim. "For the jihad."

"You gave the Russian the money?"

"Yes."

"And you made sure he returned to his hotel?"

Jamul laughed. "There was no need to accompany him anywhere. The Russian is lying in a pool of his infidel blood."

Ibrihim felt his heart skip a beat then rush to send a pounding tattoo in his ears. "What are you saying?"

"The Russian is dead."

Ibrihim's mouth filled with bitter phlegm. He choked the vile taste down. "You killed him?"

"I did not kill him." Jamul puffed up his chest. "An assassin killed him."

"You fool." Ibrihim slapped Jamul hard enough to knock him to the deck.

Jamul curled into a ball. Ibrihim's boot slammed into Jamul's left flank. The fallen man moaned and rolled toward the rail. "The Russian was an infidel. He didn't deserve to live. I heard him call to his God."

"Stupid." Ibrihim hissed the words. "So stupid."

"I brought your package. The Russian was of no further use."

"That was not your decision. Your instructions were to get the package, pay the Russian and make sure he *safely* returned to his hotel."

Jamul sprang to his feet. "Why should I have taken him back to his hotel? He didn't deserve my protection. He was an infidel."

Ibrihim grasped Jamul's cloak and pulled him close. "You have put me at risk. He was to go to his hotel. He was to fly to Dumayr in the morning."

"The Quran says..."

Ibrihim spat at Jamul and threw him against the rail.

A dull pain settled in Ibrihim's chest. His lips began to tingle, to itch. He dropped his face into his hands. How will I explain this to Al Halbi? What will he do? I was instructed to make sure the Russian flew to Syria in the morning.

Ibrihim stalked to his stateroom. He gasped for breath. His chest ached. His fingers tingled.

It is the Imam's fault. The Imam recommended him. He said Jamul could be trusted. Jamul is a disgrace.

He abuses the boy.

He steals from me.

And, he has killed the Russian.

Ibrihim's breaths finally eased. Feeling returned to his fingertips. He staggered to the bathroom and stuck his head under the faucet. Cold water. Ibrihim raised his dripping head and looked in the mirror. The reflected fear in his eyes made him tremble.

Chief of Staff, Collette Demaree, opened the door and nodded to Connor and Donovan. "The President will see you now."

"Thank you, Collette." Connor followed Donovan into the Oval Office.

The Oval Office was decorated to provide comfort and project power: soft blue walls, a cream-colored rug with the Presidential seal, marine blue drapery, Rembrandt Peale's painting of George Washington hung over the mantel. Two Queen Anne armchairs upholstered in cream and blue flanked the fireplace. A row of straight-backed Queen Anne chairs, their seats upholstered with blue and white striped damask, stood in front of the bookcases on the far wall.

President Julian sat in a Moroccan leather office chair behind the Resolute Desk. He glanced at his watch, then looked up and smiled. "Good morning, gentlemen." He gestured to the chairs. "Make yourself comfortable."

"Good morning, Sir," Connor and Donovan answered in unison.

"Donovan, good to see you. What's the occasion?"

Donovan nodded to Connor. "We've got Bushinikov."

Ed Julian straightened and pulled his chair a little closer to the desk. "Good work. How did you manage to capture him?"

"We didn't exactly capture him. By the time we got word about his phone calls, he was no longer in Berlin. We didn't miss him by much. Out surveillance started when Bushinikov arrived in Jakarta. Our people kept very close tabs on him." Connor smiled and suppressed a laugh. "We were able to make a reservation for a room adjoining his at the Mercure."

"How did you manage that?"

"Pure luck, and an agent who can imitate the horrible, high pitched, well enunciated voice so many British women are taught."

The President lowered his head, turned it to one side and winced. "She who must be obeyed?"

Connor laughed. "That's the one. She spoke to the hotel manager and insisted she had to stay at any one of three rooms. She asked for Bushinikov's room or the room on either side of it. You can imagine listening to that voice droning on and on with multiple, silly reasons for having to have that view, that floor, that distance from the elevator. There were a few other excuses I don't remember."

President Julian shook his head. "I'm sure the clerk's toes were curling by the time she was finished. After five minutes of one of her tirades, you'd kill to get her the key to the Taj Mahal."

Connor glanced down at the papers in his hand. "On the second evening a driver arrived at the hotel, picked Bushinikov up, and drove him to the warehouse district. Our agent was able to follow them. When the call to evening prayer came, the driver stopped in front of a mosque, jumped out of the vehicle, and ran into the building. Bushinikov waited for almost an hour. The driver never returned. The Russian got out of the vehicle and walked into the warehouse district. The fog was thick and it was after dark. Our agent could only to follow the sound of the Russian's footsteps."

The President tapped his pen on his desk blotter. "Hard to do." His lower lip puckered a bit. "Sound and direction are hard to interpret in those conditions."

"Yes. The agent lost Bushinikov for a short period of time. When he found the Russian, he was slumped in a doorway with his abdomen slashed."

"The vials?"

"Gone."

"Bushinikov?"

"Barely alive. The agent got Bushinikov to our Embassy's Medical Clinic."

"Is the Russian going to make it?"

Connor's lips pursed, his mouth awry, one eye closed. "They say his chance of survival is slim to none."

"Have we gotten any information about the whereabouts of his family?

"Yes, sir. The Brits have them in a safe-house near London. Right now the Russians have no idea where Bushinikov's family is."

The President stroked his chin. "Good. We have to make sure the Russians stay in the dark. Keep this information under your hats. This conversation is not to go beyond this room."

Donovan closed the thick file and. pushed back from his desk, "According to the Aussies, sanctioned export goods have been going to Syria since 2002. Syria's purchased enough equipment to establish a sophisticated level-four biological laboratory."

Anne rubbed her eyes and checked her watch. She'd worked her way through several hours of classified reports. She placed the last file on the top of the stack. "I can not find an existing building at the Syrian Scientific Studies and Research Center complex in Dumayr able to accommodate all the clean room equipment, animal cages, and laboratory apparatus necessary for a Level Four, or even a Level Three Biological Laboratory."

"We've been at this for almost three and a half hours." Connor waved toward the piles of top secret communications stashed one on top of another. "None of these reports provide evidence of existing facilities being altered in the past five years. Do you think the equipment is sitting in a warehouse gathering dust?"

"Not for a minute. There's got to be a lab somewhere in Syria. We've known about their ability to genetically engineer bacteria and viruses for years." Anne chewed at the edge of her bottom lip. "Al Halbi isn't stupid. He wouldn't have tried to get the virus before he had a laboratory stocked and running."

"I agree." Connor looked up at the ceiling. "The Islamists have sent professors, engineers, scientists, and students to live in the United States and other Western countries. They call on them occasionally... when they're needed." Connor tipped his head to Donovan. "No doubt about it. He must have a laboratory, somewhere."

Donovan's secretary knocked and entered the office. She carried a large coffee carafe in one hand and a box of bagels and cream cheese in the other. She scanned the disarray in the room. The files she'd wheeled in hours before covered the conference room table, Donovan's desk, and were stacked in random piles on the floor.

"Okay, you all. It's time for a break."

"What a great idea." Anne hadn't realized she had her fists clenched. She stood and rubbed her hands to restore the blood supply, shaking them to relieve the tension.

Connor stood and stretched. "Fresh coffee and bagels. And schmear. Perfect."

Amelia laughed. "Somebody has to make sure the three of you get some nourishment. Besides, it's one of my jobs."

"One of your jobs? I didn't know you had a clause in your contract about coffee and bagels at noon. Maybe I should check my secretary's contract again."

"No, my other job. The one that earned me a gold medal for Mother Hen of the Year." She winked at Connor, spun toward the door, and gave a flippant wave over her shoulder on the way out. "Let me know if you want me to order sandwiches for your afternoon recess."

"She's a treasure, Donovan," Anne said as the door closed behind Amelia.

"Yeah, I know. And she's right, we need to relax a bit. Maybe we'll be able to make some sense of all this info after our break. Fresh eyes always catch more detail."

Twenty minutes later, Donovan flipped through his file and read from another report. "A couple of years ago our Department of Defense said Syria has had the will and the knowledge to make biological and chemical weapons. We know they have chemical weapons. They mounted a sarin gas attack against their own people in 2013. And they used chlorine gas on the rebels in April of 2014."

He stood and walked across the room, drew a line on the white board, drew a crosshatch and labeled it '02. "The first sanctioned goods reported." A second crosshatch was labeled '08. "The Australian Center for Strategic International Studies reported the Syrian Scientific Research Center had the scientific expertise to produce biological weapons, and the technological base to develop those weapons."

Donovan drew two more crosshatches and labeled them *4/14 and 9/14*. "Chemical attack in April and the bombings in September." He extended the line and drew a fifth crosshatch. "And, this is where we are now. They have the virus, but we don't know where."

"So, now we know he has the equipment, the scientists and the will to try to make a weapon. He must have a Level Four Bio-Lab." Anne's eyelids puckered with a thoughtful squint. "The bills of lading indicate the equipment was sent to the Syrian Scientific Studies and Research Center in Dumayr. The Syrians bought all the equipment they need to build a world-class facility. It can't be far from the tech center."

Connor tossed the latest report on the table. "I don't think we can wait much longer for the answers."

January 16
Dumayr, Syria

Al Halbi's driver met Ibrihim at the airport. The chauffeur rushed him out of the terminal and into a black Mercedes coupe. The car was parked in the taxi lane. The cab drivers bowed as Ibrihim and the chauffeur passed them.

An overcooled, air-conditioned drive brought Ibrihim to the Institute.

Al Halbi, the director of the Syrian Institute of Science and International Security, a slender, hooked-nose man with India-ink-black hair greeted Ibrihim. His gaze expressed evil. Pure evil. The pale yellow irises were rimmed with flecks of deep emerald green.

He accepted the Styrofoam container from Ibrihim without a word and placed it on a narrow, glass-topped table, then pressed a button on the wall. Seconds later a lab-coated technician entered the office, grasped the Styrofoam package, bowed, and retreated. Al Halbi gave an imperceptible nod before the door closed.

He motioned for Ibrihim to follow into an adjacent room filled with expensive furnishings. Heavy velvet drapes covered the windows. Thick, hand-knotted carpets were spread beneath carved wood furniture. His glance took in the walls of shelves adorned with silver and gold cups and bowls.

Al Halbi's tight smile morphed into a malicious sneer. The hateful look lasted less than a millisecond, a momentary flicker, the sneer disappeared even as it formed, leaving the directors face bland and unwelcoming.

Ibrihim's skin prickled. The director's cold-blooded expression forced him to look away.

Al Halbi clasped Ibrihim's arm, led him to a sitting area, and pushed him toward a chair. The director's strength, flat gaze, and attitude demanded compliance.

Ibrihim tripped over the edge of the carpet and fell into the chair.

A servant wheeled a cart laden with coffee, fruit, and cakes into the room. The man kept his gaze downcast, did not make eye-contact with Al Halbi or Ibrihim. The servant poured thick black coffee into two small cups. He added a generous spoonful of sugar to each cup, then arranged marzipan, dried fruits, and cookies on plates. He straightened his spine and took two steps backwards.

Al Halbi's dismissive wave sent the servant scurrying from the room.

Ibrihim reached toward a small plate filled with figs.

Al Halbi caught Ibrihim's wrist. "Where is the Russian?"

"The Russian?" Ibrihim's words squeaked out of his mouth, gone dry from the fear.

"Yes, the Russian. The Russian who was supposed to be on a flight to Dumayr this morning. The Russian who never left Jakarta." He released Ibrihim's wrist. The director's strange eyes burned with hate.

Ibrihim reached for his coffee. Al Halbi caught his arm again. "I asked you a question. Where is the Russian?" His grip tightened, cutting off circulation to Ibrihim's fingers.

Ibrihim shivered.

Unable to speak with confidence or courage, he shrank deeper into the cushions until Al Halbi yanked him forward. "Tell me now. Where is the Russian?"

"The Russian is dead. He was stabbed," Ibrihim whispered, "near the warehouse. After he delivered the vials."

Al Halbi pulled Ibrihim closer, and spat words into his face, "The Russian was under your protection."

"The warehouse district is a dangerous place at night." Ibrihim's words were an almost unintelligible mumble, his statement hesitant, cowed.

"You were instructed to obtain the package and ensure the safety of the Russian. It was *your* responsibility to get him to the airport in the morning."

"My intermediary was instructed to get the package from the Russian and provide a means of getting the Russian to his hotel."

Ibrihim sounded, even to his own ears, like a pre-adolescent boy. Sweat coated the back of his neck.

"Your intermediary? You trusted this to an intermediary?"

"My Imam told me Jamul could be trusted."

Al Halbi grabbed Ibrihim's shirt, twisted the fabric, and yanked him even closer. "Disobey me again at your peril." He pushed Ibrihim away with a twist and a powerful shove that slammed Ibrihim into the cushions. Ibrihim's teeth bit into his tongue.

Al Halbi clenched and unclenched his hands, eyes locked on Ibrihim as if he could drill destruction into the man's heart. "You were *not* told to send an intermediary for the package. *You* were instructed to meet the Russian. *You* were ordered to protect the scientist."

Al Halbi tugged at his beard. His lips compressed into a hard, straight line, his eyes narrowed to mere slits.

"The scientist was to return to his hotel. He was to fly to Dumayr this morning."

Al Halbi's voice dropped low, and underlined his displeasure. "Get up. We are going to take a drive."

"A drive?" Ibrihim couldn't breathe. Couldn't move. Couldn't stand. Fear prevented him getting on his feet, as if he was cemented to the chair. He fought nausea, liquid churned in his bowels, haze crept into the edges of his vision. "Where are you taking me?"

Al Halbi stood. "We will go to the laboratory, *now.*" The director spat out the last word. His voice was low, quiet. "It is time to leave." The statement whispered disdain and screamed derision.

Ibrihim forced himself to stand.

Al Halbi prodded him toward the door.

Ibrihim shuffled and stumbled, forced forward by Al Halbi.

A dusty hour later brought them to a dilapidated wood building. Al Halbi stepped out of the vehicle and gestured toward the shack.

"We are here," he said in a measured, icy tone.

Ibrihim slid out of the Mercedes but kept a death-grip on the door handle. "We are nowhere. There is no laboratory." His voice sounded tinny. He tried to clear his throat and swallow his panic.

"Follow me." Al Halbi walked away, along a narrow path.

Ibrihim felt vomit well in his throat, tried to swallow the bitter taste. His left hand kept the firm grasp on the door handle.

The chauffeur stomped on the accelerator and yanked Ibrihim forward.

Ibrihim lost his grip and stumbled. He felt as if his left arm had been ripped from its socket. His right arm and left knee broke his fall.

The vehicle vanished in the trail of dust.

"Do you plan to leave me to die in the desert?"

Al Halbi looked down at Ibrihim, his eyes mere slits, the pupils constricted to a pin prick, only the vile yellow iris visible. "You should not allow fear to over-ride rational thought."

"Take me back to Dumayr." Ibrihim swallowed several more times to prevent vomit from spewing across the sand. "Find someone else to be your slave."

Al Halbi opened the cracked, wooden shed door and motioned to Ibrihim. "Get up, fool. You are not finished. You will do what I tell you. And, you will not deviate from my plan again. You still have much to do."

Ibrihim struggled upright, brushed the sand off his clothes, and followed Al Halbi into the shack.

Almost a minute passed before Ibrihim's eyes could adjust to the darkened interior. The temperature inside the shack was at least twenty degrees hotter than in the open desert. He stood in a dusty, low ceilinged room. When he tried to stand straight, his hair brushed against the ceiling. A filthy carpet covered the floor.

Despite the heat, Ibrihim shivered. His mouth was dry. His hands trembled. It felt as if all the oxygen had been sucked out of the hovel. He fought the urge to turn and run. "This is just an empty shack. The dust is suffocating. I'll wait outside."

"You will stay right here, and you will do as I say." The venom in the director's voice left no choice.

Al Halbi leaned over, flipped up a corner of the carpet, pushed it aside, and pulled open a trapdoor. Dim light rose from the pit. A steel ladder was propped against one side of the shaft.

Al Halbi pushed Ibrihim toward the opening. "Go down."

Ibrihim hesitated. A look from Al Halbi forced him down the ladder. His chest ached. *I'll be left to starve in this hole.*

Al Halbi climbed halfway down the ladder, pulled the trapdoor shut, and descended to the floor of the pit. The sandstone walls looked unforgiving. Heavy screws bolted the ladder to the concrete floor

Lightheaded and weak-kneed, Ibrihim leaned against the wall, then jerked upright as what looked like a solid stone wall slid open to reveal a hallway, wide and well-lit.

"I see you've discovered the entrance." Al Halbi's laugh echoed off the walls, piercing and sarcastic.

They stepped into the bright white-tiled laboratory.

Ibrihim watched the six inch thick, steel pocket-door slide shut. The temperature dropped thirty degrees. Perspiration that glued Ibrihim's clothing to his back turned clammy-cold.

"Welcome to my laboratory." Al Halbi's arm swept toward the passage. "Few who enter will ever leave. You are one of the chosen."

Al Halbi laughed and pushed Ibrihim forward when he was immobilized by panic. Al Halbi continued to laugh and shove the frightened man along corridor.

Ibrihim looked into rooms with stinking animal cages, laboratories, dormitories, kitchens, lavatories, storage rooms, and offices. Rooms with refrigeration units. Rooms with incubators. And, rooms filled with young children.

Al Halbi stopped in front of a double-doored dormitory. The outside door was a metal pocket door, the inside door was steel bars. He pointed at the children in the room. "These are our test subjects. Orphans from the recent disturbances."

All around them, the facility buzzed with activity. White-coated lab workers walked with purpose from room to room. Ibrihim began to perspire, despite the temperature-controlled environment. He quivered from the panic that crept along the passage with him, feeling as if the walls were closing in with each step away from the entrance.

Al Halbi slid his hand across the smooth white tile. His gesture was like a caress. "Beautiful, isn't she. Beautiful and strong. We are ten feet underground. The walls, floors and ceiling are half a meter thick. They're made from a special concrete mixture fortified with quartz and fibers." His expression became one of sexual satisfaction.

Ibrihim felt his heart pound. His breaths came in painful gasps. He fought nausea and dizziness. How can people work here, locked in a tunnel under the desert? He stumbled, fell against the wall, and looked up to see Al Halbi's malicious sneer.

Halfway down the corridor, Al Halbi opened the door to an opulent room. A window cut into the door was secured with decorative wrought-iron grill work. The room held an elaborate, carved table, surrounded by matching upholstered chairs. The table was set with embroidered linens, bone china, silver utensils and crystal. A sofa and two lounge chairs flanked a low coffee table that held a silver bowl filled with fresh fruit. An Oriental carpet covered the floor. The walls were draped with burgundy silk. "My home-away-from-home," Al Halbi boasted. "My tent in the desert."

Al Halbi laughed, closed the door and continued down the hall. At the end of the hallway, he pushed a tile, and waited as the wall slid aside. Another shove sent Ibrihim into a pit similar to the one they used to enter the laboratory.

Ibrihim sprinted up the ladder to shove the trap door open. He climbed to the last rung and found himself standing in another shack. A torn remnant of cloth hung over a small window. He walked to the window and pushed the tattered curtain aside.

The Mercedes waited outside.

Al Halbi's Office
Syrian Scientific Studies and Research Center
Dumayr, Syria
A few hours later

Al Halbi paced the length of his office and stroked his beard. There was no confirmation that the Russian was dead. Ibrihim's associate said the Russian had been stabbed. What if the Russian didn't die? Where could Bushinikov be?

The Syrian couldn't comprehend how the Russian could have survived. He stopped and stared at the dust motes floating in the slant of sunlight. The inside of his cheek was raw from his gnawing at the tissue. But, suppose the Russian survived the attempt on his life? Al Halbi paused and looked up at the ceiling.

What if the Russian made a deal with Ibrihim? What if Bushinikov went to London? Was Ibrihim complicit in allowing the Russian to escape to the west?

Al Halbi shook his head. Too many pieces of the puzzle were missing. Too many unanswered questions. The Russian's family. They might be the key. Where were they? Did they reach London? He turned on the ball of his Italian leather shoes and moved to a recessed alcove. A chessboard, dusty with disuse, was tucked into the space. He yanked the velvet drape open. The heavy fabric hit the Black King and knocked it into a Knight. The Knight knocked over a Pawn. Al Halbi pondered the pieces, oblivious to the window's reflected heat.

Of course. Adi Shamash. Adi Shamash is the answer.

January 17
Donovan's Office
CIA Headquarters
Langley, Virginia

Donovan's intercom buzzed. "Dr. Damiano and Connor Quinlan are here."

"Thank you, Amelia, send them in."

Donovan stood to greet the pair. "Anne, Connor, come in. Grab a cup of coffee." Donovan pointed to the ever-filled carafe. His office had soundproofed walls and ceiling. The entire suite was windowless and the temperature was kept at a constant seventy degrees. Pictures of Donovan with various dignitaries covered one wall. The pictures were a visual testament of his successful years in the Company.

His large L-shaped desk held several computer screens, a secure telephone, and a work space flanked with pictures of his family. Smiling faces of Hugh and Suzie Donovan on their twenty-fifth anniversary, his daughter, Erin, en pointe as the Dying Swan, and the Naval Academy graduation picture of his son, Eric.

The coffee carafe and a box of donuts waited in the center of the large conference table. Cups, ready to be filled, were grouped around the carafe. "Have a seat." Donovan gestured toward the conference table with leather padded chairs lining each side.

Seconds later Donovan's secretary, Amelia, backed into the room pulling a cart piled high with red and white striped envelopes marked "Top Secret."

"How do you keep this man supplied with fresh coffee, Amelia? It's a wonder you have time to do the work he assigns to you." Anne picked up a mug. "And you make excellent coffee."

"If I feed his caffeine addiction, he stays happy. That makes my life a whole lot easier. But, I do find the time to accomplish a few other chores." She gestured toward the mass of documents on the cart.

"Thank you, Amelia." Donovan drained his cup. He waited until she'd left the room and closed the door, then he looked across the table at Anne.

"Your comment about the Syrians having a lab made sense. I decided we should start looking for possible sites. I asked the geospatial people at Livermore to search for any signs of excavation near Dumayr. I asked them to go back twenty years. The team decided to go back thirty years."

Donovan placed a satellite image on the table. The picture revealed a wide expanse of desert and an excavation project. "This is what they found. The people at Livermore seem to think this project is a possibility. I'm not sure why they think this is significant. All I see in these photographs is tons of sand excavation."

Donovan grabbed another file from the cart. "So, I thought I'd share the files with you. Maybe fresh eyes can find what I can't see."

Anne carried a stack of the folders and retreated to one end of the large conference table. There were maps, satellite pictures, and communication reports piled at her end of the table. Each satellite image was marked with latitude, longitude, and date of acquisition. The satellite images concentrated on a specific project. It looked as if the Syrian's were building a roadway across the desert. But, the road didn't lead to any obvious village or compound.

The road moved in a straight line across the vast, arid stretch of land. Sidebar information explained that heavy machinery cleared and leveled a rudimentary roadbed.

Donovan had a batch of subsequent pictures. These pictures showed the road construction occasionally stopped while the crew built a warehouse. Approximately ten days later the warehouse would be dismantled, the road continued, and another warehouse was built. The pattern repeated itself for months. Most of the warehouses were destroyed. There were some interspersed shacks erected fifty or so feet from the road. To Anne those buildings looked to be about the size of a one-seater outdoor privy.

Two somewhat larger shacks were built about a hundred yards apart. They stood at the beginning and at the end of the original dig.

In the final images only a dirt road, the two shacks, twelve small outbuildings, and one dilapidated warehouse remained. There was a road of sorts, probably left by all the heavy equipment during their exodus from the site.

One headache and four hours later Anne pushed her chair back from the table. "I need a couple of aspirin." She reached in her purse, pulled out a small container, flipped the top open, and shook out two tablets. She washed down the aspirin with the remaining cold coffee in her cup.

Anne squinted to read the time and date markings. "These images date back to the nineties. Where did they take all the truckloads of excavated sand?"

"The Syrians were building pipelines, roads, and airports near the oil fields." Donovan bit into a donut and followed it with a sip of coffee.

"God knows they have enough sand and gravel in that country to scrape up for construction," Connor added.

Anne, skeptical about the layouts, voiced her concern. "But those construction projects were far from this area." She paced back and forth in front of the photographs. "Doesn't make any sense."

"What are you thinking?" Connor had learned to trust Anne's instincts. Her intuition had saved his life on more than one occasion.

"If all they wanted to do was excavate sand, why would they build warehouses?"

"Maybe they built the warehouses to provide living quarters for the workers." Connor put down the report he was reading and walked over to the table.

She stopped short and caught her lower lip with her teeth. The answer came in a flash, crystal clear. "I don't think so. Look at this." She pointed out several of the photographs. "Trucks filled with sand face Dumayr. That's expected if all they were doing was excavating sand." She indicated others. "But, how do you explain all these trucks filled with boxes that go toward the warehouse?"

"They would have had to bring in equipment to do the excavation, food for the workers, all kinds of machinery, and other supplies."

"Okay, if we accept that premise please tell me why we don't see any workers?" She looked up at Connor and Donovan.

Both men answered her with exaggerated shrugs.

"And, what makes no sense at all is if all they wanted was sand and rocks why didn't they just come in with heavy equipment and dig up the sand and load it onto trucks?"

"Yeah. That's what they did."

"No, it's not. They removed a lot of sand. But, according to these pictures all the truckloads of sand came from inside the warehouses." She reshuffled the photographs. "And, they pulled one heck of a lot of sand out of each warehouse."

Anne laid the images in two lines down the length of the conference table. "It looks like a hundred or more trucks loaded with sand headed toward Dumayr. And that's only the ones that were picked up by the satellite. Who knows how many more there might have been. There's no evidence of the machinery used to fill the trucks with sand. No cranes. No bulldozers."

Connor and Donovan stood and walked around to Anne's side of the table. Their faces reflected the question Anne posed.

"Who builds warehouses to dig up sand?" Anne returned to the coffee carafe for a refill. She pointed her chin at Connor, "Why would they fill trucks with sand here and carry it to places so far away? What was in the boxes they were taking into the warehouses? Where did they put whatever they had in them? And, why isn't there evidence of boxes or used equipment leaving the warehouses? The only thing in the trucks heading back to Duma is sand."

"The satellite only takes pictures when it's over an area." Connor reminded her.

"Yes. But don't you think at least one picture would have shown used equipment leaving the construction site?"

Donovan put down his coffee cup, rubbed his chin and took another look at the photographs. "Okay, point taken. Recheck all the dates. But, keep in mind that Syria signed the treaty set forth by the Biological and Toxin Weapons Convention in 1972."

"Right. And you're telling me to believe that a signature on a piece of paper has ever kept an adversary from violating a treaty?"

Donovan picked up his coffee cup and walked to the carafe for a refill. "Another good point."

Connor leaned over to get a better look at the dates on the photographs. He stood straight and arched his back and neck. "I guess no one gave these images more than a cursory glance. We were concentrating on Iraq and Kuwait."

Anne rechecked the location and date stamps, then shuffled the images. She arranged the pictures into two long lines.

Donovan returned and looked at the array. "What are you doing?"

"This excavation may have supplied sand and rock for their highways and airports, but I'm betting it also served to hide the construction of a laboratory."

"What are you talking about?" Donovan scowled. He pointed to the second row of photographs. "There's no lab there. Just some broken-down shacks a dirt road, and an old warehouse that looks like it's in terrible shape."

Anne pointed to the first line of photographs. "These show the original construction sites moving across the desert." She took a deep breath and pointed to the second line. "And this is what the desert landscape looked like when the construction was complete."

Donovan's face was getting red. "So?"

"You can't see the lab because you're not looking hard enough. It's there. I can see it. For years we've looked at these pictures. We haven't looked hard enough. What we see is nothing but some buildings left in the desert to decay. Exactly the impression the Syrians want. They don't want us to see the lab."

Donovan stared at the display. He raised his left hand palm up. "So where is the lab?"

Anne cut strips of paper and placed them across the second row of pictures. She connected the shacks at each end with the warehouse entrance in the center. Then she placed shorter lengths to reach out to each of the sheds. "The lab is right there," she paused to watch Connor and Donovan squint and look up at her with the first spark of understanding.

She gave a grim smile. "Underground."

Ambassador Fry's intercom buzzed. "Dr. Smith is here to see you."

"Thanks, Connie. Send him in." Tom Frey looked up from his papers. His office reflected items from the many cultures of the Indonesian population. Beautiful porcelain lamps from China, hand knotted rugs from India, a teak-wood floor, carved chests, and mahogany tables were in abundance.

A disheveled physician entered the room and stood in front of the ambassador's desk. Tyler Smith's eyes were bloodshot, his hair hung over his forehead, two days' worth of whiskers covered his chin, and his usually spotless, starched lab coat was wrinkled and stained.

"My God, Smith. You're a mess. You looked exhausted."

"I *am* exhausted. I've been at the clinic for forty-six hours."

"How's our patient doing?"

Smith shook his head. "He's failing." The doctor's shoulders slumped. Smith sank into an overstuffed armchair covered in a bright Polynesian print.

"What's wrong?"

"He's septic."

"Septic?"

Smith raised his hands, then let them drop to the arms of the chair. "The infection is in his bloodstream."

"Is that bad?"

"Very bad. He needs to be at a facility with up-to-date drugs and equipment. We need to send him to a real hospital. He has no chance to survive if we keep him here."

"We don't have a secure hospital in Indonesia. You'll just have to do your best."

Smith stood, put his hands on the ambassador's desk, and leaned toward him. "My best will kill him under these circumstances. *He needs a hospital.* A *real* hospital with an intensive care unit, a laboratory, and antibiotics. I can't order any of the drugs he needs. The antibiotics alone would raise all kinds of red flags." Smith straightened. "Whoever stabbed this man must have used the dirtiest knife in Jakarta."

"Move him? Move him where? I'm not sure we can move him."

"If you want him to survive you'll have to figure out something."

"Sounds like an impossible task. But, I'll call the team. Maybe someone will have a workable solution." Ambassador Frey pushed an intercom button. "Connie, call everyone on the security committee. We need to have a meeting."

In less than thirty minutes key members of the embassy staff were seated at the conference table in the ambassador's office.

Dr. Smith outlined the problem.

"We need to save this man. Does anyone have an idea on how we can help him?" the ambassador asked.

Colonel Mitchel spoke first. "The closest US military trauma center is in Hawaii. Its sixty-seven hundred air miles from here. Do you think that would work?"

Tyler Smith shook his head. "Too far away." He rubbed his right eye with the heel of his hand. "If we want him to survive the transport, the hospital has to be much closer."

"How about the Aussies? They have a great facility in Perth." the deputy chief of missions suggested. "Maybe they'll agree to help."

"How far away is Perth?"

"Less than two thousand miles."

A gleam of hope crossed Tom Frey's face. "Great idea, Robert. Connie, get the Australian ambassador on the secure phone, please."

An hour later a delegation from the US embassy visited the Australian ambassador. The cortege included Bushinikov and Tyler Smith.

Royal Perth Hospital agreed to admit Stavros Trzcynski, a member of the Australian embassy staff, to the surgical intensive care unit. They understood Mr. Trzcynski had suffered a ruptured appendix complicated by peritonitis and septicemia. An emergency transfer to the hospital in Perth was essential.

At 1330 hours, the Royal Australian Air Force took off for Perth.

The President glanced at his watch. "Good morning, gentlemen. You're both here, again. This is getting to be a habit. I hope this is good news."

"Good morning, Sir," Connor said. "We got an update from Perth a few hours ago."

President Julian looked pensive. "How's Mr. Trzcynski doing?"

Connor glanced at Donovan and tilted his head. "They're hopeful. His infection has started to respond to treatment. He's in a lot of pain. The doctors are still concerned that he'll go into kidney failure. They're administering some pretty powerful drugs. Drugs that have to be carefully titrated. These medications are a double edged sword. They will eliminate the infection. But, they might do significant damage to several organ systems in the process."

Donovan took over. "The Aussies plan to transfer him to Tripler as soon as he is able to survive the trip. He's going to have to travel commercial. And we'll have to get him another alias and the papers to go with it."

President Julian tapped his index finger on his desk. "How long will it be before they send him to Georgetown?"

"The doctors think it will be a couple of weeks," Connor said. "But, they're pulling out all the stops to make it earlier."

"I hope it doesn't take weeks." President Julian glanced toward the window. "We need to get him into a safe house. Every delay increases the chance that either the Syrians or the Russians are going to find him." The President paused. "And speaking of the Russians, have we heard anything from them?"

Connor consulted his notes. "Not much. Russia House says they don't know the whereabouts of Bushinikov, his wife, his children, or his mother-in-law."

"How much longer will we be able to keep them in the dark?"

"There's no telling. But, that might be the least of our problems, Sir." Connor continued without waiting for the President to reply. "The Syrians know Bushinikov's family made it to London."

"I thought they were in a safe house."

"Bushinikov's wife, children and mother-in-law are in a safe house. The Syrians attempted to get to the cousin in London. MI6 has put Golovin in a safe house as well."

"Won't that raise the suspicions of the Russians?"

"I thought it might, but not so far. The Brits notified the Russian government that Golovin sought political asylum. The Russians have no idea he's involved in the family's disappearance."

"Let's hope that information stays under their radar." The President shook his head. "I doubt it will."

Connor opened a second fine on the conference table. "Things are not all doom and gloom, Sir. I have some good news."

President Julian waited.

Connor smiled, "We've located the bioweapon laboratory in Syria." He spread Anne's projection of the laboratory on the table.

The three men perused the outline of the excavation.

"What evidence do we have that will verify her theory?" The President pointed to Connor.

"Not much. We have a small amount of information from a trusted source that supports the possibility of an underground laboratory. And there's lot of speculation. Scientists bragged about being chosen for a secret special project several years ago. They disappeared one by one and haven't been seen again. Lots of orphans have disappeared as well."

"Where do you suppose the children went?"

Connor cleared his throat. "The answers are vague. No one knows where the children are. There are rumors about children being kid-napped by the sex trade, other rumors about orphans being taken to a place where they test diseases." Connor ran his finger around his collar, uncomfortable with the thought, repelled by the idea.

The President frowned. His consternation evident. "That's it? Rumors about children sold to sex traders? Rumors about medical testing? I'd like to hear a better explanation—one that contains verifiable information."

"Yes, Sir. I understand. We've made contact with the owner of a company that delivers food and other supplies to this building." He pointed to the dilapidated warehouse on the satellite photo. "For the past decade he's been bringing supplies to the warehouse. Enormous amounts of food and supplies. And, he also told us the laundry he's carried back and forth has been prodigious. Sounds like a fair number of people live and work there."

The President rubbed his chin. He was quiet for a few moments. "Looks promising."

"There's more, Sir." Connor turned a page in his portfolio. "We have a few satellite images of a Mercedes parked here." Connor pointed to a structure on the west end of the diagram. "It's the same model as the Mercedes owned by the director of the Syrian Scientific Studies and Research Center."

President Julian put the intelligence report into a folder on his desk. "Continue to collect as much intelligence as you can. In the meantime, I'm going to talk to some folks at the Pentagon. Obviously we're going to need a team to take out the lab if this information is valid."

January 28
Ruth's Chris Steakhouse
Arlington, Virginia
The next evening

Anne sat at a table overlooking Reagan National Airport. Large windows in the Ruth's Chris lounge were positioned for customers to watch aircraft landing and departing. The lounge had a sweeping oval bar. Windows framed in gold drapes stretched the length of two walls. Comfortable chairs with tan-gold fabric upholstery surrounded tables scattered between the bar and the windows. Anne glanced at her watch. The fingers of her right hand beat a tattoo as she waited.

Her waiter approached. "Excuse me, ma'am. May I bring you a cocktail while you're waiting for your friend?"

"Thank you. A Perrier and lime would be great. He must be running late." Anne fiddled with her pearl necklace. *Connor Quinlan's always running late.* If he isn't at his computer, trying to solve a problem, he's talking to Donovan, or the President, or . . .

Connor stood at the entrance to the lounge and scanned the room. Anne was at their usual table, her shoulders slumped, lips pressed together. *Not a good sign. I wonder what's going on.*

He strode across the room. "Sorry I'm late." He bent down to kiss her cheek, then slid into the chair across from her and took her hand. "Really sorry."

The waiter approached. "Welcome to Ruth's Chris, sir. Would you like to order a cocktail before dinner?"

Anne pulled her hand from Connor' grasp and cleared her throat. "A Tanqueray martini on the rocks with a twist for the gentleman, please."

Connor looked up. The tone of her voice wasn't like Anne at all. *She's upset.* In the past the phrase was playful, a way to tease each other and the waiters. Tonight her voice was flat, her eyes without expression. Very upset. Connor closed his eyes, rubbed his forehead, and drew out his words.

"Let me think. A Bloody Mary, light on the spice and light on the vodka, would be perfect for m'lady." He exaggerated the required response in hopes of softening her mood.

The waiter smiled at Connor's antics. "Sounds like you two have done this before." He handed them menus. "I'll be back in a few minutes to take your dinner orders."

Anne turned toward the window. "Did Donovan make you stay late at the office this evening?" Her tone was sarcastic. "Some National emergency? Some other problem of earth-shaking importance?"

Connor shook his head. "Just a busy day and beltway traffic. Seems like there's never a break in the action."

"*Seems* like an excuse I've heard before. *Seems* as if you could have sent me a text message to let me know you'd be late. *Seems* like I'm no longer a trusted member of the team. *Seems* like I've been excluded from recent meetings at Langley. And, *it seems* like I'm being kept out of the action."

He had figured this was coming. *But, I didn't think it would happen so soon.* "Anne—"

"So, why have I been cut out of the loop?"

"C'mon Anne, you know the drill."

She leaned forward, her voice low, her words clipped and precise. "Drill? What drill? Our country is facing a huge threat and you're talking about drills?"

Connor put his palms up as if to ward off the accusation. "You're a valuable part of the team. Our lack of . . . It's not because . . . It's . . . For now—"

"Okay, I get it," Anne said. "Even though I'm a part of the team I don't have a 'need to know.'"

Connor shook his head. "No . . . That's not it. Just . . . we have to—"

"Forget about it."

"Forget about it?" Connor rubbed the back of his neck; his shoulders slumped. "You never give up so easy."

"I'm not in the mood to play games. I don't know what's going on, and at this point I'm past the point of caring. I'm going to put in a formal request to be read out of the project. There's no point in staying on the outside while whatever is going on inside isn't shared with me."

Before Connor could answer the waiter appeared, serving their cocktails with a flourish. He handed each a menu. "Would you like an appetizer? Shrimp cocktail? Crab cakes?"

Anne shook her head. "Not for me, thanks. I've lost my appetite."

Connor placed his menu aside. "Give us a few more minutes."

Anne stirred her drink. She didn't make eye contact with Connor, and she didn't open the menu.

Connor pushed the base of his martini glass in random circles. The silence stretched into long minutes. How was he going to get around this? The President said to keep the info sub rosa. Connor rubbed his right shoulder, a mindless habit from a long-ago injury.

"Stressed?" Anne said, eyebrows arched, voice caustic.

"What makes you think I'm stressed?"

"You always rub your shoulder when you're stressed."

"Yeah, or if the weather changes, or if I've overworked at the gym, or if I've carried an antique wardrobe up several flights of stairs. And, before you ask, my knee is fine."

"Even after you carried a wardrobe up to the attic?" She tossed her head and looked to heaven.

"So much for backing off," he said. "Can we at least have a truce during dinner?"

"A truce?" She drummed her nails on the tablecloth.

The doubt in her voice sent a chill from his heart to his groin. "Please be patient, you know how it is in Washington. If a clearance and a turtle were racing, the turtle would win."

Her breath caught. *It was the President.* She looked up at Connor.

He saw a flicker of understanding. Relief flooded through him, he could feel his heart rate slow to normal, his stomach unclench.

She pursed her lips and nodded. "Okay. You've got your truce, Mr. Turtle."

Three hours later Connor sank into the limo's soft leather seat and checked his watch. *Thank goodness I requested a car and driver. I'm way too tired to drive back to Langley.*

The car turned onto the beltway. Exit signs flashed by.

I hate nights like this. Anne goes to the cottage, alone, and I go back to my office. He closed his eyes. *Oh, Annie, no one knows how much I love you.* "Not even you."

"Excuse me, sir, I didn't hear you." The driver stared at him in the rearview mirror.

Conner shook his head. "Sorry, Corporal. Thinking out loud."

January 29
Jakarta, Indonesia

Ibrihim breathed in the gasoline scented air of the harbor, a familiar and comforting smell for him. A packet of powder Al Halbi had given him and his second installment of the money was locked in his briefcase. He was grateful to be alive, relieved to be away from the desert and out of the confines of the hideous underground laboratory. He shivered, his skin crawled when he thought of his walk through the lab. How can those people live underground? *It's like being buried alive.*

Back in his cabin, he unrolled his prayer rug and thanked Allah for his good fortune.

At his request the captain took the yacht out. As soon as they were beyond the harbor limits he stepped up to the flying bridge. Fresh salty air filled his lungs and cooled his body. They were far from the tainted air of the harbor.

Jamul dragged the boy, clean and dressed in satin robes, to the bridge. "I am glad you had a safe trip. It is good to be at sea, again."

Ibrihim guessed the boy to be eleven or twelve. "What is the boy's name?"

"Simi." Jamul walked toward the child.

Simi cowered and seemed to shrink with each approaching step.

Jamul pulled Simi up in front of Ibrihim. "Stand straight," he scolded, and turned to Ibrihim. "Simi has provided great value to me."

"You should feed him better and give him more time to rest. He will not be able to walk the length of the waterfront alley if you continue to *value* him."

"He's happy to be off the street. He does what I wish."

"Tomorrow you will take the powder to the warehouse."

Ibrihim started down the steps. He was tired from the long plane trip and exhausted from his time in the desert, his revulsion of the laboratory, and his encounter with Al Halbi. Halfway down the stairs he stopped, turned, and said through clenched teeth. "Come to my cabin tomorrow at dawn. You and the boy."

"I told you to be at my cabin at dawn." Ibrihim kicked Jamul's door. "It's already midmorning."

Jamul staggered onto the deck and blinked in the harsh light.

"Where's your urchin?"

Jamul tipped his head toward the cabin.

"Bring the boy to me."

Jamul returned to his cabin and a few minutes later dragged the child on deck. "He's ready to do whatever you wish."

Ibrihim's mouth flooded with disgust.

Simi stared at the deck and shifted his weight from one foot to the other.

"What I wish is for the boy to distribute the powder and return without incident."

Ibrihim checked his watch. "It's time for you to go to the warehouse."

Ibrihim cupped Simi's chin to gently raise the child's face. "You look intelligent enough. Tell me what you've been instructed to do today."

"I will take the powder to the warehouse and sprinkle it in the boxes marked with this sign." He drew a symbol in the air with his finger: Ω. The Greek symbol *omega*. "When I've used up all the powder, I'll return to the yacht."

"Very good. That is correct." He tousled Simi's hair.

The boy bowed his head and drew back from the man's touch.

Ibrihim moved to the railing. "Come here."

The child took a few steps toward him.

Ibrihim knelt to be eye-level with the boy.

"Do you have enough to eat?"

Simi raised his head and nodded, then looked down at the deck again.

"Do you like your fine new clothes?"

Simi nodded.

"Are you being treated well?"

Simi's head dipped, a slight nod.

"Speak up, boy," Jamul chided.

"I'm treated well," Simi muttered. He continued to stare at the deck.

"Wear your rags to the warehouse; leave your fine clothing here," Ibrihim said.

Simi nodded.

"When you've completed your task, you'll come to my quarters. You will never return to Jamul's cabin."

Jamul took two steps forward and opened his mouth. Ibrihim flashed a look. It froze the man's protest. "Give the boy his rags and be quick about it. You've already wasted too much time this morning. He'll carry the powder today. Follow him, and make sure he gets the powder in the correct containers. You can have breakfast when you return."

Simi jumped off the yacht and dashed to the waterfront A maze of carts, trucks, and vendors crowded the streets. Simi darted around piles of mule droppings and horse dung. He dashed into the warehouse and dodged between the containers, looking for the symbol. Before Jamul could catch up, he'd found three cartons marked with the omega.

The boy scattered a small portion of the powder over the garments in each marked carton.

When Jamul reached the fourth carton, he pinned Simi against the crate. "Tonight you will go to Ibrihim's cabin." He grabbed the boy, pulled his head close, and ground his groin against the child's face.

Simi jerked away but Jamul caught his arm and yanked him back. "Now you reject me? I found you. I make sure you are well fed. I purchase your clothes."

Jamul lifted the boy and threw him face-down over the edge of the open crate. The plastic bag slipped from Simi's hand and spilled the remaining powder into the container. When Jamul attempted to pull the boy's clothing loose, Simi kicked.

Jamul fell to the warehouse floor, gasping.

Putra strolled into the concierge room in the Hotel Kempinski. He settled in one of the leather-lined booths to wait. Another boring luncheon with his sister's husband. He'd agreed to the meetings to appease his wife and his sister. He pretended annoyance at taking time from his import-export business. Having access to an Imam with connections to the more radical elements in Jakarta was a benefit. The acceptance increased his ability to look sympathetic to their cause. There was also the chance, however remote, he would learn information he could transmit to Langley.

Putra's father, a nuclear physicist, accepted a faculty position in the Engineering Department at the University of Minnesota thirty years before. When it was time to leave for the United States, Putra's four older brothers refused to leave Jakarta. They remained in Indonesia and lived with their grandparents. His two eldest sisters had been promised and married into wealthy families in Jakarta. The three youngest children, two girls and a boy, were taken to Minnesota. Putra was born six months after his parents arrived in the United States.

His family were devout Muslims, attended mosque faithfully and followed the mandates and traditions. Both of Putra's youngest sisters were sent back to Indonesia in arranged marriages. Only Putra and his brother remained in the United States with their parents. However, the family took yearly vacations to visit Putra's grandparents and his siblings.

He was an outstanding student in high school and college, an accomplished soccer player, and an ardent fan of the Minnesota Vikings. His language skills were impressive. Putra was fluent in English and Bahasa, the Arabian dialect of Indonesia, and he had a good understanding of classical Arabic. In addition he elected to take Russian to fulfill his second language requirements in college.

He applied and was accepted into Wharton School of Business at the University of Pennsylvania. The CIA approached him during his last semester of graduate school. He jumped at the chance to be a part of the organization.

Putra completed his training at the Farm a few months before 9/11 and became an undercover agent in Jakarta. He started an import/export business in Jakarta which became very successful in record time. And, provided a reasonable cover for his multiple trips abroad.

His family made arrangements for him to marry a woman from a wealthy Muslim family in Jakarta. Putra realized the danger. If he was exposed, he would be tortured and interrogated. And, when they finished getting all the information they could force out of him, they would kill him. Still, Putra was compelled to work against the forces of the radical extremists.

Today, he relaxed and enjoyed the ambiance of the room. Larger-than-life photographs of Sukarno, the first President of Indonesia, covered the walls. Sukarno with John F. Kennedy. Sukarno with Marilyn Monroe. He expected his lunch companion to be late. Bhima, his brother-in-law, was always late. His sister's husband was the Imam at one of the local mosques.

After a wait of thirty minutes, his brother-in-law rushed into the room. Bhima was overweight, out of breath, sweating.

Putra stood and bowed. "Assalamu Alilkum Wa Rahmatulah Wa Barakatuh."

"Assalamu Alilkum Wa Rahmatulah Wa Barakatuh," Bhima responded with a slight inclination of his head. He pulled out a handkerchief and wiped his brow.

The men met for the hotel's buffet lunch once or twice a month. The food and service at the Kempinski was outstanding. Uprisings in Jakarta the previous year continued to have the population on edge. Still, the men took the opportunity to relax and share information about their families and mutual friends.

"These are strange and troubling times," Putra murmured when they were midway through their meal.

"Yes, yes. But, the violence has encouraged many men to join my mosque. A good number of young people are converting to Islam and they are joining ISIS in huge numbers." The Imam paused to swill some tea. "I'm told that even in America the numbers of converts are increasing—quite rapidly, they say."

Putra nodded. "Yes, I hear the same news. It is getting increasingly difficult for me to travel back and forth for my business."

"Many families from Indonesia are leaving for Iran to join ISIS."

Putra nodded and took another bite of fish. "Yes, that's the current news." They've gone to fight and die, he thought. Their wives and daughters will be raped. Their sons will die in battle. Putra fought the bile rising in his throat.

The Imam leaned closer to Putra. "I have some important information. You will be pleased." The Imam smiled. His excitement grew from pleasure to ecstasy. "You must not tell anyone about this."

Putra gave a short nod. *What's this?*

"You cannot tell anyone." The Imam's affect became guarded.

Putra stared into the man's eyes and gave another affirmative nod. Get on with it fool. What earthshaking news could you tell me?

"Soon many Americans will die."

Putra's astonishment was genuine. "What are you saying? That is not news. We have been praying for victory over the infidel."

The Imam raised his chin. His smile was confident. "Our prayers have been answered. The destruction of the Great Satan is imminent. Our flag will fly from government buildings in Washington. It will fly from the White House." He straightened his shoulders. "Allah has chosen one of the members of my mosque to complete this glorious task."

Putra opened his right hand palm up and shrugged his shoulders. "The destruction of America?" How could this fool have access to information about the destruction of America? "The destruction of America doesn't seem possible. There have been several small victories. But, they have been infinitesimal."

Bhīma's expression, his closed-lip smirk and the way he stroked his beard conveyed satisfaction. He lowered his voice to a whisper. "A wealthy member of my mosque has obtained a powerful weapon."

Putra could barely hear what the Imam was saying. He leaned closer to his brother-in-law. His attempt to understand what his brother-in-law whispered required him to read the Imam's lips.

"He brought it from Syria yesterday. It is a weapon so powerful, it will destroy the Great Satan."

Putra leaned closer and lowered his voice. "What is this weapon? A bomb? A nuclear device?"

"No." Bhima's eyelids narrowed. He moved his hands back and forth in a gesture of denial. "It is not an explosive. Not a bomb."

"Well, what then."

"I should not be sharing this information. But, you are a member of my mosque, you are sympathetic to our cause."

Putra waited.

"The Syrians gave him a powder. It will be shipped to America in containers. It will decimate American cities."

"How can I believe someone from Jakarta has access to a substance that would cause such destruction?"

"It's an infectious agent." The Imam leaned across the table, pointed his finger, and raised his chin.

"An *infectious* agent? A disease?"

The Imam nodded enthusiastically. "The Syrians produced the agent. It is the perfect weapon. It will be shipped to the United States from Jakarta."

"What disease could do that kind of damage?"

"I don't know. I'm told it will spread rapidly. Millions of Americans will die."

"Who is this chosen person?"

Bhima shook his head and looked to heaven, dismissing Putra's question. "A member of my mosque. He has been to Syria three times in the past few months."

"Why was he trusted with this lethal material?"

"He is well educated and very wealthy."

"Is he a scientist?"

"No, I told you, he is extremely wealthy and dedicated to the cause."

"How did you become involved in this scheme?"

"The man came to me and asked if there was anyone in our mosque who could be trusted in a business venture. Someone who was faithful, dedicated and trustworthy."

"Is this someone I know?"

Another dismissive wave. Bhima seemed to concentrate on eating.

Putra let the subject drop. He knew his brother-in-law. The fewer questions he asked the more information he would get.

Finally, Bhima leaned toward Putra. Pride shone in his eyes. "The man gives the mosque a small gift before he leaves for each trip, to insure his safety."

Putra watched his brother-in-law eat. The name. *I need the man's name.* "How many gifts has he given you?"

"He's given much in the past. His contributions to the mosque have exceeded any I've ever received. After each trip to Syria, he donates more money."

"As gratitude for his safety or for being chosen? He must feel as if he is in great danger. Is this someone I know?"

The Imam nodded vigorously raised one shoulder, let it fall, scanned his dinner plate, and chose a particular morsel. He acted as if he hadn't heard Putra's question.

Bhima chewed and swallowed the food in his mouth. He leaned toward Putra. "Ibrihim's been paid a handsome price for his efforts." The Imam's eyes shone. "A member of my mosque, chosen for such a glorious task."

"I was late for our lunch because he brought another gift. He said the weapon is on its way to the United States."

Putra pushed his plate aside, lit a Galois, and signaled the waiter to bring coffee.

He was sure the shine in the Imam's eyes had more to do with the amount of money he received from Ibrihim than from the glorious task. He watched his brother-in-law. There was no evidence the man was lying. Nor did the Imam seem to realize he'd let Ibrihim's name slip into the conversation.

Anne and Connor were ushered into Donovan's office by Amelia.

Donovan set his jaw and pushed up his sleeves. "We have valid information about the intermediary." He gestured to the conference table. "Our source in Jakarta, the man that saved Bushinikov's life, sent the information a few hours ago."

Donovan pointed to the coffee carafe and cups.

"The intermediary's name is Ibrihim. He's disgustingly wealthy. Owns a Ferretti nine-sixty yacht. An expensive little toy. It retails in the vicinity of ten mil. In all fairness, the yacht also seems to be his home. Ivy-League educated."

Donovan refilled his coffee cup.

"He has dozens of brothers and he's pretty far down in the pecking order, so it's not likely he'll take over the family business. His father owns massive holdings and provides an expense account for him. In addition Ibrihim gets a yearly allowance in the nine-figure range. He owns a Learjet and a ready to go flight crew."

Anne pulled out a chair. "Sounds promising, but Ibrihim's a common name. Are you positive he's *the* Ibrihim?"

Donovan gave a slight shrug. "About ninety-nine percent positive. In the past three months his plane has filed flight plans to Dumayr, Syria four times. We checked the records for the fifteen previous years and only brought up one flight to the Middle East. He went to Mecca for the Hajj in 2005."

Connor leaned against the cabinet that held the coffee carafe. "Substantiation?"

"Of course. We have intelligence to solidify the ID. We've been watching him for a few weeks—even before the informant gave us his name. Our Mr. Ibrihim flew to Syria on January sixteenth and was driven to Syria's Scientific Institute."

Donovan checked his notes. "He returned from his most recent trip the day before yesterday. This was his fourth trip. A chauffeur-driven Mercedes met him at the airport in Dumayr and again drove him to the Syrian Scientific Studies and Research Center."

"Sounds like he's our man."

"He's bragged to his Imam." Donovan paused. "Our informant tells us the infectious material has been placed in shipments leaving from Jakarta to the US."

Connor placed his coffee cup near the carafe. "What products do we receive from Indonesia?"

Anne sat a little straighter in her chair. "One of the major imports from Indonesia is clothing. I'm not sure about other products."

Donovan put down his coffee cup, leaned forward, and picked up his report. "Check it out—but we may already know what goods will be contaminated." He paused for dramatic impact. "Ibrihim's yacht has been under surveillance. Today it paid off. This morning a young boy and a man from the yacht sprinted to one of the warehouses." Donovan put down the paper.

"And?" Anne's eyes were bright. Her mind whirred with possibilities, anticipating Donovan's information.

"Just a hint. But it may be a valuable one. By the time our man caught up with them, the kid darted from between a bunch of containers and ran out of the warehouse."

"And?"

"The man was still inside the warehouse. He was on the ground, holding his groin and retching. The closest crate was marked with a spray-painted omega. It was full of children's clothing."

"Good morning, Connor." The President looked up. He closed the file he'd been reading.

"Good morning, Mister President."

The President gestured to Connor to have a seat in the chair on the other side of his desk. "I see you came alone today."

"Yes, sir." Connor eyes crinkled in a broad smile.

"What do you have to report?"

"We've located the intermediary in Jakarta. It looks as if some of the infectious material may be on the way to the United States." Connor related the remainder of the communication.

"I have some news for you, too. The Pentagon made a decision. They suggested Delta Force for the mission in Syria. I expected them to go with a Seal Team operation. Even more surprising, they want the selected team to work out the plan to destroy the lab."

Connor smiled. "Yes, Sir. Years ago, thanks to Charlie Beckworth, none of the Pentagon armchair commandos can run a Delta Force operation. He finally got the mandate through their somewhat thick heads that the men who actually conduct the mission should be the ones to plan it. He convinced them the best mission planning would come from the men who had skin in the game."

"Good thinking. And, if our intelligence doesn't pan out we can cancel the mission. But, if this *is* the lab we'll have to do the job as soon as possible. And, we'll have to get it right the first time."

Donovan's phone buzzed. "Yes?"

"Connor Quinlan and Dr. Damiano are here."

"Send them in."

"Good morning." Connor gave a three fingered salute to Donovan and walked to the coffee carafe. He poured two cups of coffee and handed one cup to Anne. "What's up?"

Donovan paused and pulled on his right ear lobe. "Our informants are saying Russia House thinks the missing vials might contain RAHIMA."

Anne gasped and felt her mouth go dry, her tongue suffused with a coppery taste. Connor stopped doodling and looked at the expression on Anne's face. "What's RAHIMA?"

Anne took a sip of coffee to wash the taste away. The acrid taste persisted. "RAHIMA is a strain of smallpox with a high morbidity and mortality rate."

Connor put down his pencil. "So now we think that Bushinikov stole a highly contagious form of smallpox from the lab in Russia and delivered it to an intermediate in Jakarta."

Donovan nodded. "That's what it looks like. When the Russians first checked the supplies in Bushinikov's lab, it looked as if nothing was missing. They continued their inspection to verify the contents of each vial. Evidently the vials marked RAHIMA contained an innocuous substance."

Yuri searched through the bedcovers to find the TV control.

Up until now the cable stations hadn't mentioned him or his family. There was no news about a missing Russian scientist.

Yuri didn't know if he should be gratified or fearful.

Who is hiding the information? The Russians? The Australians? He pushed the covers away. Why did the Australians send me to Hawaii? Where are Iveta and the children? Are they safe? He felt a chill. Have they been captured?

He patted the bedcovers again. Have the Russians reported my escape? What about the vials I took from the lab?

Yuri reached for the call button. Where is my nurse? He hasn't taken away my breakfast tray. Yuri grabbed the bedrails to sit up straighter. I need to get out of this bed.

He looked up. Another chill swept through him. A stranger stood in the doorway.

"May I come in?" Donovan straightened his suit jacket and swiped a palm over his thinning salt-and-pepper hair.

Yuri's stomach clenched. Politzi. He shrank back into his pillow, his mouth gone dry. "Who are you?" He struggled to keep the fear out of his voice.

"My name is Hugh Donovan. I'm with the CIA." Donovan proffered his identification.

Yuri gripped the bedrails to keep his hands from shaking. "Why are you here?"

"I wanted to meet you. I've been very interested in your recovery. You were very lucky one of my agents found you in Jakarta. He saved your life. And, thanks to some quick thinking and luck, we got you out of Jakarta."

Yuri remembered the fog, he remembered his fright and panic. He felt the knife that sliced into his abdomen. Then nothing.

"American and Australian physicians worked miracles to save your life."

Yuri had vague flashes of memory. Doctors. Nurses. He remembered the last few days in the hospital in Perth. Then nothing until he woke up in this bed in Hawaii.

Donovan walked across to the window, then turned to face Yuri. "It's time for us to talk."

Yuri looked into Donovan's eyes. "I have nothing to say."

"Mr. Bushinikov, let me be clear. Thanks to our intelligence sources, we've known about your disappearance from Russia since your first phone call in Berlin. Our agents picked up your trail there, and we watched you in Jakarta. One of our agents followed you to the warehouse."

Yuri dropped his hands from the side rails, smoothed his covers. He pulled a blanket across his chest. "Your agent tried to kill me."

Donovan shook his head. "No, you were not stabbed by one of our agents. Someone else tried to kill you. Our agent was following you but he lost you in the fog." Donovan sighed. "You were bleeding, and unconscious when he found you."

"Who stabbed me?"

"We don't know. It may have been the person you went to meet. It may have been a paid assassin. There's no way of knowing for sure." Donovan bowed his head and rubbed the back of his neck. "Whoever stabbed you was interested in killing you. You weren't robbed. Someone stabbed you and left you to die. Who did you meet? Who did you give the vials to?"

"I didn't meet anyone. I didn't give a package to anyone. I didn't get money from anyone. I was walking, and I got lost."

"Why would you decide to walk through the warehouse district in Jakarta on a foggy night? It's a dangerous place."

Yuri shrugged and made a puffing sound. "I didn't know where I was going. It was hot. I couldn't sleep."

"You couldn't sleep. And to cure your insomnia you hired a vehicle to drive you to the warehouse district?"

"I told him to take me toward the water. I thought it would be cooler there."

"You were carrying a large sum of money when we found you—far more money than anyone should carry while going for a walk in Jakarta."

"I know nothing about money." Yuri remembered the fog, the shadows, the man with the ink-black eyes, His heart began to pound. "What money are you talking about? I have no money."

"Mr. Bushinikov, your money is here."

"Here?"

"We put your money in a safe. And, what you left in your hotel room is here as well. All your clothing and possessions."

What is this man telling me? Is it possible my belongings are here? The crucifix from our kitchen? Iveta's embroidery? "Bring them to me."

"I'll see that you have access to them. However, there is a considerable amount of money. It would be prudent to keep the money in the safe. We've confiscated all the passports, all the fake IDs and your Russian passport. " Donovan shoved his hands in his pockets. "Now, about our discussion. Your cooperation will be appreciated."

Yuri looked away. Fear prickled his intestines. He crossed his arms on his chest. "Nyet. I will not talk to you." His voice was guttural. Sweat beaded his forehead. "Why should I cooperate?" He kept Donovan in his peripheral vision and stared at the ecru walls. He shifted his focus of attention and watched the morning light play across the blank television screen.

Donovan's gaze was level and unblinking. He pressed his lips together, stood a little straighter, and squared his shoulders. "It would be to your benefit to tell me what you know. You have information essential to the security of the United States."

Yuri looked away.

Donovan unbuttoned his suit jacket and shoved his hands into his pockets, again. "I think the lab in Russia was deteriorating. I think you were not being paid." Donovan rocked back on his heels. "We know Russian scientists are not being compensated adequately, if at all. You were desperate. Your family was starving. The Syrians offered you money and a way to escape."

Yuri pushed out his lower lip, then looked away. *How does this man know all this?*

"Mr. Bushinikov, you're a famous scientist. You've done valuable research in genetic manipulation, genetic engineering. You were a division director at Vektor."

"*Nyet.*" His hand slashed downward, again.

"Mr. Bushinikov, the Russians have already told us you stole vials from the lab and escaped from Russia."

Yuri felt the room lurch sideways. He clutched his abdominal bandage. What will they do to me? Will they send me back to Novosibirsk?

Donovan's voice was soft, almost a whisper, "They also told us your family and your mother-in-law left Russia."

"My family? What do you know about my family?"

Donovan rocked back on his heels. "I know they were able to get to London. Your cousin alerted the British authorities. Your family is currently under the protection of the intelligence service in Great Britain."

"Iveta? The children? Olga?" Black spots swirled in Yuri's vision. The room lurched again. It felt as if the room began to revolve around him with slow, jerky movements.

"Yes, your wife, your children and your mother-in-law. They are well. They are together in Great Britain, under the protection of the British."

"Protection? What have you done with them? Where are they?"

"They are in a compound outside of London."

Yuri sat straight up, oblivious to the sharp pain along his incision. "Compound? They are under arrest." Yuri's voice was flat.

"No, they're not under arrest. They're in protective custody."

"Arrest. Custody. No difference."

"Here, in the West, there is a great difference."

"I want to speak to my wife."

February 10
Timpano Italian Chophouse
Rockville, Maryland

What is the matter with me? Why on heaven's name am I here? Anne
glanced at Connor and traced circles with her spoon. The circles morphed to horizontal figure eights on the tablecloth.

Infinity. Infinity? Who am I kidding? What's the point of having
dinner with Connor tonight? Years ago, he made it perfectly clear that
he'd outgrown our relationship.

Another wasted evening together. Another dinner at one of their
favorite restaurants.

Dark wood, red velvet and large plate glass windows. Recorded
Frank Sinatra and Dean Martin mood music, completed the restaurant's New York-Italian feel.

Anne wanted to push away from the table, run out the door, get
in her car, and not look back. *Why am I here?*

She used the celery stick to stir her Bloody Mary. He calls and I
jump to do his bidding. Stupid. Another evening of small talk. She
licked off the few drops of tomato juice and vodka clinging to the celery.

Connor waved at the waitress.

Anne bowed her head and rubbed her forehead. This morning,
she tried to defer on the invite. But, Connor said it was important,
even though they had still not informed her of their 'secret.' Thank
you, President Julian. What on earth could be so important?

Anne and Connor were seated at the far table on the balcony. In
years past, their favorite table. Had been since 9/11. Much quieter
here, far less traffic flow. And they had a 180 degree view of the room.

Connor snapped his fingers and waved his hand. "Hey, Anne, a
penny for your thoughts."

She looked up. "You don't want to know what's in my mind. It's
worth a whole lot more than a penny, and it's not complimentary to
you, Donovan, or the President." She sipped her drink and managed
an 'I'm-trying-to-smile' smile.

"You're still angry?"

"Of course I am. If you people don't trust me with information at the highest level—*especially* at the highest level—I can't see any reason to be a part of this effort." She sat a little straighter, closed her eyes, and took a deep breath. "I've had enough."

"Enough? You've got it all wrong. You're a valuable part of the team."

"I am? Hard for me to believe. You and Donovan are still withholding information. What could be so important that a key member of the team, a *hand-chosen* member of the team, is kept in the dark? And, you've had more than enough time to get the clearance. Don't give me another lecture on how long it takes wheels to turn at the White House."

The waiter arrived with their appetizers. "Roasted mussels for the lady and clams oreganata for the gentleman. Can I get you fresh drinks?'

"I'll have another martini," Connor said. 'Thank goodness our appetizers are here. I'm starved and I don't want to eat one more peanut."

"Nothing more for me, thank you." Anne smiled at the waiter. "I have a long drive."

After the waiter left Anne's smile faded. "I'm not interested in one more stall tactic, Connor. What don't you understand about, 'I've had enough?"

Neither spoke until they were ready for the main course. Connor finished the last of his martini. He pushed his glass toward the edge of the table and jabbed his fork into one of the clams. His voice was low. "When do you plan to talk to Donovan?"

"I made an appointment for next week."

"He won't accept your resignation."

"We'll see about that. Amelia said Donovan would be out of town for a few days."

Connor nodded. "Yes, we all will."

Anne looked up, startled. "Who's 'we'?"

"You, me, Donovan. We're going out of town for a few days." Connor had a self-satisfied smile.

"Where are we going?"

Connor evaded the question. "You need to cancel any plans you have for next week. Donovan has arranged a field trip. We leave tomorrow afternoon. Be at Langley by noon."

Anne rested both elbows on the table and cradled her head in her hands. She must be losing her mind. Did she hear Connor say we're taking a trip, or were the words an echo of the past? She straightened her back, raised her head, and looked into his eyes. "I thought those days were long gone."

"Bring your passport, as well as business and casual evening wear. Make sure you wear something warm." He gave her a quick kiss on the cheek, and picked up the check.

"See you tomorrow." Connor was down the stairs and out the door before she could respond.

February 11
Al Halbi's Office
Dumayr, Syria

Al Halbi sat at his desk and waited for Adi Shamash to give him a detailed report of his mission.

Shamash stood at parade rest in an obvious effort to make Al Halbi uncomfortable.

Al Halbi tried to stamp down his fear. Adi's casual stance didn't mask the aura of danger that radiated around him. Al Halbi shivered, as if the room temperature dropped twenty degrees whenever Shamash was present.

Adi's voice was controlled, barely a whisper. Arrogance flashed from his eyes. "There was no evidence that a dead Russian was found anywhere during the time you said he was in Jakarta. There were no reports of any foreigners killed in the warehouse district that week."

"But that's impossible."

"The Russian was in Jakarta—he spent a full day at the hotel. A driver picked him up in the early evening the second day of his visit. He was transported to a mosque and left in the vehicle at sundown." Adi crossed his arms and glared at Al Halbi.

"How did the Russian reach the meeting place? The Indonesian said there was a money transfer. And, he received the package."

"I have no idea. The trail ends there. I could not find information regarding the driver. No one knows what happened to either the driver or the Russian. And," he paused, "there is no proof the Russian was killed."

Al Halbi stood, but did not move from behind his desk. Angry and frustrated, his eyes focused on Shamash. His fists clenched. "How could there be *no* information? How can two men disappear without a trace? I sent you to Jakarta to find answers, and you come back with *nothing*?"

Shamash moved closer to Al Halbi's desk.

Al Halbi reflexively took a step backwards. Shamash looked like a tiger read to spring.

Adi's eyes narrowed. His words were quiet with an undertone of hate. "You haven't heard the rest of the story." He placed his hands flat on Al Halbi's desk and leaned toward him.

Al Halbi cowered and recoiled. His back against the wall.

"As far as I can tell, no one entered the Russian's hotel room." Adi's mouth twisted into a hideous sneer. "In the morning the maids went in to make up the room. It was empty."

"Empty?"

"The Russian's belongings were gone."

"Who would have taken them?"

"I looked at the surveillance tapes. No one entered or left the room after the Russian went to meet the man who drove him to the warehouse district. The hotel couldn't provide any information. The Russian was given one key. No other key was issued for the room. And, the Russian's key was never returned."

"Did the security cameras provide any information?"

"The adjoining room was occupied by an elderly couple from Great Britain. They checked out several days later. They weren't connected to the Russian. She had white hair and wore a horrible hat and one of those awful British capes. The man wore a fedora and a woolen coat. The hat was pulled low on his forehead. I never saw his face."

"Could it have been the Russian?"

"No. He didn't move like a man who had been injured, and he was much thinner and taller than the Russian."

"So, either the Russian was being followed or someone gained access to his room after he was injured. *Or* the Russian wasn't stabbed and the story Ibrihim told me was a lie. Could the Russian have left the country?"

Shamash's level gaze chilled the director of the institute. "It is a possibility. However, no one named Bushinikov left. And no one using any of the false identities you provided purchased a plane ticket."

Al Halbi's shoulders drooped. His vacant stare locked on the papers on his desk. "Were you able to find his wife and children?"

"They are in a compound near London, under heavy guard."

Al Halbi glared. "I want the Russian *and* his entire family."

February 12
Marriott Hotel County Hall
London

Anne, Connor, and Donovan, dragged through the first jet-lagged day, cloaked in the foggy cold of London.

In the evening, with still no indication of what the trip was about, Anne joined Connor and Donovan for dinner at Chez Bruce. At the elevator Donovan suggested a good night's rest.

"A driver will pick us up tomorrow. Expect a call early in the morning."

A little before seven a.m., Anne's phone rang. A woman told her a driver would be at the hotel in two hours.

Anne remained confused. They'd been in London for twenty-four hours. As far as she knew there was still no reason for traveling to London. She was convinced the trip was connected to the Bushinikov family. But, why did they have to travel to London? It made no sense. Donovan could have briefed us on the status of the family in his office at Langley.

Anne chose black wool slacks, a lavender turtleneck sweater, and a lilac and pale blue plaid jacket. She pushed her feet into cordovan loafers and picked up a brush to smooth her hair. Secrecy. "Need to know" She was so sick of hearing that phrase, she wanted to puke.

Beyond annoyed and confused, she fumed. Why would the family's whereabouts be kept under wraps?

Anne swiped some powder on her nose, brushed a faint glow of pink on her cheekbones and applied pale lip gloss. She zipped up her make-up kit, then opened it again. She gave a single spray of perfume above her head and waited for it to settle on her hair and shoulders.

A scattering of people sat alone at tables in the breakfast room. Most of them held newspapers turned to the financial pages. She rejected the table the waiter offered her, and instead chose a table with four chairs in a corner.

Connor arrived. "That coffee smells good." His lips brushed her cheek. "You do, too." He sat to her right, with the same 180° view. A waiter hurried over to fill his coffee cup. A few minutes later Donovan joined them. He chose a chair to Anne's left.

"What's on the agenda for today?" Anne asked.

Connor nodded to Donovan and opened his hand as if to say, 'It's in your court now.'

Donovan waved away Connor's hand-off with a dismissive gesture. "I've planned a short drive into the country."

The morning fog was accompanied by a persistent drizzle and brisk breeze. "Oh, sure," she said in mock agreement. "It looks like a lovely day to drive through the English countryside."

Their driver, Percy Raines, met them in the restaurant a few minutes before nine. In addition to his military bearing and haircut, he wore a blue suit made of serviceable fabric, a white shirt, blue tie, and a black driving hat. His dress and demeanor marked him as a British intelligence officer.

An hour beyond the London city limits Percy pulled into a long driveway and stopped at a locked gate. A man stepped from the guard shack next to the gate.

Percy flashed his ID.

Seconds later the electric gate opened. Percy turned into a compound encircled with ivy-covered chain-link fencing. He drove down a lane lined by tiny thatched-roof houses and braked to a stop at a picture-perfect English country cottage.

Percy helped Anne out of the car. No umbrellas, everyone but the driver hurried to the door.

Connor knocked. Footsteps sounded from inside. A woman in her late twenties opened the door. Two little boys peered out from behind her, their hands clutched in the folds of her skirt.

"Come in, Mr. Quinlan." Her chandelier-bright smile welcomed him. She held her index finger to her lips. "The baby is asleep." She pointed toward the back of the house. "Please, come to the kitchen."

The narrow entry hall opened into a large country kitchen. A round oak table held a blue pitcher. Green-checkered curtains hung at the windows. Beautiful, polished cherry-wood cabinets lined the wall over the sink. A pine chair rail encircled the room. Wallpaper printed with rows of tiny yellow roses covered the upper walls, wooden paneling below.

Donovan made the introduction. "Anne, I'd like you to meet Iveta Bushinikova. Iveta, this is another member of our team, Doctor Anne Damiano."

Anne fought to keep her composure. "I'm happy to meet you." The name, Bushinikova. Was Yuri Bushinikov here, too? Is that the big secret?

"Yes, thank you, it's good to meet you, too."

Iveta turned toward the stove and gestured to an older woman. "This is my mother, Olga Chasova."

Olga gave a brief nod to Anne. Her high cheekbones, almond-shaped eyes, and chestnut-colored hair with just a hint of gray were telltale evidence of their relationship. Olga's hair was held back by a babushka tied behind her neck.

"And those two," Connor pointed to the boys, "are Ondrek and Josef. I don't know which one is which."

Iveta covered her mouth and giggled. "This one is Ondrek." She placed her hand on the head of a boy wearing a green and white sweater. "And this little trouble maker"—she patted the shoulder of the smaller boy—"is Josef."

Connor explained the arrangement to Anne. "Iveta, her children, and her mother are guests of MI6. Vaux Hall decided to house them at this compound to ensure their safety. The area is well guarded, and the children can play outside."

Donovan turned to Iveta. "Yuri's recovery is practically complete. We hope you'll be able to join him in a few weeks."

Anne drew in a deep breath. *We have Bushinikov? He's recovering? What's he recovering from? Obviously he's not here. Is he in the United States?* Her mind was flooded with questions. *Is this what they've been hiding from me?*

Iveta walked to the counter and pulled cups and saucers from the cupboard. She placed them on silver tray.

Olga brushed her away. "Sit, sit, I will take care of the tea."

Connor held a chair for Iveta.

"I spoke to Yuri yesterday." She sat and smoothed her skirt. Her voice was soft. "He said he was feeling much better."

"He's improved over the past few days," Donovan said. "I think it's because he knows you and the children are safe. Peace of mind makes a big difference in the healing process."

"Yes," Iveta agreed. "All he has to worry about is getting well."

London
Later the same afternoon

Anne and Connor accompanied Donovan to Heathrow. They remained in the lounge until his plane took off, banked to the right, and disappeared into the clouds, then they turned and walked out of the terminal.

"Why aren't we flying home with Donovan?" Anne asked.

"Just trust me on this one." Connor took her hand and led her toward the taxi stand.

"Why did we come to London?" Anne stopped short. "You or Donovan could have briefed me about all of this at Langley."

Connor shook his head. "Could you just relax and go with the flow for once in your life?"

He steered her to the taxi line, stepped into the drizzle, and signaled for a cab.

"Searcy's Grand Brasserie," he told the driver.

Anne slid to the far side of the taxi. "What other surprises do you have in store for me?"

"We're going on a holiday. To Paris." Connor smiled.

"You've planned a side trip to France?" Anne did not smile.

Connor reached across the seat to hold Anne's hand. Anne shook her head, pulled her hand away, and gave Connor a long, hard look. "Another surprise? Who are we going to meet this time?"

"No one. I said we're going on a holiday. Just us."

"A holiday." She adjusted the creases in her slacks.

"Yes. Time alone. Together."

Anne stayed glued to the door as far from Connor as she could get. Nothing made sense.

"A holiday."

"Yes. I wanted to surprise you."

"Surprise me? You didn't think it might be appropriate to ask me if I wanted to take a week off to be with you."

Connor's shoulders slumped. He sighed and bit his lip. "Okay, I'll take you back to Heathrow. We can book the next plane to the States. We don't have to go to Paris. I was hoping..."

Anne rubbed her forehead. *Damn it! What am I thinking?* "I didn't... I don't... Connor? What's this about?"

"I wanted some time alone with you, far away from the Company."

"Did you think you might have asked me if I wanted to go anywhere with you"

"Yeah, but I was afraid you'd say no. And, I guess I was right."

"You tricked me." She crossed her arms.

"I couldn't think of any other way to get you away from..." Connor raised his hands. A gesture of helplessness. "I wanted a few days alone with you. With no chance of intrusion." Connor slid across the seat and put his arm around her. "I know you're confused. Please listen. Let me explain."

Anne nodded and uncrossed her arms.

"I've wanted our relationship to be different for years. But . . ." He closed his eyes and rubbed his forehead. "For all kinds of reasons" His smile reflected years of weariness. "Probably all stupid reasons, but . . ." He kissed her forehead. "I'm having a hard time explaining. Are you okay with going to Paris, with me? I mean, Valentine's Day is the day after tomorrow. It's a day for lovers."

"You were the one that ended our relationship. You came to me years and years ago and made it quite clear that you didn't want me. You were the one that told me not to wait."

"I know what I said. But, it was because ... Oh, never mind. I wish I could erase that night. What I said and what I meant were all mixed up. I've never stopped loving you. I wanted you to wait for me. But, I knew my love for you could put you in danger. Then you were in danger and it was because of me."

Anne caught her breath. "And then I was recruited and became an agent."

"That made double danger for both of us. Is there any chance that you still love me? If you don't want to go it's okay. But, I was hoping—"

"Oh, Connor." She felt heat move up to her face. Her cheeks burned. She rested her head on his shoulder and took a deep breath. "If you wanted to knock my socks off you've succeeded. Of course I want to go." She blinked back tears. "I never stopped loving you. I've loved you forever."

He kissed her forehead, again.

She snuggled against him. "Let's go to Paris. I think it's a wonderful idea."

"We've got a few hours before our train leaves. How 'bout a trip to a pub and drink a pint in honor of St. Valentine."

"A pub and a pint? Sounds more like St. Patrick's Day. You get a pint. I'll settle for tea."

At Searcy's they were handed off to a waiter by the maître d'. The waiter escorted them past the champagne bar to a small table by a window. Beveled glass partitions, filigreed metalwork, globe lamps, and reflective ceilings completed the art deco setting. Indirect lighting gave a golden glow to the room. Through the windows the ribbed-metal roof of St. Pancras Grand Station arched high over the train tracks.

Anne's hopeful highs swooped down to fears of rejection. Where is all this going? How many more times am I going to be surprised? She pushed all thoughts of disappointment aside.

"Paris!" she said. "I've been through Paris more times than I can count." A kernel of doubt planted itself in her mind. The attack in Paris was fresh in everyone's minds. Wrinkles crossed her brow. "Donovan's approved this? Even after the ISIS attack?"

Connor nodded. "The French have tightened their security. Donovan wasn't excited about the plan. He reluctantly approved it."

"I'm excited. I've never gotten closer to Notre Dame or the Champs-Elysees than De Gaulle International. There was always some place I had to get to in a hurry. And, I was almost always traveling under an assumed name."

He laughed. "I can relate." He squeezed her hand. "It's time we slowed down." He leaned close and whispered. "I hope you..."

"A before-dinner cocktail?" Their waiter interrupted, cutting off Connor's declaration and breaking the mood.

Anne scanned the wine list. "I'd like a glass of the Louis Roederer. Demi Sec, please."

"I'll have the Chateaux Deville Bordeaux," Connor said.

The waiter peered down his nose at Connor. "What quantity, sir."

"The 250-milliliter, of course." Connor rolled his eyes, and the waiter hurried off.

"Will I get to meet Iveta's husband any time soon?" Anne asked. "Now that I know the *big secret* you've been keeping from me, you'll have to fill me in on all the details."

Connor let a few seconds pass before he answered. "Iveta arrived here about a week ago. She, her children and her mother braved a very long, hard trip. They are guests of MI6 for the time being. At the President's request." Connor nodded his head, made a small gesture of uncertainty. "Vaux Hall thought the compound would be the best place to insure their safety. They will be joining her husband as soon as he's recovered."

This gets more intriguing with every new piece of information. "What's he recovering from?"

"He was stabbed. Someone tried to murder him. We had to keep it from you because the President didn't want the information released."

Anne's head snapped up. "The President said I couldn't know?"

"No, it wasn't that he didn't want you to know. He didn't want *anyone* to know. All of the discussions about Bushinikov, his condition, or his whereabouts went unrecorded. The information had to be kept sub rosa. *No one* could know."

Connor went quiet as the waiter approached their table. "I'll tell you the rest of the story later."

The waiter poured their wine and made a few suggestions for their meal.

"I'll have bangers and mash," Connor said with a horrible imitation of a Cockney accent. "And a dozen oysters on the half shell, please."

The waiter frowned, "Excellent choice, sir. A dozen British rock oysters followed by the Cumberland sausage, mash, and red onion gravy. And for the lady?"

Anne suppressed a grin. "I'll have the char-grilled chicken salad, followed by the double-baked cheddar and spring onion soufflé, please."

When the waiter left, Connor raised his glass, peered down his nose with a superior expression, and in the formal tone of the waiter, said: "To a romantic few days in Paris, madam."

Paris
Four hours later

Anne was more than a bit overwhelmed when the taxi dropped them off at the W Hotel Paris Opera. "A champagne bar in London and a five-star hotel in Paris. You certainly know how to impress a girl."

Grecian columns, swirled tubular neon light, and art-deco gates led to the entrance.

Gray and gold dominated the contemporary furniture, walls, and drapes of their suite. Antique black iron fireplace lintels set in white brick enclosures contrasted with the avant-garde art hung on the walls. Views of Paris tempted them from every window. An ice bucket with a magnum of champagne and a basket filled with cheese, pâté, and other delicacies waited on a side table.

"Oh, Connor, it's perfect." Anne felt warmth blossom through her body. *Good grief, I feel like I'm sixteen.* She looked up at Connor and felt her face flush again. His eyes were warm, his look soft. It was a look she hadn't seen in thirty years. Not since the night he'd told her he was going away and might not return. The night he told her not to wait for him.

"Where to, madam? Perhaps a street café, where we can drink coffee and watch the world swirl around us?" He extended his arm.

Anne slid her hand into his. "Sounds wonderful. Let's stroll along the Champs-Élysées. I want to see Notre Dame."

"Whatever your heart desires. We have four days all to ourselves."

They walked along the Seine, drank coffee, munched on flaky pastries at a cafe, and bought a loaf of bread. Later, they strolled hand in hand back to the hotel. Connor uncorked the champagne and poured a generous glass for each of them. He fixed a tray with the cheese, foie gras, and the crusty bread, then sat next to her on the couch and lifted his glass. "To us."

"To us?" Anne held her breath and snuggled close.

He put his arm around her and pulled her even closer. "Anne, we've been best friends forever, and we've been a good team for years."

Anne answered with a skeptical smile and a nod. She caught her breath. *Is this going where . . .?*

He nuzzled her ear. "Anne, I want—"

His cellphone buzzed. "Damn."

Connor stood and walked over to the fireplace. "Damn." he spit out the word when he saw the caller ID.

She exhaled. *Whatever Connor planned to say was gone.* "Donovan?" she whispered.

He shook his head and mouthed *'President.'*

Connor turned on his heel and walked into the bedroom.

He returned carrying their bags.

"Seems like we've been abandoned by St. Valentine, Anne. They've sent a car for us. It's waiting downstairs."

"Good Morning, Connor." Chief of Staff, Collette Demaree, accompanied Connor to the door.

Connor nodded at the woman. "Good morning, Collette."

"I hope you have some good news today. The President's been pensive all morning."

Connor gave a wry smile and shook his head as she opened the door. "Security briefings are seldom filled with good news. I'm afraid today's news won't make him feel any better."

President Julian looked up from the papers on his desk. "Good morning, Connor. Come in." The President stood, walked toward the fireplace, and stared at the picture of George Washington that hung over the mantle.

"Good Morning, Mr. President."

"Sorry we interrupted your leave. Hope it didn't inconvenience you."

Inconvenience is not the word I'd use, Connor thought. "I'm sure there was a good reason."

"I received information from the French President regarding an imminent threat. You and Dr. Damiano are too important to lose. Couldn't take any chances."

"Thank you for being concerned for our safety."

The President gestured, palms up. "You must have some news for me. What's happening now?"

Connor's mouth was set in a straight line. There was no way to soften the information he was about to relay. "We've received credible information from multiple reliable sources that indicate the Russians are convinced Bushinikov survived his attack."

The President nodded. He glanced at the portrait of George Washington again. After a few moments he shook his head, turned, and sat in the leather chair facing the hearth. He gestured for Connor to sit in one of the upholstered chairs beside him. "It was inevitable. I'm surprised it took this long."

"That's not the worst of it. It's not just the Russians. The Syrian's have investigated the official reports from Jakarta. They don't know where Bushinikov is. But they know he didn't die the night he was stabbed. No dead Russians were reported in the warehouse district. No reports of Russian deaths anywhere in Jakarta on the night of January thirteenth."

The President took a deep breath and exhaled forcefully. "Go on."

Connor nodded. "MI6 has reported a Syrian operative in Great Britain. He attempted to capture Bushinikov's cousin. I'm happy to report it was a failed attempt. However, the Syrian got away. They've been watching the airports and the borders—they're convinced he's still in England."

"How safe is Bushinikov's family?"

"According to MI6, the Syrians have determined their whereabouts."

President Julian rubbed his forehead and squeezed his eyes shut for a moment. "I'm sure the Syrians are going to try to capture them. They have to be protected at all cost."

"MI6 realizes the danger to the family. They've assured me all safeguards are in place."

"What's the update on Delta Force?"

"Delta Force is ready." The tension in the President's face relaxed a little. "The teams have practiced the mission over and over. Delta Force and the Israelis have coordinated their movements. Of course, there's no telling what glitch might occur at the last minute. There always seems to be a malfunction. A plane doesn't land where it's supposed to... one of the vehicles breaks down... someone leaks info . . ." Connor shrugged. "But, these guys are adaptable. They'll be able to deal with any hiccup. The Department of Defense is getting all the ships in place to extract the team when the mission is complete. And, they have a backup plan to make sure they can get the teams out."

February 23
Nine days later
Ibrihim's Yacht
Jakarta, Indonesia

Simi lay on his small pallet at the foot of Ibrihim's bed. The child's breathing was shallow. A soft sob pulled Ibrihim to the boy. "What is the matter, my little friend?"

The slow, obviously painful movement of Simi's head and a gasp of pain were the only answers. Ibrihim could feel the heat radiating from the child's body. Every touch brought a moan from Simi, as if his entire body ached. He scooped the boy into his arms and carried him up the stairs to the flying bridge, placed him on a lounge chair covered with an Egyptian cotton sheet, and arranged a soft bamboo blanket over the child's legs. "Perhaps the breeze from the sea will cool you."

"Thank you." Simi's lips were dry and chapped, his exhaustion clearly overwhelming. Any attempt to swallow caused pain. A grimace pulled at his features. Pain coursed through his body.

Ibrihim called to request ice and bottled water. "Have Bakti come to the bridge. I want him to stay with the boy while I go into town." Minutes later a young crew member appeared.

"Here are the bottles of water you asked for, sir." Bakti placed a tub of bottles and ice on the deck.

"Thank you, Bakti," Ibrihim said. "Please, stay with Simi. Make sure he's comfortable. I have to go to the bank. I won't be long."

Ibrihim felt Simi's forehead again. "The boy is ill, very ill. I'll call the physician as soon as I return."

Ibrihim ran down the steps and across the deck.

Bakti pulled a deck chair close to the lounge chair, poured a glass of water, and held the rim to Simi's lips.

He choked and pushed the glass away. "Hurts."

Bakti nodded and soaked a rag with water to bathe the boy's face. He fed Simi one sliver of ice at a time.

Simi managed to let the melted water slide down his throat.

A few minutes later Jamul stepped onto the upper deck and leered. "Simi, I am surprised to see you on deck."

Simi turned his head away.

Bakti slipped another sliver of ice between Simi's chapped lips. "The child is ill. Mr. Ibrihim brought him up here to see if the sea breeze would cool him."

"Where is Mr. Ibrihim?" Jamul pushed the young crewmember aside.

"He went into the city." Bakti moved to the other side of the chair, grabbed Simi's hand and patted it. "I was told to stay with the boy."

"Go back to your regular duties. I'll watch the boy."

Bakti stood beside the deck chair and continued to pat Simi's hand. "Mr. Ibrihim told me to make sure he was comfortable. He needs bits of ice. He can't swallow."

"I told you to leave. You are not needed here." Jamul stood and pointed to the stairs.

"Don't go, Bakti," Simi croaked. "Stay with me." Fear of Jamul was written in Simi's expression. He took a ragged breath.

Bakti looked at Simi and turned his head to stare at Jamul. He straightened his spine. "No, I will stay. Mr. Ibrihim told me to care for Simi."

"I'm in charge when Mr. Ibrihim is away," Jamul shouted. "Go!"

Bakti didn't move. His eyes never left Jamul's face.

Jamul's arm shot out; a quick chopping blow sent Bakti to the deck. "Leave."

Bakti crawled to the chair and pulled himself up. Defiance burned in his eyes.

Jamul stood, grabbed Bakti, and threw him against the rail. "I said go."

Bakti dodged another blow and ran down the stairs to the lower deck.

Jamul turned, pulled his chair closer to Simi, and stared out at the harbor. After a moment's silence he turned to Simi. "I haven't seen you for two weeks."

Simi raised his chin and narrowed his eyes. His hatred for Jamul was unmistakable. Jamul moved the lounge chair closer. "I'm happy to see you."

Simi stiffened and pulled his arms tight against his body. "Go away. Leave me alone," he rasped.

Jamul rested his hand on the boy's shoulder. "You're feverish."

Simi shook Jamul's hand off, struggled out of the lounge chair and took a step. "Don't touch me."

Jamul caught the boy's shirt and yanked him back to the chair. "Ibrihim thinks the ocean breeze will cool you." He pulled the child onto his lap, then tucked the blanket around Simi.

"No. Go away." Simi kicked and struggled to loosen the blanket.

Jamul reached into his pocket and pulled out a bottle containing a reddish-brown liquid. "This is very special oil. Soothing." He held the bottle and stroked Simi's face with the back of his hand.

A burst of energy fueled by fear flooded Simi. He jumped off Jamul's lap, the tangled sheet dragging behind him. He was able to stagger a few steps toward the stairs before Jamul grabbed the sheet.

"No!" Simi pulled the sheet from between his legs and ran.

Jamul dove and caught the boy's ankle.

Ibrihim stepped on deck in time to see the boy pitch forward and tumble down the stairs.

Simi lay sprawled on the main deck. A large gaping scalp wound slowly oozed blood. His neck was twisted, his head rotated to an abnormal position.

Ibrihim forced his gaze from the child and looked up. Jamul stood at the top of the stairs.

"Slime." Ibrihim's word hissed hate.

Jamul opened his mouth, but no sound came out.

"Allah will reward the boy." Ibrihim's eyes narrowed.

"P-Praise Allah," Jamul murmured too many seconds later.

"Your mission is complete." Ibrihim's gaze focused on Jamul's eyes, like a raptor swooping in for his prey. He threw the heavy canvas bag he carried onto a table, where it landed with a clang. Two gold coins rolled out. "Your reward."

Jamul jumped to the main deck and leaned forward to kiss Ibrihim's right cheek.

Ibrihim jammed his dagger into the soft flesh of Jamul's stomach and gave the blade a vicious twist.

Jamul's look of surprise stayed frozen on his face as he wrapped his hands around the haft and sank to the deck. Ibrihim shouted orders, "Take the yacht out to the reefs."

An hour later, he shoved Jamul off the deck and saw the body tumble into the churning motor blades and watched the mutilated remains rise to the surface of boat's wake. Ibrihim smiled.

May the ray sharks make short work of you.

After they had covered another twenty nautical miles he ordered the captain to shut down the engines.

Ibrihim gently lowered Simi into the water. The small body floated on the surface for few minutes, then slowly sank into the Java Sea.

"May you walk in paradise, my little friend."

"The route to moral horror is never direct."
—*The Crime of Julian Wells*, Thomas H. Cook

February 24

Al Halbi's phone call had been short. "Come to Syria tomorrow. Your payment is ready."

Disgust washed over Ibrihim. I hate the desert. I hate the heat, the endless stretches of sand, the dust.

Al Halbi gave him no choice. He had to return to Syria to get his final payment.

Ibrihim's plane seemed to float to Syria on the wave of intense heat from the desert floor.

He stretched his neck and upper back, searching for a position to ease his discomfort. The muscle and joint pain he woke with this morning seemed to double every hour.

A flick of his wrist brought the flight steward to his side. "Bring me two aspirin."

He watched the he attendant go to his station, open the first-aid box, and shake two tablets into a pill cup. The attendant placed the cup on a tray along with a small bottle of water from the cooler, and carried it to Ibrihim.

"How long before we land?" Ibrihim asked

"Several more hours."

"Bring me the bottle of sleeping pills."

Ibrihim pulled three sedative capsules from the plastic container. He tried to swallow the two aspirin tablets and the sedative tablets with a swig of water. He choked and gagged, unable to swallow. The pills dissolved in his mouth, leaving an acrid taste. Ibrihim couldn't wipe the bitterness away.

The steward brought him several lemon candies.

Ibrihim leaned his seat back, elevated the footrest, and slipped into a restless sleep. Dreams of Simi's body sliding out of his arms into the clear water of the Java Sea, troubled him. Visions of Jamul rising from the deck, pink froth spewing from his mouth, repelled him. And, dreams of Al Halbi laughing and taunting left him horrorstruck.

Ibrihim's yacht
The same day

Adi Shamash and his team loitered in the marina until Ibrihim left for the airport. A nod of Shamash's head sent one team member to make sure Ibrihim and his plane took off for Syria.

Thirty minutes later Shamash boarded the yacht.

"Excuse me, sir," the captain said, "This is a private yacht. If you have come to visit Mr. Ibrihim, he is not on board at this time. He will return in two days. Three days at the very most. I must ask you to leave."

"I'm aware the yacht is owned by Mr. Ibrihim. I'm from Ferretti. I have come to evaluate the yacht's efficiency. The routine inspection of the motor was scheduled for today, according to company policy."

"I'm sorry. Mr. Ibrihim did not provide authorization for your visit. I must ask you to return when Mr. Ibrihim is present."

"Mr. Ibrihim gave us specific instructions. He wanted the inspection done today."

"I was not told about an inspection. Mr. Ibrihim would have informed me."

Shamash reached into his briefcase, produced a paper, and handed the sheets to the captain. "Please review this document. It states our authorization to inspect the motors. Here is Mr. Ibrihim's signature. As I said, he specifically requested today's inspection." Shamash watched the captain's eyes shift left then right, as he read the papers.

Shamash snatched the paper from the captain. "We've come a long distance. What are you are trying to hide from the company?"

"No. No. I am not hiding anything. It is just . . ." The captain's confusion was apparent.

"Are you having some problem with the engine? Have you tampered with the control mechanisms?" The light in Shamash's eyes conveyed a honed threat. Violence simmered in his gaze.

The captain shivered, took a deep breath, and stepped aside.

"When we are finished with our inspection you will take us out to sea. It is essential that I evaluate the motors at full speed."

The captain nodded.

Shamash smiled. "Please have the crew assemble on the main deck. I don't want any interference with our work. I will come to your cabin when we have finished the maintenance."

Later the same day
Scientific Institute
Dumayr, Syria

Ibrihim arrived in Dumayr feeling tired and weak. His drug-induced sleep left him with a hangover. And, it seemed, all his symptoms had gotten worse. He shivered uncontrollably in Al Halbi's air-conditioned automobile.

He stepped out of the automobile into the blast of heat of Dumayr and walked the short distance to the artificial chill of the institute.

"Come in. I'm happy you are here." Al Halbi's eyes reflected cunning, hatred, deception. He led Ibrihim to a divan. "You've had a long flight."

A white-coated servant arranged platters of fruit and sweets, poured two cups of thick coffee, added a generous spoonful of sugar to each, bowed, and left the room.

"I had refreshments prepared for you." Al Halbi looked at him through eyelids narrowed to mere slits. "You were successful?"

"The powder was distributed as you directed."

"Who distributed the powder?"

"A street urchin." Ibrihim gagged on a wave of vomit, at the memory of Simi lying on the deck, the hideous angle of his head.

"You trusted this important task to a child?"

"He was intelligent and could do the chore, and he posed the least amount of suspicion. No one would question a homeless child wandering through the warehouse district. At most they would have chased him off."

"You observed the distribution?"

"Of course not. My presence would have raised questions."

Al Halbi slammed his hand on the table. "This was the most important part of the assignment."

Ibrihim winced. "My associate went with him to make sure the powder was put in the correct boxes." Ibrihim tried to swallow. "The warehouse people would have reported my presence. They would have followed me and asked questions about why I was there and what I was doing."

Al Halbi nodded. "Where is this child now?"

"He's dead."

"Dead?" Fright shimmied across Al Halbi's face. "How did he die?"

Ibrihim shook his head. "He slipped and fell on the stairs. Broke his neck."

Foul smelling perspiration ran from the back of Ibrihim's scalp, down his neck, and under his collar.

"Are you ill?" A hint of pleasure tainted the director's voice.

"I'm not used to the desert. The dust. The heat. I'm more comfortable near the sea." He pushed his plate aside.

"Perhaps this food is too rich for you." Al Halbi clapped his hands and asked the servant to bring figs, stuffed dates, marzipan, and tea. "While we are waiting, the hot coffee should help."

Ibrihim sipped the sweet brew. The liquid soothed the intensity of the pain in his throat.

When the servant returned with a new tray of delicacies Al Halbi grabbed a plate and filled it with rose-shaped marzipan. "Suck on these. They will melt and coat your throat."

Ibrihim attempted to swallow a bite of the citron flavored almond paste. The candy stuck to the roof of his dry mouth. A sip of tea did not dislodge the confection. Ibrihim covered his mouth with a napkin and gagged.

"It seems my hospitality does not please you." Al Halbi sneered. "Now, tell me about your friend, Jamul."

"Jamul was not my friend. He was an intermediary. Nothing more than a tool." Ibrihim rubbed his forehead. "I hired him to go to the warehouse to get the package from the Russian. He was also tasked with making arrangements for the Russian to get from his hotel to the warehouse and back."

"Where did you find the urchin?"

"Jamul found him. I sent Jamul out to find an orphan who would be capable of accomplishing the simple task of salting the containers." Ibrihim worked his tongue to remove marzipan from the roof of his mouth.

"I hired you to meet the Russian. I gave you specific instructions: You were told to make sure the Russian would be on the plane to Syria." Disdain was reflected in Al Halbi's expression. "You say your friend killed the Russian. How do you know he's dead?"

Ibrihim ground his teeth. "I was told the Russian was stabbed and left to die. Why would Jamul lie to me?"

"You didn't confirm the Russian's death? You didn't go to see for yourself?"

Ibrihim shook his head, eyes closed. "No. I can't go to the waterfront at night; it is a dangerous place."

Al Halbi smirked. "How do you know he's dead? Maybe he made a deal with your intermediary." A frown pursed his lips and pulled a deep crease between his eyebrows. "And where is this *intermediary* now?"

Ibrihim shrugged. "He's dead. I killed him. He was a liability. He hired the assassin. He responsible for the boy's death."

Al Halbi's voice became light, playful. "So, both are dead?" He relaxed into the divan pillows and stroked his beard. "How convenient."

"Convenient? Why would it be convenient? I put both bodies into the sea."

"I think you wanted to keep all the money. He accomplished the mission I assigned you."

Ibrihim tried to protest, but Al Halbi wouldn't listen.

"And, now you are here to collect the remainder of the money because you think your mission is complete."

"Yes. You told me to come here to collect the payment. Please, give me my money so I can leave. I must return to Jakarta today."

The director stood and gestured to the door. "We will go to get your payment now. But, what is your hurry?" Al Halbi's eyes narrowed. A triumphant smile added to Ibrihim's unease.

What is Al Halbi up to? Ibrihim's stomach cramped. I don't want to stay here another minute. "I prefer the sea breezes. I will feel much better in Jakarta."

Al Halbi stood. "We must go to the laboratory."

The thought of returning to the tunnel made Ibrihim shiver. "My flight crew filed the flight plan for Jakarta. I expect to leave in the next few hours."

"Oh, but you must come to the laboratory and see the progress we've made. You have time. We'll be back before your flight. You have been essential to the success of this venture. None of it would have been possible without your assistance." Another glimmer of the triumphant smile.

"I do not want to travel into the desert. I know the importance of your work. I don't care to see the children. I don't want to learn about your techniques. I would prefer to leave. My work is done. I want to return to my yacht and recover there. The sea breeze will help." Ibrihim stood, his hand resting on his knife. He towered over Al Halbi.

"I cannot give you your payment." Al Halbi stepped back, eyes narrowed, back straight. He pursed his lips and shook his head. "Your reward awaits at the laboratory. I have no place to keep large sums in this office."

Thirty minutes later, Al Halbi's Mercedes roared through the checkpoints on their way out of town. Ibrihim tried to relax into the plush leather upholstery of the vehicle. The rutted road and blast of cold from the car's air conditioning made it impossible.

The Mercedes bounced over the now familiar dusty desert road.

Ibrihim tried to ignore his joint pains as he walked from the car to the shack. Even with the trap-door open, the confines of the small room seemed to suck the air from his lungs. He climbed down the ladder, his hands slick with sweat. His muscles twitched. The thought of the tunnel triggered his fear of enclosed spaces.

Al Halbi pushed on the stone wall of the pit, the door swung open.

Ibrihim staggered backwards, blinded by the light reflected off the white tile.

Al Halbi grabbed his arm and pulled him into the tunnel.

Ibrihim's shoes felt lead-boot heavy. He wanted to rush back through the door but felt cemented in place. The pit and the desert shack were preferable to the long passageway. He watched the heavy steel door slide shut.

The laboratory stank of ammonia and death.

Al Halbi tightened his grip on Ibrihim's arm and dragged him along the corridor. Al Halbi stopped along the way to point out the sickest innocents. At each stop, he praised Allah for giving him the opportunity to create the laboratory. "Each of these subjects are infected with a different organism." Al Halbi's smile grew demonic.

The empty-eyed children made no sounds. None smiled. Some rocked, others thrashed convulsively.

Ibrihim shook his arm free. He shivered. He shoved his hands in his pockets so Al Halbi couldn't see the tremors radiating from his chest to his fingertips.

Midway along the corridor the director stopped in front of the elegantly carved door with the decorative wrought-iron grill window. Plush carpets, elaborately carved mahogany furniture, and silk cushions enhanced the room.

"You must remember my apartment. Wait here." He opened the door and swept his hand in a dramatic gesture. "Please, sit down, relax." He pushed Ibrihim into the room.

A servant arrived with a tray holding several small cakes, cups and a pot coffee. He placed them on a low table, bowed, left Ibrihim to serve himself, and backed out of the room.

Ibrihim sank into the soft down-filled cushions of the divan. He tried to relax. In a few hours I'll be back in Jakarta, he thought, and I will never have to deal with this man again. The thought gave him enormous comfort. *I'll be out of this dreaded tunnel.* Away from the desert. Far from the heat, far from the sand, back in Jakarta, on my yacht.

Al Halbi stepped back into the hallway and closed the door. "I have a small bit of information for you." He said through the window-grille. "The Russian was not killed in Jakarta. You have failed miserably. This is all the reward you will get. Enjoy my apartment. You will never see your precious yacht again. You are suffering from the same disease I've sent to the Great Satan." His smile of triumph was no longer hidden.

The metal-on-metal screech of the door's bolt echoed through the laboratory.

Donovan's office
Langley, Virginia
The same day

Anne sat in a chair across from Donovan. "What's up, boss?"

"Just got more news. I thought you'd both like to hear it."

"Okay, we're here, what's the news?" Connor was puzzled. Donovan almost never called him to his office for an urgent meeting.

"I knew Anne was going to be in town today. So, I thought it would be good to share the new information now instead of waiting for the meeting next week." The boss was clearly happy about something.

"Our Mr. Ibrihim made another trip to Dumayr. As usual, he was picked up at the airport by Al Halbi's chauffeur. They went to the institute, and a half hour later Ibrihim and Al Halbi left and got into the Mercedes. They headed east. Forty-five minutes later, the Mercedes turned off the highway onto an unpaved road. The observation ended there. Our agent couldn't follow them into the desert without being seen." Donovan sat back in his chair and looked pleased.

"That's it?" Connor had been drawing circles on the top sheet of a pad.

"Of course not. That's hardly earth-shaking news." Donovan took a breath." Four hours later the Mercedes dropped Al Halbi off at the Scientific Institute."

Connor's latest page of doodles hit the rim of the wastebasket and fell to the floor. Donovan pointed to the crumpled paper. "I see your skills at basketball haven't improved."

Connor waved the comment away. "So, what happened to Ibrihim?"

"Don't know. We're guessing he's still at the laboratory."

All conversation stopped when Amelia came into the room to make more coffee. "Should I take lunch orders?"

Donovan laughed. "No, I'm letting them off early today, Amelia. But, you can send out for a roast beef sandwich for me, if you don't mind."

"You got it," she said on her way out the door.

"Oh, Amelia, wait."

"Yes?"

"Add a Boston Cream Donut to that order."

"I always do." She laughed as she stepped away from the desk.

Connor waited for the door to click closed. "What about his plane and crew?"

"Another question I can't answer. The plane is missing. The crew is missing. They filed a flight plan to return to Jakarta, but the plane never took off."

"So, we're assuming Ibrihim is at the lab."

"That's right. There was a report about his plane being wheeled into an empty hanger. But, we can't substantiate that information."

"How's the Delta Force team doing?" Connor refilled his coffee cup, and gestured toward Anne and Donovan with the carafe.

Anne shook her head. "No more coffee for me right now. I'm in town for a meeting with a class at the National Intelligence University. I'll drink enough to keep me awake for the next week while I'm there."

Donovan pushed his cup toward Connor for a refill. "Thanks." He waited until the cup was full.

"The team is somewhere in New Mexico or Arizona. I don't know which. All they said was southwestern desert. They've built what they hope is a replica of the underground lab. We at least know where the air-vents are and where the delivery entrance is located. We're taking a chance with those shacks—in the end, they'll be destroyed along with the rest of the laboratory. We have reconnaissance photos with evidence of Al Halbi's Mercedes parked near each of the shacks. We haven't been able to confirm their exact function, but we think they're entrances to the lab."

He paused to swill more coffee. "The President and the Prime Minister of Israel made a workable plan. Israel provided a dozen men from Shayetet 13 to work with an equal number of Delta Force for the mission. The teams are together. They'll perfect their timing until they can pull the mission off blindfolded."

Anne pushed her chair back. "Shayetet 13. Twelve well-trained Israelis and twelve men from Delta Force: now *there's* an awesome group. Who planned the mission?"

Connor placed the carafe on the table. "The team did." He noted the look of amazement on Anne's face. "They have the training and the experience. They know their capacity. And, they're the ones with the most to lose if the mission fails."

Donovan blew on his coffee and tentatively took a sip. "The damn desk jockeys from the Pentagon weren't pleased. They wanted to change the strategy. Tried to muscle their way into the plan. Thank goodness the President and his military advisor had the team's back. The mission will go down the way the men planned it."

"Have they decided on a staging area?"

"I haven't heard. I know they ruled out Italy, Greece, Kuwait, and the United Arab Emirates. I'm guessing they'll go out from Israel."

"Israel would be the best choice if Shayetet 13 is involved."

February 25
Al Halbi's office
Syrian Institute of Science and International Security

Al Halbi unlocked the door to his office and stepped inside. A lead weight seemed to settle in his stomach.

Adi Shamash, his head wrapped in the traditional black and white checkered kufiya, stood next to Al Halbi's desk. Neither the loose grey bisht nor his casual parade-rest stance masked the man's jaguar-like capability to spring.

Al Halbi's forced shallow breaths. The door had been locked. How did Shamash get in? He shut the door and turned. "May the peace, mercy, and blessings of Allah be with you."

Shamash sneered. He stood next to a carved wooden chest centered on the director's desk.

The thought of Shamash's strength and killer reflex left Al Halbi's mouth dry.

Shamash opened the lid: gold, silver, and gemstones sparkled in a shaft of dusty sun-light. Al Halbi smiled and rubbed his hands together. "You had no problems?"

"None. We boarded the yacht. The captain was suspicious, but he accepted the signature on the fake work-order. The captain was very helpful. He gathered the crew, restricted them to the bridge, and allowed us access to the engine room. We were able to place the explosives without interruption."

"Was the entire crew on board?"

"All were there." Al Halbi rubbed his hands together again and circled his thumbs on his index fingers. He wasn't interested in the details. He was anxious to run his fingers through the riches in the chest.

Shamash stepped in front of the chest, cutting off Al Halbi's view of the contents. "I asked the captain to take us on a test run. As soon as we were beyond the harbor limits, we dispatched the entire crew, sailed to the reefs and dropped the anchor. Our recovery team met us there."

Hot with excitement, almost salivating, anxious to check the contents of the chest, Al Halbi shivered in anticipation.

Shamash did not move, but narrowed his eyes and smirked. He leaned back, put his hands on the edge of the desk, and crossed his legs.

"We were some distance away when the charges went off." He yawned.

"Are you sure the yacht was destroyed?" Al Halbi knew Shamash was taunting him.

"Yes." Shamash shot him a look of disbelief. "Of course. We watched the explosion. The water spout was incredible. Whatever remains of the crew has been reduced to shark food on the floor of the Java Sea."

"A shame. A Ferretti 960. I would have liked to keep it for my use." Al Halbi shrugged. "What about the plane?"

"Dismantled and buried in the sand."

"The crew?"

"Dead — and buried beneath the aircraft."

The stylish Capitol Hill restaurant buzzed with activity. Dealers, donors, and diplomats enjoyed the ambiance and the French cuisine. Bistro Bis was a place to make deals, exert influence, and most important, be seen.

Maria sipped her tea and waited for Mary-Katherine.

Always in a hurry and always late, the senator dashed through the door of the restaurant and across the dining room to Maria's table. She hugged Maria, pulled off her trench coat and draped it over an empty chair. Her questions began nonstop. "Where have you been? Why haven't you answered your cell phone? I've been trying to call you for weeks."

"I was out of town."

"You didn't tell me you were going out of town the last time I saw you."

"It sort of came up at the last minute."

"Where..."

Maria didn't let her finish the question. "Fort Dietrich and Aberdeen Proving Grounds."

"Wha..."

This time Maria didn't let her finish the first word. "I attended the US AMRIID course on Biological and Chemical Warfare."

Mary-Katherine's eyes went wide, making them look bluer than ever. Her lips formed a heart shaped *O*. Her auburn hair was a mass of tangled curls from the rain. Maria laughed at the sight. "You look just like Aunt Anne's Christmas angel."

Mary-Katherine pursed her lips and waved off her friend's comment. "When did you decide to do that? You never said you were going to Fort Dietrich. You never told me that you wanted to take the course."

"If I told you how much I wanted to take the US AMRIID course, we would have gotten into another long discussion about bioterrorism. You would have said all kinds of horrible things."

"I would not..."

Maria cut her off. "Besides, I didn't have time. Your uncle Connor and my aunt Anne put my name on the list and wrote letters of recommendation. The approval came through at the last minute. I had a few hours to pack and get there." She crossed her arms on the table top. "Come to think of it, why didn't you ever tell me your Uncle Connor was Connor Quinlan?"

Mary-Katherine gave Maria an incredulous look. "I thought you knew."

"Did you know about Aunt Anne and your Uncle Connor? Did you know they were sweethearts in high school?"

"No. I didn't know they dated. I only knew they'd been friends for a long time. Mom and Dad and Uncle Connor still reminisce about the good times they had down the shore. Dances at St. Benedict's, the whole gang going somewhere to drink Awful-Awfuls. Fond memories of their teenage years."

"What's an Awful-Awful?"

"Some kind of enormous milk shake, I think. So, how was it?"

"How was what?"

"The course."

"Oh, I got lost in your details about the reminiscing." Maria's cheeks burned. She rubbed them and laughed.

"The course was fantastic, but intense." She talked faster and faster, and her hand gestures became more pronounced. "I learned so much. On the last day we searched the woods for victims of all sorts of bio and chem weapons. We made diagnoses, gave primary treatment, got them to the decontamination area . . ." She opened her bag, took out an envelope, and placed it on the table.

"Wait, wait, *wait*." Mary-Katherine waved her hands. "Slow down. Are you telling me *you* ran through the woods? *You* searched for casualties and transported them to the decontamination facilities . . . and you *enjoyed* it?"

"Yes. It was great." Maria's gestures became even more pronounced.

"Calm down, Maria. Everybody is looking at you."

Maria glanced at the closest tables. Diners from adjoin tables stared at her. "Oops, Sorry. I guess I got carried away." She folded her arms again and forced herself to calm down.

"But, it was so great. I wore full chemical gear and carried a backpack, and I wore a gas mask through the entire exercise. We got everything right." Maria could still feel the exhilaration of working with Antonio.

Mary-Katherine knitted her brow and reached out to Maria. "Keep your voice down. I'm sure the other diners don't care in the least about your experience. You're causing a scene." She paused. "I don't understand, you aren't making any sense. You hate hiking and camping. And who is the 'we'?"

""Me and Antonio." she forced a whisper. "This wasn't some kind of back-to-nature vacation. It wasn't like a hike up some rocky trail in the Poconos. It was important." Maria kept her voice low and tightened her gestures. She leaned across the table and looked into Mary-Katherine's eyes. "We had to find the victims, diagnose, treat and transport them to the decontamination tents. Antonio was great."

"Who's Antonio?"

"I told you, Antonio Ulibari, my field buddy. Everyone was assigned a field buddy for the duration of the course."

"What kind of criteria did they use?"

"I have no idea. Maybe they pulled the names out of a hat. Antonio is a doc at Ft. Hood. We studied together, planned our mission. It was really intensive."

"Sounds exhausting."

"Mary-Katherine . . ." Maria tried to find the right words to describe how empowered she felt. She closed her eyes and thought for a long moment.

"Do you remember the lengthy hours you worked when you were clerking for Justice Breyer? Remember how you felt when your work resulted in a favorable decision?"

"Yes. But what I did was real." Mary-Katherine tossed her auburn curls.

"And you think because this wasn't *real*, it wasn't important?"

"I didn't say what you did wasn't important. But it was an exercise, not a response to a real attack." An irritated expression crossed Mary-Katherine's face. "The work I did at the court was for real people involved in real situations. My research directly affected people all over the United States—it wasn't some abstract exercise."

"I don't know how you can maintain that attitude. How can you deny the reality of something that *could* be very real? After 9/11, the anthrax attack, the Ebola scare, and now Zika virus, you're calling the exercise abstract?"

"Look, Maria. No matter how many times you run through the woods in all your gear, you won't convince me we're going to have a biological or chemical attack in the US. I just don't think it's going to happen."

"I think we need to stop talking about this. You're doing exactly what I knew you'd do." Maria pursed her lips and turned her head away.

"What am I doing?"

"Being so damn negative."

Mary-Katherine reached for the envelope Maria had placed on the table and pulled out a photograph. "What's this?"

"You said you didn't want to talk about it anymore." Maria reached for the picture.

"Well, you can tell me about this." She squinted at the image.

"It's a photo of my class. Sort of our graduation picture. They took it on the last day." Maria pulled Mary-Katherine's arm back to the center of the table and pointed at the image. "Here I am."

"Right in the center of the crowd, as usual. Who's the guy next to you? And why is he looking at you, not the camera?"

Maria knew her cheeks had turned bright crimson. "That's Antonio. I told you, he was my field buddy." She grabbed her menu and held it in front of her face.

Mary-Katherine cleared her throat, reached across the table with one finger, and eased the menu down a few inches.

Maria peeked over the edge of the leather folder. "Don't look at me like I've hidden a deep secret from you. I told you, Antonio was my field buddy. By assignment."

"Uh-huh. Tell me more."

"He's an army doc. He's stationed at Fort Hood, in Texas."

Mary-Katherine caught her lower lip with her teeth. "I know where Fort Hood is. I want to know more about your Doctor Antonio."

"He's not *my* Doctor Antonio. The assignments were random."

"From the way he's looking at you in the picture, he *wants* to be your Doctor Antonio. And judging from your reaction to my question, you want *him* to be your Doctor Antonio, too." Mary-Katherine shook her curls. Her look conveyed certainty.

Maria made a face. "Okay, okay, enough already. Even if I wanted there to be a relationship. Even if I hoped there could be. It would never happen. I'm in Maryland and he's in Texas." She slapped her menu closed. "There's no way for this to develop into a real relationship. We would have to travel two thousand miles just to go out for pizza." She paused for a sip of water.

"I don't want to discuss Antonio." Maria covered her eyes with her hands.

"I'll change the subject, for now. But only because I have some good news."

"Oh? Have you passed a bill on the hill that affects real people in some wonderful way?" Maria's tone was condescending.

Mary-Katherine lowered her head and glared at her friend. "No, this doesn't have to do with the Senate. I wanted to invite you to your favorite godchild's First Communion. But, forget it. You have the uncanny ability to pour cold water on the most innocent information."

A feeling of shame filled Maria's chest and dumped into her belly. "You're right. I'm sorry."

"Brittany's First Communion is June ninth. I hope you'll help me pick out a dress and headpiece for her."

Maria forced down the lump in her throat. "I'm really sorry for being so bitchy. Of course I'll go shopping with you. She'll look so innocent with a headpiece and veil over her wild, strawberry-blond curls. Nobody will realize she's a devil in disguise."

"Believe me, the teachers and Mother Superior all know she's a devil."

Maria laughed. "The headpiece and veil will be my treat."

"She'll love it." Mary-Katherine signaled to the waiter. "Oh, and while we're there you can help me pick out some new maternity clothes and a few—"

"Maternity clothes? Mary-Katherine?!"

Anne and Connor took the elevator to Donovan's office at the George Bush Center for Intelligence. "What's this all about?" Anne stepped out of the elevator and waited for Connor.

"Don't know. He called me yesterday and said we should meet him here this morning."

"Yeah, he told me that, too."

Amelia was at her desk, smirking. She picked up the phone and dialed Donovan's extension. "The newlyweds are here."

"The newly-weds?" Anne looked at Connor. "What's she talking about?"

"I haven't the faintest idea." He leaned down and whispered in her ear, "Do you think it would be such a bad idea?"

"God'll get you." Anne laughed. "Don't ask me again unless you're serious. I might say yes. What'll you do if that happens?"

Connor opened his mouth to respond, but Donovan opened his office door and greeted them with a grin. "Come in. I want to congratulate you in person."

Anne looked at Donovan's grin, Amelia's smirk, and Connor's expression of total confusion. What on earth?

As soon as they shut the door Donovan handed an envelope to each of them. "Your packets are complete: tickets, hotel reservations, papers. You leave for Jakarta in a few hours."

"Jakarta?"

Donovan ignored the interruption. "The story is, you were married three hours ago at St. Francis Xavier Church in Leonardtown, Maryland. My good Jesuit cousin, Father Michael Callahan, has documentation to support the story. And if necessary, he'll make it available."

Donovan grabbed a paper from his desk. "You're flying to Jakarta, where you'll be staying for two days. Then on to India for a week, followed by a few days in Eastern Europe to visit Anne's cousins, and finally to Vienna for four days."

Connor looked up, "Might I be askin' ye' why ye' haven't included me cousins in Ireland?"

Donovan covered his eyes with his left hand. "I wouldn't recommend you trying to impress any of your cousins with that horrible brogue. And, please remember that you didn't really get married today."

No, but it would have answered my prayers if we had, Anne thought.

"As usual, we've provided several extra identities for you to use, just in case." He pointed at the envelopes. "We included cell phones in the packets. They'll connect you to the folks if you need to be pulled out in a hurry. I don't expect that you'll have any trouble."

"Problems always pop up. I can't think of a single assignment we didn't have to alter on the spur of the moment."

"So, you're covered. You know what to do if there's a problem." He walked to his desk. "I don't expect any problems. This is not a secret ops trip. Neither of you are on the dark side of the Company anymore."

Donovan took a sip of his coffee and made a face. "Damn. Cold coffee." He put the half-full cup down, grabbed a clean cup, and poured fresh coffee from the carafe.

"You'll be traveling under your real names. Doctor Anne Damiano, an expert in the international transport of disease and Connor Quinlan, a lawyer who does frequent consulting for the International Association of Ports and Harbors." He took a swallow of the fresh brew. "You just got married. You're going on your honeymoon, and you'll stop and see old friends and family along the way."

"All the more reason to go to Ireland. I'd be sure to be bringin' me fine bride to show off to the family in County Wicklow."

"Well okay, I'll cancel the Vienna trip and send you to Ireland if you'd like." Donovan shook his head and picked up two thick files from his desk.

Anne and Connor spoke at the same time: He said "Vienna" and she said "Ireland."

"Enough of the foolishness." Donovan handed one folder to Anne and the other to Connor. "Have a seat, and memorize the information. As usual, the folder stays here. Only you and your travel papers and the cell phones leave this office."

Donovan walked back to his desk, pulled out his chair, and cleared his voice. "Be careful. Jakarta is a dangerous place even for the casual visitor. Several bombs were planted there in the past few years. The JW Marriott and the Ritz-Carlton were both bombed on several occasions. Even though I don't think you'll have a problem, there are no guarantees. Stay sharp."

"The reports that cross my desk at Dietrich are filled with information about Indonesians leaving for Syria." Anne stared at the unopened file. "The last report I read said more than three hundred men left each month. Most were going for military training in the Saudi army."

Donovan's office chair creaked as he sagged into the leather seat. His voice reflected weariness and frustration, "Their government has the same problem most democracies have. They've declared the Islamic State an illegal organization and denounced its ideology. But the pronouncement has no force of law. They can't arrest anyone unless they're carrying firearms or can be proved to be actively plotting an attack."

Connor read through the first few pages. "You want me to locate the shipping containers?" He pursed his lips and wrinkled his nose. "The containers aren't in Jakarta. I'm sure they're on the high seas."

Donovan nodded. "No doubt. See if you can find out what ships they're on and where they plan to off-load their cargo." He turned to Anne. "Keep your eyes open for any sign of disease. Pay a visit to the Minister of Health in Jakarta. If you can, find out why he wasn't at the last International Seminar on Bioterrorism Preparedness. His absence raised some flags for the analysts."

"I wondered about his absence too," she said. "He has never missed one of our meetings."

Anne opened her packet. "I've been watching the bulletins from the World Health Organization. There's no indication of any orthopox outbreak anywhere in the world."

"Orthopox?" Donovan and Connor chorused.

"Monkeypox, cowpox, camelpox, mousepox."

"Are you serious?" Connor started laughing. "Camelpox?"

"Mousepox?" Donovan looked to see if she was teasing.

"No, I'm not kidding. Mousepox is an actual disease. Of mice. Camelpox and monkeypox are actually better named than chicken-pox. Camelpox occurs in camels and monkeypox attacks monkeys. Chickens don't get chickenpox—humans do." She took a sip of her coffee. "The World Health Organization is reporting Ebola cases in West Africa. And—"

"Ebola?" Connor interrupted. "I haven't heard a word about Ebola in months."

"The American press just hasn't bothered to report Ebola deaths. You know how it goes. When the public gets bored with a story, the press doesn't talk about it." Connor and Donovan both nodded. "Cholera's a huge problem in the Libyan refugee tent cities. But, I did find reports of new cases of MERS-CoV in Syria and in many other countries, including South Korea."

"MERS? What's MERS?" Connor asked as Anne sipped her coffee.

Anne made a face. "Yuck, how old is this coffee?" She slid her cup away. "It's the virus *du jour*: Middle-Eastern respiratory syndrome coronavirus. We all worried when it first showed up, thought it was going to be a pandemic. But it hasn't turned into a huge problem—at least so far."

"The only virus of concern to the Americas, right now, is the Zika virus." She paused and straightened her shoulders. "There's been no sign of smallpox anywhere in the world. If even one case existed,

WHO would have put out an alert immediately. The media would be fighting to find experts to give them dire warnings, and they'd be putting out any and all information they could get their hands on, whether it was true or not."

Connor pushed his chair back from the table. "I've been thinking. What if Bushinikov didn't hand them smallpox virus? Maybe he brought some other virus." He tipped his chin at Donovan. "What kind of information have you gotten out of him?"

"Not much. He was sick for a long time. He admitted exchanging vials containing some kind of virus for money, but he didn't identify the contents of the vials. We don't want to push him too hard. We'd like him to come over to our side willingly. If we can get him to join us, he'll be a treasure-trove of information. But we have to gain his trust first. And he and his wife will have to decide if they want to become a part of the American way of life."

"You know, it is possible he gave the Syrians an inactivate virus." Anne's voice came low and quiet.

Connor stopped midstride. Donovan's head snapped up. They each turned toward Anne, and stared at her, waiting.

Anne grabbed a clean cup and poured fresh coffee from the carafe. She took a sip. "If he stole smallpox from the lab at Vektor and handed those vials to the courier in Jakarta, the virus might not have been viable." Anne returned to the table, put down her cup, and pulled out her chair.

"Are you saying he intentionally brought them inactive virus?"

"No, he may not have known the virus was inactive. The vials could have been mislabeled at Vektor. Considering the state of their labs, it's possible the temperature of the refrigeration units didn't remain constant." She spun her chair to face them.

"Even if they were viable when he left Russia they could have become inactive. If the vials got too warm during his travels . . ."

Donovan threw up his hands. "I get it, I get it! How many more 'maybes' can there be?"

"Lots. But I want to warn you of one other important consideration."

Connor gave a sigh of exasperation. He returned to the table and refilled his empty coffee cup. "What else?" He sounded bored. Uninterested.

Anne's jaw was clenched. She took a deep breath and exhaled. "There hasn't been enough time."

"Time for what?"

"Time for Syria to make a weapon."

"Come on, they have the virus. They have the lab. We're told they have the know-how. What else do they need?" Connor gave a dismissive wave.

Anne's foot tapped against the table leg. "They need time. *If* we assume Bushinikov gave the Syrians viable virus. *And* we assume the Syrians are going to produce a weaponized form of smallpox." She pushed her chair back, stood and paced the length of the conference table.

"We have to realize how much time it will take. Al Halbi would have had to replicate the virus, then activate the virus and use some method to increase the amount of infectious material. A multitude of controlled steps are necessary in the process. They haven't had the virus long enough to get a weapon ready for primetime. And, he certainly wouldn't have had a weapon ready to send to the United States."

Donovan leaned forward, an inquisitive look on his face. "What else would he have to do?"

"Test the weapon, somehow. He would have to infect a population of humans. There's no other way he could be certain the virus would work."

"What kind of time frame are we talking about?"

"Many months. More than a year."

March 1
Jakarta, Indonesia

Connor and Anne struggled through the Soekarta-Hatta International Airport. Lines to clear customs were tediously long. Anne held tight to Connor's hand. She feared they would be separated on their way to collect their luggage. People shouldered and shoved their way through the crush of bodies packed into the reception area.

"Heck of a way to start a honeymoon. I feel like I've been squished," Anne said when they reached the taxi line.

"Can't think of anyone I'd rather be squished with." Connor smiled and pulled her close against his body.

Once they were seated in the cab, Anne rested her head on his shoulder. This feels good. Nice to at least "play" married folks. She smiled at the thought. St. Francis Xavier, a wonderful touch. Donovan covered all the bases. Too bad it's not real.

When Connor kissed her forehead, she smiled and gave a satisfied sigh. Warmth spread through her body and sank to a place that made her realize how much she wanted Connor.

She grinned. A nice topping on my thoughts.

"What's with the smile?" he asked.

"Just savoring the moment." She snuggled closer. "I'm exhausted. I don't like long flights."

"Exhausted? We're on our honeymoon. I can't wait to explore this beautiful city." He gestured out the taxi window. Enormous ferns in the entire spectrum of green filled the public spaces. Modern buildings rose to the sky, fountains bubbled over, apartment buildings with purple, white, scarlet, and yellow orchids draped from their balconies. Silvery white and green vines climbed trellises and garden walls. Vehicles filled the streets, horns blared, brakes screeched, voices raised in anger shouted from open automobile windows.

A uniformed porter greeted them at the door of the Jakarta JW Marriott, the sleeves of his navy blue jacket were enhanced by three gold bands. The quiet lobby offered relief after the clamor of the street. A much younger bellhop with a single gold band on his sleeve ushered them to their suite on the twenty-fourth floor.

A wall of windows stretched the length of their sitting room and bedroom. The view encompassed the cityscape. Gold silk drapes. Beige walls. Brass lamps with white silk shades. Chairs covered in gold and white damask. Thick beige carpet. Luxury and comfort.

Connor scanned the room. He found three listening devices. One on each phone and one in a lamp in the bedroom. He pointed to each device and covered his lips with one index finger.

Anne nodded. They would have to guard their conversation and stay in "honeymoon mode." The devices remained in place.

"You better call your brother to let him know we arrived safe and sound," Anne said.

"It's almost nine a.m. here, so it's going on ten p.m. last night in Maryland. I'm sure he'll be awake and anxious to hear from us."

Connor pulled out his personal cell phone and called Donovan. "Hi, we're here. Just got to our hotel. The flight was smooth. No problems."

He listened for a moment. "Okay. Be sure to let Anne's sister know you heard from us. We'll call again when we get to New Delhi."

"I'm going to take a shower and crawl into bed. I'll unpack later." Anne heaved a sigh. "I didn't get much sleep on the plane. And, if it's nine p.m. in Maryland, it's close to my bedtime." She grabbed a terrycloth robe from the closet and headed for the bathroom. "I wonder how long it'll take me to catch up with the jetlag."

About an hour and a half later Connor whispered in her ear. "Hey, sleepyhead, time to get up."

Anne's eyes flew open. "What time is it?"

"Time for lunch. Do you want to go down to the restaurant or get room service?"

"The restaurant. I want to check out the pool and the spa. I'd love to get a massage."

A wall of floor-to-ceiling windows in the Pearl Chinese Restaurant provided a magnificent view of the city. Elegant, high-backed chairs upholstered in gold velvet surrounded each table. Crisp white linen cloths were placed over full-length burgundy table cloths. Each table held a graceful vase that held a single white orchid. White linen napkins. Silver flatware. And, white china plates on gold chargers. The pea-green carpet woven with dinner-plate-sized oriental medallions of white, gold and burgundy, stretched across the expanse of floor.

The maître d' escorted Anne and Connor to a table next to the windows. Connor feigned an aversion to heights and pointed to an empty table for two along a side wall. The table he chose provided a 180-degree view of the room.

Anne scanned the menu. Her stomach lurched. "Oh, yuck!"

Connor's head jerked up. "What?" He scanned the room.

"How does barbecued jellyfish sound to you?"

"Not high on my list of favorites. I'm not into exotic."

Anne wrinkled her nose. "The menu's a challenge. I don't imagine you want roasted pork belly either. I know it's not something I'd order."

"Maybe we should be more adventurous. We're not going to get another honeymoon trip to Indonesia. You could try the asparagus and crab soup."

"That sounds okay, but let me check out the rest of the menu." Anne flipped the page. "Oh, this sounds good. Pork loin with satay sauce and steamed rice."

"Sounds like a safe choice. I'll try the wok-fried shrimp with XO sauce. I think I've had XO steak at the Asean Restaurant in Ellicott City. Let's see if this is as good."

Connor reached for Anne's left hand and caressed the wedding band. "While you slept, I met with the director of the Jakarta Port. He told me all the shipping lines associated with the Indonesian Ports of Authority are in close contact with the Muslim Trade Network. It's impossible to do business any other way."

Anne pressed her lips into a straight line and gave a slight shrug. "Doesn't surprise me. Islamic terrorists have taken hold of the entire region. The reports I've been getting say Indonesia is a prime recruiting ground for the Islamic State."

Connor scowled. "Couples are leaving Indonesia on a monthly basis to join ISIS."

Their waiter arrived and took their orders. "Shall I bring tea?"

Anne nodded. "Yes, please."

When the waiter returned to the kitchen, Connor leaned a little closer to Anne and murmured, "The director had some interesting information about Ibrihim's boat."

Anne looked up, waiting for the rest of the story.

"The yacht exploded somewhere in the middle of the Java Sea."

"His boat exploded? When?"

"About three weeks ago."

"How convenient. Too convenient if you ask me. Do they think it was an accident?"

"The director didn't comment either way. But, convenience certainly is a consideration. He said the report wasn't detailed. Some tourists reported the explosion. He received statements from a few fishing boat captains about an explosion. No one could tell him which boat exploded. None of the fishing boats were close enough for the crew to provide a positive ID. They all agreed it was some kind of luxury craft. Ibrihim's yacht never returned to its berth. So, they've made the assumption — there's no way to know for sure. From the missing persons complaints the director is pretty sure the entire crew was on board."

Connor paused when the waiter brought the tea. He waited until the man was out of ear shot.

"The authorities are sure no one on board survived the explosion. If the initial blast didn't get them, the sharks would. The director had no idea if Ibrihim was on the boat. But, he hasn't been seen in Jakarta. And they're pretty sure he left for Syria a few hours before the boat left its slip." Connor poured tea for each of them. "His pilot filed a flight plan for Dumayr the same day."

Another pause to give the waiter an opportunity to serve their dinner. He snapped the white linen napkins and placed them on their laps.

Anne watched the waiter make his way back to the kitchen. "Let me get this straight. The boat exploded a great distance out in the Java Sea?"

"Yes. The port director said his reports indicated the yacht was near the reefs."

She folded her arms. "And, the entire crew is presumed dead?"

"Yes."

She tilted her head. "So, now the boat and all aboard are at the bottom of the ocean." She pursed her lips. "That's way too convenient." Anne took a bite of the pork. "This is good."

He nodded. "You're right, way too convenient."

"Where's his plane?"

Connor shrugged and raised his eyebrows, and speared a shrimp. "No one knows. The plane didn't return to Jakarta. And, the plane isn't at the airport in Dumayr."

"You said the pilot filed a new flight plan?"

"Yes, they filed a plan to return to Jakarta. But the plane never took off. It disappeared."

Anne sipped her tea. "Planes don't disappear. At least not when they're on the ground in an airport. What else have you pieced together?"

"Our informant tells us Ibrihim hated the desert. On previous trips, when he would visit his Imam, he brought gifts, monetary gifts, to insure a safe return."

"But not this time?"

Connor pursed his lips and shook his head. "Nope. He didn't return to Jakarta. There hasn't been any sign of him, his plane or his flight crew. Not in Syria or Indonesia, and not anywhere else."

Anne checked her watch and drank the remaining tea in her cup. "This was good. We'll have to return to try some other things on the menu." She pushed back from the table. "If I'm going to make it to my meeting with the Minister of Health, I'd better get a move on." She stood and kissed Connor's forehead.

"See you later my dear, sweet husband. See if you can make an appointment for me to get a massage later today. And, see if you can get more information about the elusive Ibrihim."

Connor stood and hugged her. "The port director said he'd get back to us later today. He's going to check with the shipping, who might be able to get the delivery addresses of the goods. If we're lucky we'll have answers before dark."

Three hours later Anne met Connor in the lobby. They strolled toward the bank of elevators. She stood on tiptoe, kissed his cheek, and murmured, "I've got a strange story to tell you—later. Did you make my spa appointment?" The elevator door opened.

He held his hand against the elevator door and waited for Anne to walk in. "No. I tried. But they kept asking me questions I couldn't answer. Did you want a herbal wrap? Did you want a stone massage? Did you want a pedicure? The list of services and types of massage and wraps and . . . ."

Anne giggled. "Not a problem. I'll call to make the appointment from our room." Still smiling, she turned and pushed the elevator button for the twenty-fourth floor.

The high speed elevator zoomed up the shaft, making Anne's ears pop. They stepped out of the elevator. The corridor was empty, no maid's carts cluttered the halls. Connor pulled his room card key from his pocket.

Anne leaned her shoulder against the wall. Connor pushed her away from the door and mouthed, "Someone's been in the room." The 'Do Not Disturb' sign was still in place, but a hair he tucked in the door jamb was curled on the carpet. He pointed to her and then pointed to the emergency exit.

She nodded, understanding his directions, grateful the powers that be always made sure the rooms they booked for agents were steps from an emergency exit. Anne ran to the exit, stepped onto the landing, and held the door open and watched Connor.

He stood as far to the side of the door as he could, slid his cardkey into the slot and immediately pulled his hand away. He sprinted to the exit. The electronic click triggered a storm of bullets that Swiss-cheesed the door's wooden panel and slammed through the opposite wall.

Connor grabbed Anne's hand. She let go of the exit door. A second burst of gunfire. Connor and Anne flew up the stairs. They reached the twenty-sixth floor landing before the gunmen fired again. Anne and Connor waited with their bodies pressed against the wall. Two floors below them the door crashed into the cement brick wall. After a moment's silence, heavy footsteps echoed on the narrow staircase.

Connor dared a careful look over the railing. Two men dressed in grey bisht, with hoods thrown back and white kufiya covering their heads, ran down the exit stairs, guns drawn.

When the echo of their steps faded Anne gestured to the door. He twisted the handle, and they jogged along the hallway of the twenty-sixth floor toward the next exit staircase. About halfway down the hall Connor broke the glass on the fire alarm and pulled the handle.

They continued to the exit at the far end of the corridor. Anne ran down one flight to the twenty-fifth floor, while Connor ran up the stairs. She sprinted along the hallway, pulled the handle on the first fire alarm she passed, then continued to take a different stairway to the twenty-fourth floor. Ear piercing alarms sounded, interspersed with directions in a variety of languages to remain calm and leave their rooms by the closest exit.

"The elevators are not operating," the announcement declared. "Please use the staircases to exit the hotel."

Anne set off two more fire alarms. Connor came around the corner and met her at the door to their room.

"By now they should be good and confused," he said.

The door, shredded from the automatic weapon's fire, stood open. They stepped over the rubble and slid into the room. Connor checked the bathroom and gave her a thumbs up.

A hubbub of voices rose in the hallway. Guests scrambled from their rooms. Men shouted. Children screamed. Mothers barked orders at their families. Fire warning announcements and fire-alarms continued to blare.

Within minutes Anne was dressed in red slacks and a white jacket. She tugged a medium-length blond wig over her dark hair. Connor chose khaki slacks and a muted green sweater. He dusted his hair with a platinum hair spray, then pulled a sling out of his carry-on, secured it on his left arm, and topped off his new ensemble with a Greek mariner's cap and a feigned limp.

"See you in DC," he said, brushing her cheek with his lips.

"Hell of a honeymoon," she responded. We can't even have a fake honeymoon. *Talk about star crossed lovers.*

They wheeled their suitcases into the hallway and walked toward separate exit doors.

Twenty minutes later Anne burst into the lobby, pushed by the frightened crowd behind her.

Worried and angry hotel patrons filled the area. Anxious guests screamed at the desk clerks. Others pushed and shoved their way out of the hotel. Firemen elbowed through the crowd and thrust guests aside as they forced their way into the hotel.

She watched Connor move through the crowd and exit the hotel through the front door. He wormed his way between the fire trucks, and walked to the taxi stand.

Anne took a firm grip on the handle of her suitcase and moved in the opposite direction. She left the hotel through a side exit and skirted a tree-lined path to a wrought-iron gate. Although the Ritz-Carlton Mega Kuningan was a few minute walk from the Marriott, Anne meandered to the Caffe Bene Café. She ordered a Spanish Latte and a blueberry and cream cheese waffle. Her corner seat provided a good view of the shop, the street and the exit.

Anne pulled out her emergency phone, and dialed the code for "need emergency evacuation." The CIA operation headquarters' response was immediate. "First alternate ID, call back in twenty minutes."

She chose a route that circled around the rear of the JW Marriott, then turned right to bring her to the Ritz-Carlton Hotel. Futuristic furniture, huge marble columns, and intimate seating areas contrasted with the lobby of the JW Marriott. Long lines of people waited their turn at reception.

I'll bet most of them are evacuees from the Marriott.

She strode across the lobby, head up, smiling. If you act like you belong no one will question your right to be here. She walked through the posh hotel to the elevator without incident. The legend beside the fifth floor elevator button said SPA.

Perfect.

Outside the spa entrance, Anne pulled out her cell phone a second time and called the CIA Operations Center. Again the reply was immediate, the message abrupt: "Qantas, eight-twenty p.m. flight to Sydney."

She checked her watch. *Almost five hours before I have to be at the airport.*

The spa, nestled in a lavish tropical garden, five stories above the city, continued the hotel's color theme. Pools and hot tubs were lined with gold-and-white tile. Floors reflected a subtle golden glow. Shades of cocoa, sepia and bronze provided a restful atmosphere.

An appointment for a massage was available in one of the private pavilions.

Anne shoved her luggage in a locker, undressed and snuggled into a thick French terrycloth robe, then wrapped her hair in a matching towel. Soothing new-age music, low lighting, and a cup of herbal tea lulled her through the twenty minute wait for her appointment.

Two hours later Anne, now an auburn-haired, green-eyed woman with a slight lisp, walked out of the hotel, climbed into a taxi, and requested a ride to the Sheraton Bandara Hotel. Her dinner at the Linjani Restaurant was excellent.

A few minutes after seven, she arrived at Jakarta International Airport. A sign written in multiple languages read: DEPARTURE FEE. Crowds pushed and shoved. Brute strength prevailed in her struggle to get to the window. Two men were in the booth; one wore a kufiya and a grey bisht. He stood behind the departure fee clerk with two pictures in his hands.

Anne held her breath, smoothed her long red hair, and slid the 150,000 rupiah fee to the clerk. The man in the gray bisht gave her a passing glance and immediately scanned the crowds behind her.

First hurdle accomplished without incident. I hope Connor is okay.

Anne checked her watch. Thirty minutes before her flight.

She smiled and handed the passport with her first alternative ID to the clerk at the Qantas desk.

"Hello Ms. Fullerton, how can I help you?" The Qantas clerk checked the picture of a smiling red-haired, green-eyed woman, and looked up at Anne.

"I'm scheduled to leave on the Qantas flight this evening."

The woman checked Anne's alternative ID. She typed the information into her computer. "Yes, Ms. Fullerton. Do you have baggage to check?"

"No, I just have a carry on."

"Have you been in contact with livestock of any kind in the past month?"

"No."

"Have you been in contact with anyone with a viral or bacterial illness in the past six weeks?"

"No."

"Australia has some additional restrictions. There is a limit on the amount of cigarettes you can bring into Australia. We also prohibit wood objects, food products . . ." The attendant rattled off an extensive list of restricted items.

Anne smiled, acknowledged the information, and assured the clerk she wasn't carrying any contraband."

Her flight was scheduled to board in twenty minutes.

The clerk tapped 'enter'.

The machine next to Anne spit out her ticket.

"You will have to go through customs in Sydney. They'll check your luggage when you deplane."

"Of course. Thank you for the warning."

The attendant smiled. "They'll repeat all the questions as well."

Anne nodded, slipped the ticket into her passport, walked to security.

The departure lounge was crowded. Women sat on benches, stared at the walls, looked out the windows, and gazed at undefined nothings. Some of the women wore western clothing, some wore burkas. Men in business suits, men in casual clothing, and a few men who wore kufiya roamed the corridors, cellphones glued to their ears. The men smoked incessantly. The acrid stench of Turkish and Syrian tobacco permeated the lounge.

Anne stood with her back to the wall and appeared to be one of the many disinterested and bored travelers. But, in reality she watched and waited, tense and alert.

March 2
Sydney, Australia

Anne deplaned at six-thirty in the morning. The Sydney customs area had roped off partitions and long queues of travelers.

She called the evacuation line. Again the reply was immediate. "Qantas, 1:10 flight this afternoon. Fiji. Second ID."

Fiji. I can handle that.

After assuring the customs clerk she hadn't brought any of the restricted items into the country, she waited through a perfunctory search of her carry on, then walked the concourse until she found a bathroom.

Twenty minutes later she wore brown slacks, a red-and-brown plaid jacket, and cordovan flats. A change of wigs and contacts and she'd become a lavender-eyed brunette.

Five-and-a-half hours to kill.

Qantas had served a continental breakfast and it was too early for any of the shops to open. No point looking for food. She did find a small coffee shop where she ordered 'a cuppa'. The strong Australian coffee lifted her mood.

I'm getting as bad as Donovan with my coffee addiction.

Fiji, she thought. *Fiji.* I think a shopping junket is in order.

Anne wandered through the airport until she found a glassed-in partition that protected the money exchange and shielded the Travelex clerk. There were no customers waited in line and no gray-robed watcher waited inside.

"I'd like to exchange American currency for Australian, please." Anne smiled at the man.

He did not smile back. His name tag read H. Bland.

She placed seven-hundred dollars and her second alternate ID in the open drawer. The clerk pulled the drawer to his side of the partition, checked her appearance against her passport picture, and counted the one-hundred-dollar bills.

Still unsmiling, he placed a voucher in the drawer and slid it to Anne's side of the partition. "Thank you, Mr. Bland."

She mustered the sunniest smile she could manage. Your *countenance* lives up to your name. Anne signed the voucher with the name on her second alternative ID, 'Courtney Wentworth'.

The clerk pulled the drawer through to his side and compared the signature on the voucher to the signature on the passport. Satisfied, he counted Australian currency, placed it in the drawer, and sent it back to her along with her passport and a copy of the voucher. Still no smile.

She roamed through the airport, browsed through a book store, and asked directions to a travel agency.

The pleasant and smiling young clerk walked her to the door. "Down the concourse to the left, miss." He pointed to the general area. "G'day."

As Anne approached the travel agency a woman unlocked the gate and pushed it open. She unlocked the front door. The lights in the office flashed on when Anne was still two doors away.

Anne stopped in the entrance and watched while the agent put her briefcase on the desk, and grabbed a green linen jacket from the back of a chair.

The woman smoothed her hair, shrugged into her jacket, then turned. Her face lit with surprise to see someone at the door. "Hullo?"

"Sorry, I didn't mean to startle you," Anne said. "I hope you can help me. I'm in a bit of a quandary."

"Welcome to the Down Under Travel Agency, I'm Sally Miller." The woman extended her hand. Sally had a pronounced Australian accent. "I'll do my best. How can I help you?" She gestured to a chair near her desk.

Happily, the chair offered a view of the concourse. "I'm flying to Nadi in a few hours. My corporate office just threw a monkey wrench into my plans. Do you think it would be possible for me to find a hotel in Nadi on such short notice?" Anne slid onto the proffered chair. "I was supposed to attend a meeting in Arizona tomorrow. But, I just got a text message saying the meeting has been rescheduled for later this week. If at all possible I'd like to check into a hotel in Nadi this afternoon and stay for three nights."

She rested her elbow on Sally's desk and swiped at her forehead with her fingers. *A meeting in Arizona? What on earth made me think of Arizona?*

"Oooh . . . I don't know. Let me see. It's such short notice." Sally started clicking the keys on her computer.

"I'd rather relax for a few days in Fiji than waste three days in Phoenix." Anne made a face.

Sally's sudden smile and look of satisfaction erased all doubt. "You're in luck. The Westin Fiji Resort and Spa at Denarau Island has an opening. It's one of the newest resorts. And, it's close to the airport." A few more clicks on the computer. "They have an ocean-front room available, on the first floor with a balcony and a view of the sea."

"Sally, you're a genius. Thank you. It sounds wonderful." Anne handed her the Courtney Wentworth credit card.

Sally read the card and continued to key in the information. "Thank you, Ms. Wentworth."

"Do you think I'll be lucky enough to get a full day at the spa?"

"Right-o, let's see." Sally's fingers danced across the keyboard. Anne stood a little straighter. She felt the muscles in her lower back relax. *I took a whole week off from Dietrich for my 'honeymoon', thanks to Donovan. No sense in wasting all my vacation time.*

Anne pictured Donovan. She was sure she was not the only covert operative who'd experienced his wrath. Agents were expected to return for an immediate debriefing. She shrugged off her guilt. *I deserve a few days of R&R after someone tries to kill me.*

Connor's face pushed its way into her consciousness. *Hope you made it back safe and sound, my dearest friend. You can give Donovan the debriefing.*

She shook off her musings and turned toward the travel agent. Sally stared at Anne, eyebrows raised, fingers poised over the keys.

"Oh. Sorry, Sally. I was daydreaming. Did you say something?"

"The spa doesn't have an open appointment for tomorrow. But, they do have an opening for a full day at the spa for the day after tomorrow. You'll start with a wrap in the morning, lunch, then a heated rocks massage in the afternoon. They claim it's guaranteed to relax a stone monolith."

"Sounds perfect." Anne's smile matched Sally's. "I guess I better pick up some beach clothes before I go."

"Right-o. There's a Billabong Shop just down the hall to your right."

At the Billabong Beach Wear Shop Anne chose a simple black bathing suit with a gentle drape effect across the front. Unobtrusive enough. She piled a black-and-white sarong beach wrap and a broad-brimmed white straw hat with a black ribbon on the counter near the cash register.

"Oops. One more thing."

Anne fetched a pair of black sandals to add to the selections.

March 4
Langley, Virginia

"Hi, Amelia."

"Hello, Mr. Quinlan. Are you sure you want to go in there? He's not in the best frame of mind."

"Guess I'd better see what I can do to calm him down."

Amelia picked up the phone receiver and pressed a button. "Mr. Quinlan is here."

Connor stepped into the office and gently closed the door.

Red-faced and glaring, Donovan sputtered, "She's in Fiji."

"Good for her. Wish I was there with her."

"She's staying for three days!"

Donovan's outrage turned his face an even darker shade of red.

Connor tried to smother a laugh. "Not a bad way to celebrate our honeymoon even if I'm not there with her." He sat in one of the leather chairs. "Why are you so angry? You're the one who sent her there."

"The stop in Fiji was to change planes. It wasn't a destination." Donovan paced to the coffee carafe and grabbed a donut. He bit into the cream filled confection. "She knows better. She was supposed to come back to the States. Fiji was a transit point." Donovan's voice was stern. "She knows better." He wiped the icing from his lips with a paper napkin.

Donovan did a double-take at Connor's smile. "Don't you laugh at me."

"I'm not laughing *at* you. I'm laughing about Anne."

"Anne? You're laughing *about* her?"

"Yes. Let me tell you what else she's done. The Jemaah Islamiyah militants have got to be in a state of total confusion. They think she's in Japan."

"Japan?"

"Before she left Jakarta she booked a flight online to Tokyo. She used her own account."

"You've heard from her?"

"I got an text message from her that said she was going to check out Hiroshima."

Donovan rubbed his forehead and slumped into his chair. "She's more than I can handle." He shook his head again and adopted a look of strained patience. "I'm glad to see you. And, as much as I hate to admit it, I'm glad to know she tripped the bad guys up, again, and she's safe. Even if she is taking a vacation in Fiji."

"When will she be back?"

"On the sixth. Late." Donovan closed his eyes and shook his head. "It's good to know you two haven't lost it." His color gradually returned to normal.

"Once you learn how to ride a bicycle you don't forget. No matter how long you've been away from the action, you just jump back on and do your best. Thank goodness there's no re-learning curve. We didn't have time to re-learn anything."

"She has an uncanny ability to come up with strange turns and twists to confuse people. And I'm sorry to say I'm at the top of *that* list."

Connor gnawed on his upper lip. "She knew how to dodge, pivot, and deceive long before she joined us. As I remember, her ability to confuse and deceive pursuers was why you recruited her in the first place. Remember how long she stayed hidden in 1989? Nobody could find her. Not me, not you, not the CIA, the FBI, or the South American Cartels."

Donovan threw his hands up. "Okay, okay, I surrender. I guess I should be pleased she let us know where she is *this time*." The muscles in his face relaxed, his skin tone gradually returned to normal, and the frown lines on his forehead disappeared.

Connor smiled.

Smile crinkles appeared at the corners of Donovan's eyes. He started to chuckle.

The laughter built until both he and Connor were holding their sides.

Donovan finally caught his breath and sank into his chair. "Okay, now fill me in. What happened in Jakarta?"

Connor leaned forward. "The plan was going according to schedule. I check the room for bugs – found several and left them in place. She took a nap and I met with the port director. We had lunch. Then, Anne went to the health minister's office. We were on our way back to our room. Anne was going to make an appointment at the spa." Connor paused.

"And . . . ?"

"And," Connor took a deep breath and exhaled, "we were lucky."

"Living through an attack takes more than luck."

"I think the people sent to kill us were inexperienced. Whoever sent them thought we would be an easy kill. The shooters didn't seem to know much, other than how to point a weapon and pull a trigger."

"Then what?"

"Then we used the fire alarms to create a distraction. We went back to our room and changed into our alternative personas. Getting out of the hotel was easy. We never had time to unpack, none of our belongings were disturbed. We joined the hotel patrons fighting their way out of the hotel and were home free."

Anne heard a tap on her door. She looked over her computer screens. "Yes?"

Connor peeked around the edge of the door. "Should I throw my hat in first?"

"You know the rules," she pointed to the sign. "If the door is open, enter at will. If it's half closed, knock. If the door is closed, I can only be disturbed if my end of the building is burning."

"Well, it was half closed." He stepped into the room. "I wanted to see how you were doing."

"You came all the way from Langley just to see how I'm doing? I'm fine. Why didn't you call?"

"I was afraid you'd hang up on me."

"Why on earth would I hang up on you? I haven't given up on you, yet."

"Did you enjoy your sojourn by the sea?"

"I did. Shame you weren't there. It was our honeymoon, after all . . ." She gave Connor a world-weary smile, a playful wink, and gestured to an overstuffed chair. "Have a seat."

"Thanks." He walked across the room and sank into the voluminous cushions. "I'm sure you know how upset Donovan was with your protracted visit to Fiji."

Anne waved the comment away. "He'll get over it. And, I'm supposed to meet with him tomorrow." She pushed back from her desk, stood and stretched. "So, I extended my return by a few days. After twenty-six years he should know I'm not going to run right back to Langley after a near-death experience."

Connor shifted and sank lower in the cushions. "The men who interrupted our trip . . . they—"

Anne raised her hand, right index finger pointed up, walked around her desk, and shut the door. "Even secure buildings aren't secure."

As soon as the door was closed he continued. "Muslim Brotherhood, Indonesia style. Saudi Wahabism is alive and well in the form of the Jema'ah Islamiyah. Because of the JI, the Islamic State is *gaining ground* on a daily basis."

"Is there a chance this was the result of independent actors wanting to take out Americans? Any Americans?"

"No. JI makes up the larger part of an Al Qaeda-linked group. I think any American in Indonesia faces increased danger. But, we've learned that the Minister of Health's assistant contacted JI to tell them we were in town. His brother-in-law has a seat in the People's Representative Council. I'm sure the JI knew exactly who we were, and probably guessed why we were there."

Anne picked up a box of Earl Gray tea from the table behind her desk and showed him the label.

He gave her a thumbs up.

"The ambiance at the Jakarta ministry was strange." She shivered at the memory. "The Minister of Health wasn't there. His secretary introduced me to the minister's assistant. It didn't feel right, so I made my apologies, told them to give my best wishes to the Health Minister, and left." She held up a yellow packet of artificial sweetener.

He shook his head. "You should have told me."

"Told you? When? Between bullets?" She carried Connor's teacup to the side table by his chair, then she walked back to the table to get a spoon and a small teapot-shaped china dish for his used teabag.

"You've got a point. One of our informants told us three young men from Ibrihim's mosque have disappeared. One of them was the hotel desk clerk."

"Do you think they were the men who tried to kill us?"

"I'm almost certain it was. I'll bet the desk clerk gave the shooters a key to our room."

"Where are they now?" She carried her tea to her desk and sat.

"Our contact can't find a trace of them. Failure to complete a mission is not looked on with kindness in the JI."

"Is Ibrihim also bound to the Muslim Brotherhood?"

"Ibrihim and his Imam are members of the JI."

Anne leaned back in her office chair and nibbled at her lower lip. "Did they find Ibrihim?" She pivoted to turn off her desk lamp.

"There's no sign of him. They've established that he wasn't on board the boat when it exploded. And, by the way, we were able to retrieve pieces of fiberglass that conform to the standards of the Ferretti Corporation. According to a flight plan, Ibrihim's plane left Jakarta for Syria. The paperwork indicated Ibrihim was on board. Airport officials in Dumayr claim the plane landed without incident. We have security-cam proof Ibrihim was picked up at the private airfield by Al Halbi's driver."

Connor picked up his tea cup, blew across the hot liquid, and took a sip. "The plane can't be found. There's no evidence the plane ever left the airport. We have an unsubstantiated report that the plane was wheeled into one of the remote hangers. And, stranger still, no one has seen or heard from the flight crew."

She swiveled to face Connor. "Do we know if Al Halbi took Ibrihim to the laboratory?"

"Our informant reported Al Halbi and Ibrihim left the institute late in the day, got into the limousine, and drove into the desert. Several hours later Al Halbi came back . . . alone."

"Looks like Al Halbi's eliminating everything and everyone exposed to the virus. The boat is gone, the crew is gone, Ibrihim is gone . . . and no one has seen his flight crew or the plane."

"You got it."

"Drowned crew, sunken boats, lost aviators, and a vanished plane can't provide information or spread infection. I'm sure Al Halbi received the vials. Now he's doing whatever he can to make sure the first case of smallpox occurs in the United States. His plan won't work any other way. Al Halbi will not allow the disease to start Indonesia or in Syria." Anne spooned the teabag out of her cup and plunked it into the wastebasket. "What have you learned about the shipments?"

"They're on two different container ships. Both left Jakarta on February fourth. One went to Long Beach. The other is bound for Oakland."

"Have the ships reached their destinations?"

"The first ship docked in Oakland a few days ago. As far as I know the other one hasn't docked yet. The Coast Guard told me they would let me know when it comes in."

"Does the Coast Guard know the reason you want the information?"

"No." Connor put his cup on the side table. "We've kept it vague. Reports of possible illness on board. We're still under the President's no-leak directive."

"What's happened with the Oakland shipment?"

"A suspicious container went by truck to a warehouse in Seattle."

"Suspicious?" Anne swirled her tea.

"A crane operator in Oakland reported lifting a container marked with Greek letters. He didn't know what they were called, so he drew them for us. Omegas. The letters were spray painted graffiti style. One on the top and one on each side."

"Have we found the container?"

Connor shook his head. "Nope. One more missing piece of the puzzle. We haven't found a shipping container, crate, carton, or cardboard box anywhere in the United States marked with an omega. Except for the one's going to fraternity and sorority houses." He took another sip of his tea. "How do you get the water to stay so hot?"

Anne laughed. "The mugs are all insulated."

"What do you know about the import house?"

"The import house in Seattle is legit. It's been operating for more than ten years, and it's owned by a family descended from Russians who settled in the area around 1800."

"How about the merchants who received the clothing?"

"All have either emigrated from the Middle East in the past ten years or are of Middle-Eastern descent."

"What about the clothing?" Connor tapped his fingers on the arm of the chair.

"A few cartons of children's clothing went to a distributor of Indonesian-made garments. The CDC checked them for contamination."

Connor's head jerked up. "What did you tell the CDC?"

Anne raised her right hand, palm up. "We told them we had reports of possible contamination."

"Did they find any biologicals?"

Anne shook her head. "The malls, kiosk personnel, and the warehouse were clean."

Safe House
Burke, Virginia
The same day

Yuri paced the garden walk. He'd take a few steps, wait a few seconds, then looked over his shoulder to glance at the envelope stuffed with documents on the wrought-iron table. A few more steps. Another stop. *How can I make this decision alone?* No answer came for the question he asked himself.

He dropped onto a garden bench and stared at the flagstones. His outlook was as barren as the trees, his mind as cloudy as the leaden sky. Saliva filled his mouth. His tongue tasted like the morning after too much vodka at the tavern. A headache began to take hold. If only he could speak to Iveta. *I can't make this decision without her.*

The documents outlined changes to his identity and the identities of Iveta, the children, and Olga. New names. New nationalities. They would be from the Republic of Slovakia, from a place called Trnava. He would no longer be Yuri, his name would be Alexi. Iveta's new name would be Jana. Ondrek . . . What do they want to call Ondrek?

Yuri stood and walked to the table. Shaking the papers out of the envelope, he searched through them to find Ondrek's new name. Ondrek would be Jarek. And Josef . . . Josef . . . Again he searched through the papers. Josef would be Stashek. Maruska's new name would be Alena.

"Alexi Ondo, Jana Ondova . . ." Yuri tried the new names aloud. He repeated the names several times. The bitter taste gagged him.

"Nyet. I cannot make this decision without my Iveta." He shook his head and shoved the papers back in the envelope. So much change. How could they explain this to the children?

Yuri stood and paced the length of the garden again. It seemed as if he'd walked a hundred miles inside these walls.

Over the past few days, Donovan had brought several scientists to meet Yuri.

Russian émigrés who brought casserole dishes filled with

home-cooked foods. Some brought salad, some vegetables, some made roast chicken. One woman made bread. And, one family brought soup.

Pot luck, they called it. An American tradition, they said. Yuri grunted. An American tradition with Russian food. Borscht. Babka. Slivovitz. Chicken Paprikash. None as good as Iveta's.

The past few days had been filled with the newness of America. His Russian guests had been cordial, informative. They were happy in the United States. It was better than Russia, they said. Safer. Freer. Their children were doing well in school. They enjoyed their positions and their research. Some retained their birth names. Their only complaint was the traffic on the Beltway.

What is a beltway?

Yuri's recovery was complete. Some residual weakness remained, but the infection was gone, his wound was healed. He'd lost fifty pounds and gained some gray hair. But he was able to get out of bed and walk in the garden.

He had a housekeeper who came in every day to made tasty, healthy meals.

Yuri longed for Iveta's cooking. He stopped, put his foot on a bench and rested his elbow on his knee.

What am I to do? The Americans have treated me well. They saved my life.

So many questions.

No answers.

He stared at the patterns of swirls and cracks in the wall.

If I become Alexi Ondo, Yuri Bushinikov will no longer exist.

Connor, Anne, and Donovan each had full cups of black coffee and piles of papers in front of them. Donovan pulled out a fresh yellow pad.

"All I can see are dead ends. It might help if we recap what we're sure of." He pointed at Connor. "What's happened to the shipments?"

Connor ticked off the information. "The first ship docked in Oakland. One container allegedly had Greek letters painted on it. The containers were sent by rail to Seattle."

"Wait." Donovan walked to the white board and wrote Ship #1 and underlined it, then wrote Oakland, Ω, and Seattle under the number. "Go on."

"The second ship docked in Long Beach. No reports of Greek letters on any of the containers from the ship. The containers were sent to the East coast by rail, along the Alameda corridor."

Donovan wrote Ship #2 and listed Long Beach, ø, and East Coast under it.

"Do you think the lack of symbols means anything?"

Anne shook her head. "No, not necessarily, the omegas may have been painted over or passed over as graffiti."

Donovan took two steps back and squinted at the information. "Connor, did the port director in Jakarta send you the list of merchants who ordered the clothing?"

"No, I called his office when I got back to the states. He wasn't in. I left a message. He hasn't returned my call."

Donovan turned. "Give him another call. It's eight a.m. here, so it's seven p.m. there. A little late, but give it a try."

Connor stood and picked up his coffee cup. "Okay. If it fails, I can check with the Seattle port director in a couple of hours. Maybe he'll be able to provide some information."

"Let's meet back here in thirty minutes." Donovan stood.

Anne checked her watch. 8:05 a.m. She pulled her shoulders back, straightened her spine, and pushed her coffee cup away. Donovan had called her at four that morning. Her breakfast had been a protein bar and way too many cups of coffee.

"I don't know about you guys, but I'm hungry. Any orders?"

Thirty minutes later Connor returned to Donovan's office. An accumulation of donuts, juice, breakfast sandwiches, and fresh coffee sat in the middle of the table. "I'm impressed. Where'd you get all the food?"

"I can't take the credit for this one. Amelia beat me to it. She had a whole cart loaded and ready."

Donovan came through the door and walked directly to the table. He reached for a Boston cream donut.

"Were you able to get the Jakarta port director?" Anne asked and opened a container of Almond Milk French Vanilla cream to pour into her coffee,

Connor shook his head. "I tried his office. No answer. I did some calling around and got some information. It wasn't good."

"What?"

"The Jakarta port director *couldn't* answer his phone. He was gunned down outside his home the same day they tried to eliminate us."

Anne closed her eyes and sighed. "Have we been able to track the containers from the second ship?"

Connor consulted his notes. "As far as I can tell, some are scheduled to go to DC and some will go to the Garment District in New York."

"What about the ships?" Donovan said through a mouthful of donut.

"The ships have left their ports. One unloaded in Oakland and is on its way to Hong Kong. The one from Long Beach is on its way to South America. That ship will dock in Columbia, then go on to Peru."

"Has the CDC given you any further information about the goods transported to Seattle?"

"Just what we already know. No evidence of any kind of biologic contamination." Anne took a sip of her coffee. "There was one interesting piece of information. The Seattle shipment went to import businesses. Most of it was children's clothing." Anne paused to take another sip. "The final destination of the clothing was businesses owned by people with Middle Eastern heritage."

Donovan nodded. "The information the Russian gave us corroborates your findings. Bushinikov told me Al Halbi said he wanted one of the weapons sent to the United States in cartons of clothing made in Indonesia."

Connor refilled his coffee cup. "We know Ibrihim traveled to Syria and back several times. From the reports our contact gave us we can assume Al Halbi received the vials of smallpox." He returned to his seat at the table. "As far as we can tell, Ibrihim took the virus to Syria on the fourteenth or fifteenth of January."

Donovan added another line to the white board and notated: Jan. 15. Vials in Syria.

"We know Bushinikov was stabbed on the thirteenth." Another line went on the white board to the left of the one he just drew. Jan 13. Vials/ Bush. $\rightarrow$ Ibr./ Bush. Stabbed."

"And, we know that several weeks later Ibrihim flew back to Dumayr. He returned to Jakarta and the next day we received the information regarding the boy going through the warehouse. A day or two later our informant gave us confirmation that the weapon was on its way to the United States."

"What day was that?" Connor drew a large X across his current page of doodles. He ripped the page from the pad and mashed it into a ball.

"February third?" Anne wasn't sure. She looked through her notes. "No it was the fifth. February fifth."

Donovan made another line and some cryptic notations.

Connor pulled his folder open. "It wasn't until the twenty-fourth of February that Ibrihim disappeared. That was the same day his yacht exploded."

"Yeah, it stands to reason—"

"Nothing stands to reason." Anne cut Donovan's sentence off, stood, and crossed her arms. "It was barely six weeks from the time Al Halbi received the virus to the time he contaminated the shipments."

"So?" Donovan grabbed another donut and took a huge bite.

"So, Al Halbi couldn't have produced weaponized smallpox in six weeks. It would take far more time to make the weapon."

"Our source in Jakarta reported he watched a man and a boy run from Ibrihim's yacht to the warehouse a day after Ibrihim returned from Syria. The containers were there, ready to be sealed and loaded on to the ships."

Donovan popped the last bite of donut in his mouth, chewed, and swallowed. "We're sure they put infectious material into the containers." He wiped a bit of cream off the edge of his mouth and gave a dismissive wave.

Anne shook her head. "Who's sure? What makes you think we're sure? Do we have definitive proof the material is infectious? Do we have definitive proof that whatever they put in the containers is smallpox? Do we have definitive proof of anything?"

Donovan and Connor stared at Anne. The looks on their faces couldn't have been more amazed if she'd demanded an explanation of Einstein's theory of relativity.

Anne stood, hands on hips, feet wide apart. "In reality, all we have are suppositions. You're reaching conclusions that ignore scientific fact. The intervals don't add up, Donovan. *And*, there hasn't been enough time, Connor. The important point is that *no one* could produce weaponized smallpox in six weeks."

Anne rubbed her eyes, glanced at the clock, and pushed her chair back. Seven p.m. Time for a break. *I'm missing something.* Some clue. It's here somewhere. Why can't I see it? It's probably right in front of my eyes. I need to focus.

Maps of New York, New Jersey, Connecticut, and the District of Columbia were pinned to the corkboard next to her desk. She stared at the maps for so many hours, the highways began to look like a tangled blue-and-red second grade knitting project.

According to Connor, the clothing from the second ship was divided into two groups. Some went to warehouses in the District of Columbia, and some went to the Garment District in New York City. Which import companies got the clothing? Which shopping centers had vendors to sell the goods? Could they stop the deliveries before anyone comes in contact with the contamination?

Anne stood and stretched, her back and neck muscles tight and painful. She went through another set of stretches. Her stomach rumbled. She grabbed a protein bar and turned on the hot water kettle.

Six weeks isn't long enough to produce weaponized smallpox.

She unwrapped the protein bar and placed it on a saucer, opened a packet of Earl Grey tea, put it in her cup and added a packet of sweetener. The electric kettle clicked off.

What if Al Halbi used an organism other than smallpox? Was this a test run? She massaged her temples. If I was a terrorist what would I do?

Anne poured the hot water into her cup.

If I wanted to start an epidemic in the United States, how would I accomplish it? She lowered her head then dunked the tea bag up and down in the hot water. I wish I could come up with answers as easily as I can come up with questions.

"Okay. Start at the beginning. Again." *Talking to empty rooms —* that can't be a good sign.

The Seattle shipments went to shops specializing in children's clothing. All the shops had owner-operators of Middle Eastern birth. All the shops were in popular malls — malls considered weekend destinations — malls with huge numbers of customers.

She stretched, fingers locked and arms pushed as high as she could reach above her head. She arched her back, then bent over to touch her toes. She dropped to the ground. A few full body push-ups.

Her muscles felt no relief.

Anne shook two Aleve out of a container and washed them down with cold tea, then grabbed a box of pushpins and walked to the maps.

Meadowlands Mall in East Rutherford, New Jersey. "Possible." Anne pushed a red pin into the map.

Somerset Mall in Somerset, New Jersey. "Also possible." Another red pin.

Jackson Outlet Mall, New Jersey. Anne shrugged and shook her head. A yellow push pin.

Westfield Mall, Maryland. Red pin.

Rehoboth, Delaware? Probably not. Connecticut and Long Island malls? "NO." Black pins.

Anne grabbed a blue marking pen and outlined the perimeters of Mount Vernon Square and the Garment District. This was where the import houses and distributers operated.

The telephone buzzed. "Anne Damiano."

"Why are you still at the office?"

"Connor, hi. Silly question. I'm working. How did you know I was here?"

"It's close to eight p.m. I've called you on your house phone and your cell phone. You didn't answer."

"Where are you?"

"At my office." His answer sent them both into the kind of laughter that results from exhaustion.

"Any progress?" he asked through his last choked laugh.

"Only if you count theories and possibilities."

"I need a time line." Connor said. "If the clothing is contaminated and it has already been delivered to vendors, when would we start to see cases?"

"If the merchandise hits the racks within a day or two of arriving at the warehouse, then we're looking at ten days to two weeks. If the goods sit in cartons on the loading dock or at the warehouses . . . there's no telling."

March 13
Garment District
New York City

Johnny Emmons pushed his battered grocery cart down Fortieth Street toward Bryant Park. The day looked to be a good one. He was glad to see the bright sunshine and the pale blue sky. A light, breeze promised warmer days to come. A few Garment District workers smiled and nodded hello.

Johnny was tall and slender, ruggedly handsome, muscle-bound with veins roping his forearms and hands. But, he had far too many creases and age lines for his thirty-five-year-old face. A head injury from a roadside bomb blast in Iraq left him blind in one eye and permanently disabled. The physical injury was healed, but the emotional scars remained. His long blond hair was pulled back to the nape of his neck. A ten-inch braid, a little off center, hung down his back, the tail secured with a small silver barrette.

He was one of New York City's mole people. His home was a small shack in an abandoned subterranean tunnel beneath Manhattan. Most New York City dwellers were unaware of the city beneath their city.

More than a century ago, during the original subway excavation, deeper shafts were dug, rails were laid, and electric lines run. The city planners envisioned the subway system would expand as the population grew. But, the tunnels were never utilized. Now they formed a cavernous homeless-people-warren beneath the busy New York subway.

The mole people didn't consider themselves homeless. They had post office boxes to access their disability and welfare checks. The hovels they created underground were 'home.' The underground dwellers created their living spaces with throw-aways from their above ground neighbors. Their improvised 'apartments' weren't fancy, but most had all the basics.

They were protected from the elements and they had ample electricity.

This morning, Johnny, happy to be above ground, breathed deep and relished the sunlight. Winter was over. He knew the short weeks of pleasant spring weather would soon turn into a hot, humid New York summer. On those days, it was a relief to return to his underground home. But, today, his face to the sun, he smiled and stepped onto Eighth Avenue.

The Garment District swirled with activity. Runners pushed racks of clothing from warehouses to showrooms. Some pulled cartons out of trucks and loaded the merchandise on handcarts to transport the clothing to the warehouses. Trucks blocked the streets. Horns honked. Taxi drivers shouted.

One of the runners stopped and reached into a cloth bag. "Here you go, Johnny." Three soda cans tumbled into Johnny's cart.

Johnny gave him a two-fingered salute. "Thanks, man."

The young man grinned and waved to Johnny. The runner's smile faded into a look of determination as he struggled with the cumbersome rack of clothing. The frame, overloaded with thick wool coats, veered away from the desired freight elevator as if it had a mind of its own.

Ruthie Moore, darted across the street. She pulled Alice, her four-year-old daughter behind her. The little girl stumbled and jumped in her effort to keep up. Ruthie's son, Ethan, had jumped on to the back of one of the racks. The runner, a frame loaded with lacy dresses, and Ethan flew across the avenue.

"Ethan. Get off that cart. You're going to fall off and break your neck."

Johnny watched the scene, unsure which child to rescue first.

Ruthie stopped short in front of Johnny to catch her breath. "Ethan is going to be the death of me." She pulled Alice into her arms. "Ethan. Come here, *right now.*" Her no-nonsense mother voice was boosted by breathless exasperation.

"Wait here, Ruthie. I'll get him." He ran to catch the boy. Johnny carried a kicking and laughing Ethan back to his mother. "What are we gonna do with you, soldier?"

"Aww, I was just playin'. I didn't touch the clothes."

Johnny set Ethan down in front of him and leaned down to be at eye level with the child. "You know your Ma doesn't want you to ride the carts. You're going to fall off and get hurt one of these days."

"Oookay." Ethan pouted, dropped his shoulders, and hung his head, his lower lip protruding.

Johnny stood. "I'm on my way to the food kitchen, Ruthie. Want to come along?"

"That's where we were headed before Ethan decided to ride the rack." She fell in step with Johnny. Alice and Ethan ran alongside.

Alice grabbed the hem of her mother's coat. "Slow down, Mama." Alice's sweet voice brought the adults to a halt. "My liddle legs can't go so fast."

Johnny leaned down and looked into Alice's emerald green eyes. She was a miniature of her mother. "Okay, mini-mite, how 'bout a ride on my shoulders?"

Alice nodded, grinned and squealed as Johnny swung her up.

Ethan brightened and looked up at Johnny. "When we finish lunch, will you tell me a story about the war an' you bein' a soldier n'all?"

Ruthie stopped short, pulled her thick dark hair back and stooped down to the boy's height. "Young man, is that how you talk to adults? Can you put a *please* in that sentence."

Ethan lowered his head again. "Okay." He kicked at an imaginary pebble. "PLEASE tell me a story, Johnny?"

"Maybe, but not until we finish eating. And only if you eat a really good lunch."

"Okay." Ethan jumped up and down and ran around Johnny. "I'll eat real fast."

Ruthie put her hands on her hips. Her shoulders slumped. "Ethan, what else are you going to say to Johnny?" A scowl pulled her lips in a straight line. A mother's sigh of frustration.

One look at his mother made Ethan snap to attention and salute. "Thank you, Johnny."

Alexandria, Virginia
Fischer and Son

Melanie Lipscomb turned off her computer. "Billy, Juana, it's almost five o'clock. Time for us to get out of here."

Billy Mack and Juana Herrera straightened.

Billy looked at the big clock by the rack of time cards. "Right you are." He had just returned from taking packing boxes to the dumpster. "And, it's time for me to head to Alexandria." A glow of pleasure highlighted his dark skin.

Juana checked her wrist watch, shook some of the wrinkles out of the dress she was about to iron, and put it on a hanger.

"I've got your paychecks ready." Melanie waved two envelopes, and handed one to Juana and one to Billy.

"I've been waiting for this day for a long time." Billy flushed with pride.

Melanie and Juana turned toward Billy with big smiles. Juana's dark eyes twinkled. Her smile was spontaneous. "You've been clean for a long time."

"Yes, ma'am," Billy said, straightening his spine. His smile matched hers. "I have. No drugs, no alcohol. It's been almost eighteen months."

"You're doing *so* well Billy." Melanie's voice conveyed the same happiness as Juana's.

"I promised my sister I was going to get it right this time."

"And, you did. You kept your promise. Mr. Fischer has been pleased with you. I know he's proud of you, too."

"He took a big chance on me. He had faith in me. So did my sister, Janine."

"Will you see her soon?"

Billy nodded. "I called Janine last night. She said I could come to visit her and the kids. She invited me to dinner tonight." He checked the clock. "I gotta date in Alexandria." He grabbed his envelope, used it to wave goodbye to Melanie and Juana, and walked out the door, whistling an old blues tune.

Subterranean tunnels of New York City
The same day

Late afternoon brought dark clouds and a drop in the temperature. It was going to be a damp evening. Johnny hurried down the staircase that lead to the subterranean passages.

City engineers tried to find and seal off all the long forgotten stairways. But, the mole people were able to remove some of the seals and find the doors the engineers missed.

Johnny ran through the tunnels to his discarded packing crate-and-cardboard hideaway.

Most of his furnishings were curbside throwaways. He roamed the streets before dawn to collect discarded blankets, furniture, cardboard boxes, bricks and wood.

Johnny was continually amazed at the useful household items his wealthy above ground neighbors put in the trash. He had to hunt for useful salvage early in the morning, before the streets were alive with people. Once the refuse trucks made their rounds the treasures would be gone.

The back wall of his space was a length of heavy canvas attached to an eight foot angle iron that was nailed to upright 4x4s. The bottom of the canvas was held in place by several rows of bricks. Johnny collected all the bricks he could find. He hoped he would eventually have a solid back-wall.

His mattress and box spring sat on a metal frame.

A scarred wooden cabinet held his meager supply of clothes.

Canned goods and a few plastic containers filled with cereal stood on a battered bookshelf.

The floor was covered with a threadbare, swept-clean rug.

A dark-brown gooseneck lamp sat on a wobbly end table that had three scarred legs and a fourth leg of stacked bricks. A faded and torn overstuffed arm chair, a milk-carton-footstool, and a small electric heater, completed his possessions.

It was enough.

Johnny snapped on his lamp and turned on the heater. The mole people had learned how to tap into the city's electricity long ago. He rummaged in his backpack and pulled out a few discarded paperback novels he found this morning in a box left on the curb.

Alexandria, Virginia
The same afternoon

Billy Mack smiled and patted his pocket. Payday. Good to have extra cash. No more booze. No more drugs. Gonna stay clean.

He stepped off the Metro at the King Street Station in Alexandria. Can't wait to see Janine and the kids. It's been almost two years. He rolled down his sleeves. Billy didn't want his sister to see the scars that were remnants of drug tracks on his arms.

Janine had told him he couldn't come to visit her family until he'd been off drugs and alcohol for at least a year. Johnny was clean.

It had been hard at first, but each succeeding month away from the drugs was a little easier. He still had days he had to fight the pull of the cocaine. But, he'd promised Janine when he checked into the rehab center that this would be the last time. She believed in him. He vowed not to fall back into the world of drugs. AA kept him off alcohol. And, Frank, his AA buddy, had been there to keep him clean through the hard times.

He'd also managed to get off the Xanax. Stopping alcohol was difficult. Stopping Xanax was even harder. But getting rid of his longing for booze or xanies was child's play compared to the lure of the cocaine.

Now, a year and a half out of rehab, alcohol and drug free, Johnny had a job. He had a job with a good salary. Not the best job in the world. But a job. His job. He swept floors, cleaned the bathrooms and the small kitchen area, and carried out empty crates and boxes.

He patted his pocket again and swung the plastic bag he carried. Janine's gonna love this album.

A bus approached. Billy moved away from the bus stop, shook his head and took a deep breath. He turned to walk down King Street. The winter had been cold and wet, but today the sun shone and made Arlington look clean and bright. Pretty soon we're all gonna be complaining about the heat and the humidity. Especially the humidity.

Billy laughed. Lord, it feels good to laugh. He laughed again because it made him feel so good.

King Street led to Waterfront Park. Each block closer to the water left a little more of the hustle and bustle of rush-hour traffic behind. Janine lived a few blocks from the park. Mom had left the house to Janine. No point in leaving the house to a drug addicted son. He shrugged. That's in the past. Not goin' there anymore. It was a good place for Janine and the kids. She was the one who took care of Mom all those years. Janine deserved the house.

Johnny straightened his spine, leveled his shoulders, and turned toward the river. He lengthened his stride. This was his neighborhood. He wanted to live here again – someday. Lots of good memories.

Many of his childhood friends had returned to the neighborhood. Some from college, some from trade school, some from prison. A few of his old friends had been in the military. He remembered the good times. The pranks they played on each other, on their teachers and on the neighbors. But, there were also bad memories.

Rebellion.

How upset his mother had been on the day he dropped out of school.

Petty crimes.

Gang membership.

The start of his addictions.

Gotta check out the park. Janine won't mind if I'm a few minutes late.

He walked across the park and stared out across the river. The familiar smell of brackish water, clean wind, and fresh cut grass.

Guess I better get to Janine's. If I'm late for dinner she'll have my hide.

He took one last glance at the water then he turned to walk along the tree lined path to Prince Street.

Two young toughs stepped in front of him and blocked his way. They looked to be about fifteen and twelve. Wanna-be gang members. Studded belts, wife beaters, open denim shirts, tennis shoes, and jeans that clung to their skinny butts. Each had a red scarf tied around his forehead. No tats . . . yet.

"Whatcha got there?" the older boy asked.

"Whadda you care?" Billy matched their rough speech. He'd seen replicas of these two during his years on the street. If you stood up to them and let them know your weren't afraid, the young punks would fold.

"Gimme your bag."

"You ain't getting nothin'. Get outta my way."

"Gimme your bag! And your wallet, too." The older boy took a step toward Billy.

Billy brushed the boy aside. "Wha's the matter wid you? Ain't you got no sense?"

"Shut up, man. You better do what I'm tellin' you."

"Go home. Your momma's got supper ready. You're too young to get into this kind of crap—you're goin' to end up in juvie."

The older boy pulled out a knife and gestured at the empty park. "You and who else is gonna make me?"

"Put that thing away." Billy blew out a long breath. He shook his head and pointed at the weapon. "That knife is gonna bring you a shitload a trouble."

"Oh, yeah, right, like you know anything." The boy swung the knife.

It took a few seconds for Billy to realize he had a deep cut on his right arm. There was no pain. Billy's mouth opened. His eyes grew wide. His entire body stiffened with surprise. "Get away from me."

"I told you to give us the bag and your money."

"Go to hell." Billy stepped forward and swung the bag close to the older boy's face.

The boy lunged. His knife pierced Billy's chest.

Billy grabbed for the knife. The sharp blade sliced the palm of his hand. He doubled over, and his forehead smacked the sidewalk. Pink froth erupted from his mouth.

The boy glanced around the park. They were still alone.

"Get his wallet." The knife-wielding tough bent down and ripped the handle of the bag from Billy's wrist. He opened the bag and tossed the sack and its contents into the bushes.

"You sure are stupid. You made me cut you for some stupid CD?" The boy kicked Billy's head. He kicked him again and started to laugh. The younger boy joined in. The two boys kicked Billy's inert body until they were out of breath.

"I told you to get his wallet. Check his pockets, see if he has any cash."

"I ain't touchin' no dead guy." The younger boy took several slow steps backwards.

"He ain't dead."

"He ain't breathin'."

The older boy nudged Billy's still body with his foot. "Now look what you done."

"I done?" The younger boy continued to walk backwards until he was under the trees. "*You* stabbed him." Tears streamed down the youngster's face. "You said this was gonna be easy. You said you done this lots of times. You said nobody'd get hurt."

He hiccupped, covered his mouth, turned, and bolted.

Juana Hererra's apartment
Ward 5
Washington, DC
The same evening

Juana Herrera struggled up the four flights of stairs to her apartment. The elevator hadn't worked for weeks.

She juggled three bags of groceries and a half-gallon milk jug. In order to open the stubborn deadbolts, she had to put the groceries on the landing and juggle the locks.

As soon as the door opened, she grabbed the groceries and pushed her way into the apartment. The door shut behind her. Not satisfied, she pressed her entire weight against the door. A satisfying click reassured her. She gulped in air and blew it out, relieved to be home.

Spring was coming, the days were finally getting longer. She was afraid to be on the streets of DC's Ward 5 after dark.

Still not satisfied, she turned back to the door and secured two dead bolts, one at waist level and one at eye level. Now she felt safe.

She smoothed her long black hair away from her face, and picked up the milk jug and grocery bags to carry them into the kitchen. The worn Formica counter, once buttery bright was now dull yellow. The fresh paint on the pale blue walls and the windows with their new bright white curtains contrasted with the blue and white linoleum that suffered from decades of scrubbing. Gray splotches defined paths from the door to the sink and from the sink to the refrigerator. Juana covered the worst spots with rag rugs from the thrift store.

Her tiny kitchen table sported two woven straw placemats and a bouquet of plastic flowers in a cracked ceramic vase.

A handsome Miguel smiled at her from a snapshot taped to the refrigerator door. A few days after the picture was taken, an IED blew up the truck he was driving. Tears filled her eyes as she reached out an index finger to stroke his cheek. She swiped at the tears with the back of her hand. Gone. Miguel would never return. The future they dreamed of since their childhood in Casas Grande vaporized in the sands of Iraq.

Miguel left Mexico to join the United States Army. He wanted his children to be American citizens. He took his oath of citizenship a few months after he completed basic training. They were married in Casas Grande, happy to have their families present. The next day they drove to Fort Hood, where he resumed his duties with the 4th Sustainment Brigade.

She had to move out of military housing a year after Miguel died. A relative from Casas Grande lived in Washington, DC. Juana moved to Ward 5 to be near her cousin and to make a new life for herself. But now, she planned to move to a better part of town as soon as her lease was up. Somewhere closer to work. Somewhere safer. Somewhere within walking distance of St. Francis de Sales Church.

Shootings, robberies and stabbings occurred every night in Ward 5. After dark the streets were a war zone. Ward 5 was not a safe place to live.

Work had been busy. Easter was several weeks away. She'd unpacked and inspected hats, purses, shoes, dresses, and pashmina by the dozens. She steamed or ironed the garments and organized the racks before the shipping department at Fischer and Son sent the goods to the vendors.

Juana looked forward to a weekend of rest.

She checked the clock. *Almost 6:30. Better get dinner started.*

Juana pulled leftover chicken out of her ancient refrigerator and put rice in the steamer to cook. She put her groceries away, opened a can of pinto beans, poured them into a pan and added chopped tomatoes, onion and green peppers. The chicken was set aside so she could warm it when the rice and beans were ready.

Father John, the priest at St. Francis de Sales Church, said he'd start the Stations of the Cross at seven tonight. Friday and Saturday nights were the most dangerous in Ward 5. She wouldn't be going to church.

Juana knelt by her small shrine to Our Lady of Guadalupe. The statue stood on a hand embroidered doily under an arch of plastic roses. Juana lit the votive candle in front of Our Lady, crossed herself and began to pray. Her crystal and gold rosary beads moved automatically through her fingers.

Miguel gave her the rosary for her birthday before he left for his last deployment. When she held them and closed her eyes, she imagined Miguel kneeling beside her.

Her faith and the prayer garden at St. Francis de Sales had sustained her after Miguel's death. She stopped by the church on her way to work each morning to pray for his soul. She knew he had to be with Jesus. He was so brave and strong.

She had just started to eat dinner when the phone rang.

"Juana, you must come home." It was her sister, Lena. "Father is ill. The doctors say you should come before it's too late."

"Si, si, Lena. I'll be there as soon as I can."

Her father was a well-respected man. He was trusted by his neighbors, and gentle toward his wife and daughters.

Juana called the airline. A plane was leaving for Juarez in the morning. She booked a flight on one of the three remaining seats.

Dinner forgotten, she packed her bags and placed them by the door, then called Fischer and Son and left a message for Melanie Lipscomb.

A picture of the warehouse flashed in her mind. A big shipment came in late this afternoon. Billy Mack helped her unload some of the cartons. A few had a strange mark on them. Some kind of a Greek letter.

Melanie called it an omega. She said it meant 'the end'. Like Jesus was the alpha and the omega. The beginning and the end.

They shook out the wrinkles and hung the clothes on racks. It was tedious work. She'd only had time to steam a few of the dresses before quitting time. There's so much work waiting at the warehouse.

Melanie Lipscomb, the secretary at Fischer and Son, told her one of the shopkeepers had been calling on a daily basis demanding the goods. Easter was coming, and he needed the clothing right away. The delivery was important.

Mr. Fischer and Melanie would be disappointed if she didn't show up on Monday.

Juana smothered a flash of guilt.

The moment's hesitation passed quickly. Her father was dying.

March 15
Fischer & Son
Washington, DC

Harvey Fischer bustled into the warehouse at noon. "How are the deliveries progressing? Did the goods leave for Westfield Mall yet?"

"No deliveries have gone out," Melanie Lipscomb answered. "I've called you at least ten times this morning and left messages. You never answered your phone, and you didn't call me back."

Harvey Fischer pulled his cellphone out of his pocket. "Darn, I'm sorry, Melanie. I had an appointment with my dentist this morning and forgot to turn my phone back on. I had to run a couple of errands for my wife."

"It's been a bad day. Juana left for Mexico on Saturday. Her father is dying. She hopes to be back before Easter. But, she was sure she would be gone at least two weeks, maybe more."

"We have to find someone to cover for her."

"Yeah, I'm already on it. I haven't been able to reach Clarita, the woman who usually fills in for her."

"How many trucks went out this morning?" Harvey pulled off his jacket and hat and hung them on the hooks next to Melanie's cubicle.

"I told you that no deliveries have gone out today. None of the merchandise is ready to go anywhere. The shop owners have been calling non-stop all morning. They're not happy. The merchant over in Chevy Chase hasn't missed a day without calling for two weeks. He called this morning and demanded the clothing *today*."

Harvey started toward his office.

"And, Billy hasn't shown up for work."

Mr. Fischer stopped short. "Billy wouldn't miss work."

"No, he wouldn't. He hasn't called. And I haven't been able to reach him."

Harvey frowned. "Billy hasn't missed a day's work since I hired him. I wonder what's going on. Has Frank heard from him?"

"I haven't checked with Frank. He's been a great AA buddy for Billy. I'll call down to the loading dock to see if he knows anything."

"Do you think Billy fell off the wagon?"

Melanie shook her head. "Billy's worked too hard to stay sober." She took a sip of her tea. "And, if he was tempted to start on either drugs or alcohol he would have called Frank right away."

"How was he on Friday? It *was* pay-day."

"Billy was excited when he left work on Friday. Happy. He was on his way to his sister's house. He bragged about it all day. I guess he told you that she refused to see him until he was clean for at least a year. It's been almost eighteen months. He even bought a present for her during his lunch break, a blues album. Bessie somebody, I think. No . . . not Bessie. Sippy. Sippy Wallace."

"Have you tried to reach his sister?"

"Yeah, there's no answer. He put her home number on the contact list. I don't have her work number. And, he didn't listed her place of employment on the contact form. I figured I would try to try her home number this afternoon."

Harvey checked the rack of dresses. "These don't look too bad. Call the man in Chevy Chase and apologize, then send these dresses over ASAP. Thank goodness we sent a partial delivery on Friday." Harvey walked into his office and slammed the door.

"You got it boss." Melanie said to the closed door.

She left her desk and opened one of the boxes, pulled out several dresses, shook them out, and hung them on hangers. When she emptied three boxes she wheeled the rack to the loading platform and gave the address to the driver. "Sorry to make you take this partial shipment, Frank. But, the shop owner is anxious to get this merchandise. He's pretty angry. He's called at least six times already this morning."

Frank looked over Melanie's shoulder. "Where's Billy? He always brings the racks down." Frank's expression reflected concern. "Who's answering the phone?"

"Mr. Fischer's covering the phone right now. There's no one else in the warehouse."

"If you hear from Billy tell him to give me a call. He's supposed to go to the AA meeting with me tonight."

"Okay, but I wouldn't count on it. Billy hasn't shown up for work, he hasn't called, and I can't reach him. To make today worse, Juana isn't here either."

Frank's shoulders slumped and he shook his head. "This could be bad. I didn't hear from Billy all weekend. He didn't come to meeting on Saturday night and he wasn't at church on Sunday. He never misses church on Sunday." Frank hunched down. His face collapsed into a frown. "Do you think . . . ?"

"Come on, Frank." Melanie tried her best to look more confident than she felt. "Billy was proud of his sobriety. I'm sure he's okay."

"Maybe you're right." Frank's voice wasn't convincing. "But, he's always called when he felt like he needed a drink. Something bad must have happened."

"I have to get back inside." Melanie started for the warehouse door. "I have a lot to do." The door whispered closed behind her. Melanie ripped open another box, shook out the first dress, and hung it on a rack.

The phone rang.

"Fischer and Son."

Melanie buzzed Harvey Fischer. "Call for you on line one. It's the Virginia Medical Examiner's office in Manassas."

"This is Harvey Fischer."

"Hello Mr. Fischer. This is Dr. Weller from the Office of the Medical Examiner in Manassas. Do you have an employee named William Mack?"

"Yes. Billy, I mean, William Mack works here."

"A person bearing Mr. Mack's identification was murdered in Alexandria on Friday."

Harvey tried to swallow through the tightness in his throat. "Murdered?" He couldn't breathe. "Did you say a person with Billy's ID was found murdered?"

"Yes, sir. I'm sorry to be the one to give you this information. We need someone to identify the body. If you could be here..."

"You want me to come and identify...?"

"Yes, sir. A man's body was found in Waterfront Park. His ID was in his wallet and he had a pay stub from your company in his pocket."

"Shouldn't his family come to identify the body? His sister lives in Alexandria. Did you contact her?"

"We tried to find next of kin. But there's about a hundred people with the last name of Mack listed in this area. Two are named William. We called them, and they're both alive and well. They denied knowing this man. One said he thought there used to be another William Mack living around here somewhere. He was pretty sure that William Mack left years ago. He thought the guy was in prison or drug rehab somewhere."

Harvey Fischer rubbed his bald spot. "We have his sister's address in the company files. I know she lives in Alexandria; Billy was going to see her on Friday. Her last name isn't Mack." Harvey's hands were shaking.

He buzzed Melanie. "Please get Billy Mack's sister's name, address, and phone number for me." Harvey Fischer moved papers around on his desk. He put a pencil in his top drawer, but took it out again. "Dr. Weller?"

"Yes?"

"D-do they know who did this?"

"We couldn't find any witnesses. A woman was walking her dog and discovered the body."

"What time did she find him?"

"About six o'clock. From the deputy coroner's report it couldn't have been more than a few minutes after he was killed."

"My secretary should have his sister's information in a few minutes." His sister should go to the morgue, he thought. *She's a nurse.* "Was it a robbery?"

"No, I don't think so. His wallet was still in his back pocket. The wallet hadn't been disturbed. And, there was still money in it. Pretty close to the amount on the pay stub."

Harvey leaned over and rested his forehead in his hand. "When he left work on Friday he said he was going to bring a present to his sister." Harvey's voice was gravely.

Dr. Weller cleared his throat. "The police found a package close by and think it might have been his."

Harvey's insides jangled. "I think his sister has several children. I'm sure she's gonna take this pretty hard. Billy's been through a lot in the past few years, but it seemed like he was getting his life in order." He paused. "Billy's been off drugs and alcohol since he was discharged from the rehab center eighteen months ago. He was going to his sister's house to celebrate his success. He said his sister had a dinner planned."

Melanie walked in the office and put Billy's personnel file on Harvey's desk.

"Dr. Weller. Do you have a pencil? I have the information."

Ten minutes later Harvey walked out of his office. He took a deep breath and exhaled as he passed Melanie's desk. "Billy's dead."

Melanie looked up. "Billy? Dead? What's happened?"

Harvey grabbed his jacket and hat from the pegs, slammed the hat on his head, and walked out the door.

'Rebellion to tyrants is obedience to God.'
American motto suggested by Thomas Jefferson

March 18
Manachim Airbase
Rosh Pina, Israel

Twenty-four men and two helicopters completed two months of planning and practice. They were ready. Colonel Sam Williams went over the plan again. His team kept it simple. Each man had a job to do, and each man had his movements timed down to the second. They understood their roles and the importance of the mission. More important, his team was dedicated to success and confident it would be completed without a hitch.

Williams checked his watch. A little after one a.m. It would be six p.m. in North Carolina. Jenny's probably cleaning up the kitchen. Pretty soon she'll get the twins in the bathtub. *Wish I could be there.*

He took a deep breath and pushed Jenny and the girls into the recesses of his mind. This mission required exact timing and total concentration. He pulled his shoulders back and walked into the briefing room. Windowless. Beige walls. He took a deep breath. Twenty-three men, his team, waited.

"Okay guys, it's about time. We've had two months. Two months of hard work."

Williams walked toward the first row of men. "Every one of you knows your job. You're ready." He looked at his watch. "We'll load at 0-200. The flight will take twenty-eight minutes. The weather's good. The aircraft carriers are in place and prepared to get us the hell out when our mission is accomplished." He glanced around the room.

"We were given a task. The President told us what he wanted done. Our order was to figure out the best way to accomplish the task. He realized the best people to design this mission were the special ops people invested in the outcome."

"We are the twenty-four most dependable, bad-ass guys in the world. Are you ready?"

"Yes, sir!" The twenty-three men shouted in unison.

"This is *our* mission, start to finish. The pencil pushers in Washington were told to stay out of the planning and give us whatever we needed. And, they provided exactly what we requested. We've got a couple of the quietest, most technologically advanced stealth helicopters ever built. We ran the mission more times than I can count. We know it inside-out and backwards. The mission lives and breathes inside each of us."

"Yes, sir."

He pulled a map down and used a laser pointer to identify a spot east of Duma. "The trucks will meet us here," the laser flashed a few inches to the right, "behind this rise." He flicked the beam again. "We've secured the cooperation of the man who brings supplies to the labs. Another Delta Force team will extract the drivers' families in about three hours.

Two trucks will wait here." Again he used the laser pointer to show the exact location. "The trucks will signal as we approach, the helos will land and we'll move our men and equipment into the trucks. Two men from each team will go by chopper to the lab."

"Shermann and Goldmeyer from Shayetet 13 and Ianelli and Olson from Delta Force."

The four men stood. "As soon as you hear the first vent explode take out the guards at the entrance. The other ten men from each team will ride on the trucks."

Williams walked the length of the room, straightened, turned with military precision, and checked his watch.

0-200.

"Let's roll."

The team left the briefing room and jogged across the tarmac. Two UH-60 stealth helicopters waited.

Twelve men climbed into each chopper: Shayetet 13 in number one, Delta Force in number two.

Within three minutes the helicopters were in the air. Each man carried a shortened M-16 carbine, an M-9 Beretta pistol and two M-67 grenades. They wore full chemical gear and each man was issued an FR M-40 full facepiece respirator with a FR C241 Filter attached. Twenty-four minutes later the pilots flew over the landing site. Trucks blinked their headlights on and off below them.

Colonel Williams breathed a sigh of relief. Their presence assured him. If the Syrian truck drivers didn't buy into the mission they were screwed. So far, it looked like the truckers intended to keep their part of the bargain. The two Syrian truck drivers were the one possible weak link. They were promised huge amounts of money for their co-operation. In addition the truck drivers and their families would be extracted from Syria.

He said a silent prayer. If any one of the Syrians or their families even hinted at the mission it would fail. The result would be death or capture for every member of his team.

The helos landed without incident.

Williams checked his watch. *Right on time*. He breathed a sigh of relief.

It took less than ten minutes for the men to load the trucks.

Ianelli and Olson, remained in the first helicopter, Goldmeyer and Shermann joined them.

Ten men from Shayetet 13 in one truck, ten from Delta Force in the other. In addition each truck carried six sand bags and six DM canisters.

DM (Adamsite), a riot control agent that produces vomiting, as well as nose and throat irritation, would cause confusion and fear. A grenade would be dropped down three different vents on each side of the laboratory to destroy the exhaust baffles. The DM canister would be dropped with a second grenade to insure dispersion of the Adamsite. The sand bag would block any of the riot control agent from escaping from the vent into the desert air.

Williams, Wilson, and the remainder of the Delta Force team rode in the forward truck. The vehicle swayed and jounced over the rough terrain. Williams checked his watch again.

Intelligence reports indicated no sentries or other security assets above ground. Aerial photos had confirmed the area of the lab was unguarded. But still . . .

He glanced at Wilson, got a smile and thumbs up.

Colonel Williams' molars slammed together when the truck hit a deep pothole. He blessed himself and said a short prayer for the safety of his men and the success of the mission.

Another quick look at his watch. If everything went according to plan, Goldmeyer, Shermann, Ianelli, and Olson had just landed. Williams chewed his lower lip.

Ten minutes later, the remainder of the team approached the laboratory. To Smith it felt like half his lifetime. *No matter how much we practice, no matter how many times we go over the plan, no matter how well my team is coordinated, it's never like the real mission.*

The familiar sensation started. Every mission elicited the same excitement and fear at this point. He felt like an elephant was tap dancing on his chest and a flock of ravens was flapping their wings in his gut.

Their truck slowed. Each man checked his respirator. Coles would roll off the Delta Force truck in two minutes and forty-two seconds to cover the entrance shed at the other end of the laboratory. If the Shayetet 13 truck was on time, Zimmermann would roll off the second truck at the same time and secure the entrance shed on the left. No one would escape from the lab.

Williams continued to glance at his watch. *Still on schedule.* He had pride in the plan. Pride in his team.

The truck slowed to a stop. Colonel Williams watched Peterson, Jones, and O'Neill run toward the exhaust vents. Each man carried two five pound canisters of DM, two 30 pound bags of sand, and four grenades. They ran toward the exhaust vents on the left side of the facility.

The plan called for Shayetet's Samuels, Schwartz, and Lester to cover the vents on the right. There were a total of twelve vents, six on each side. Each man would drop a time-delayed fragmentation grenade, a DM canister, a second time-delayed fragmentation grenade, and a sandbag into the first, third and fifth vents on each side. The remaining vents received time-delayed fragmentation grenades but no DM or sandbags.

The grenades would detonate seconds before the remainder of the squad reached the main entrance.

Williams checked his watch again. *Three seconds behind.*

Damn, the explosives are going to go off just about the time we'll arrive.

They stopped a few yards from the entrance. Everyone pulled on their gasmasks. One team member from Delta Force and another from Shayetet 13 slid out of their respective trucks. Ianelli, Olson, Goldmeyer, and Shermann placed the plastic explosives at the entrance to the warehouse, and dove for cover. The door imploded. A shower of metal, concrete, and sand exploded into the night sky.

Seconds later, the four advance men entered the facility. The remainder of the team exited the truck. Shots echoed from the enclosed space.

Williams had been correct. The three second delay caused the explosives to detonate in the air shafts as the two teams ran to the open entrance.

Another few seconds wasted.

Shit.

Williams held up his hand to halt further movement.

Now their mission was off by five seconds.

Five seconds could make the difference between a successful mission and total devastation.

Delta Force covered the corridor to the left. Shayetet 13 covered the right. They could hear the amplified curses echoing along the tiled corridors. Doors slammed and bolts clanged shut.

Williams and the lead Israeli moved forward.

The mirrors mounted on the walls had been destroyed, and three dead men lay in the foyer.

Williams waved his team on, relieved to see the devastation. The advance assault team had done their job. He let out a breath and focused, peered around the corner. Bodies littered the corridor.

Ianelli and Olson, halfway down the hall, approached the entrance to a lateral hallway. Olson turned his weapon to the left the same time Ianelli turned his weapon toward the right. Several members of his team ran to cover the remaining lateral hallways.

A deafening thunder of gunfire.

Bullets ricocheted off the tiled walls, ceilings, and floors.

Screams.

Sobs.

Sudden, sinister silence.

Donovan's Office
Langley, Virginia
The same evening

Connor and Donovan stood when Anne entered the room. Each man flashed a shit-eating grin. "Hi, Anne, glad you could make it," Connor said.

"No problem. I had a late afternoon meeting with the secretary's Vaccine Committee."

"This won't take long. I'm sure you're anxious to get some dinner and drive back to Frederick."

"I'm not going to Frederick. I'm going to my cottage at Swan Cove—I need a few days to rest. With the kind of hours I've put in for the past two weeks, I decided to get a jumpstart on the weekend."

"Are the crabs in yet?"

"Soft shell, maybe." She sat down. "Maryland blues won't be in for another month or more. But, it doesn't seem to make any difference these days. Most of the restaurants serve fresh crab all year round. Offseason, they ship it up from South America. The mussels come from Australia . . ."

She looked at the two men. Neither had a cup of coffee in their hands. Their grins remained in place.

"What's up with you two? I don't think you asked me to stop by so we could talk about what the Chesapeake Bay shellfish are doing this week."

Donovan's grin spread wider. He dusted off his hands. "We got 'em."

"We got 'em?" Anne looked from Connor to Donovan. The grins remained. "Who'd we get?"

"The underground lab in Syria as well as whoever and whatever was in it. The combined Delta Force and Shayetet 13 teams, along with two modified stealth helicopters, were successful. All the men from Shayetet 13 are back in Israel, safe and sound, and the entire Delta Force team is on its way back to the states."

"Tell me more." Anne's grin matched Donovan's. She poured a cup of coffee.

"The mission went as planned." Donovan paused, grabbed a stale Boston cream donut from a platter, and filled his cup with coffee. "The underground lab no longer exists. The entire operation went off without a glitch. Took the team less than fifteen minutes to place explosives and implode and incinerate the structure. What was left is a trench in the sand. Fighter planes followed up with MOPs. And best of all—no casualties on our side."

Anne rescued the last sad looking donut from the tray. "MOPs?"

"Maximum Ordinance Penetrators. They're fourteen-thousand kilogram bombs, bigger and stronger than any bunker buster we've had in the past."

"Repercussions?"

Donovan shook his head. "The Syrians reported a minor earthquake in the area followed by a series of after-shocks."

Hugh Donovan looked pleased enough to dance an Irish jig.

Anne thought maybe the Irish Washer Woman was playing in Donovan's head as he rocked back and forth, heel and toe, heel and toe.

"The President has listed the mission top secret. We're remaining silent. There can't be any leaks on this one."

"And there won't be from me." Anne took a seat at the table. "I have news, too. But my news leaves more questions than answers."

Connor gave a twist of his wrist. "So, what's happened on your end?"

"A marked carton went to a distributor in Mount Vernon Square. A company called Fischer and Son received at least one of the omega labeled cartons. The CDC tested the warehouse."

"And?"

"We're still waiting for the results."

"Did any of the clothing go to the malls?"

"A few pieces were delivered to Westfield Mall. The CDC confiscated the vendor's stock."

"What about the warehouse employees?"

"We might not be able to tell if the people who work there were exposed. We have a few complicating factors."

Donovan looked up from his notes. "Complicating factors?"

"The man who owns the warehouse is a Vietnam vet, so he's been vaccinated. His secretary is in her sixties, so she's probably at least partially immune as well. Their delivery man was also in 'Nam, so he was vaccinated before he left the country." Anne paused to take a sip of her coffee.

"That doesn't sound like complications."

"No, they're all clear. It's the other two employees who present some problems. The janitor and the woman who preps the clothing to go to the stores. The janitor, William Mack, was murdered in Alexandria after he left work the day the box was delivered to the warehouse. He unpacked the carton, hung the clothes on racks, broke the boxes down, and carried them to the cardboard recycling receptacles."

Donovan tapped his pencil on the table. "If he was killed on the same day he was exposed he wouldn't have had time to develop the disease. So, I'm guessing he's not the problem."

Anne nodded. "True. Mr. Mack could not have transmitted the disease."

"What about the cardboard boxes?"

"The cardboard boxes were long gone. The chance of the cartons transmitting disease is slim. If someone raided the cardboard supply in the trash there's a slight chance they could acquire the disease."

"And, I'm assuming the cardboard boxes are untraceable."

Anne nodded again. "The biggest worry is the other employee. The woman who steams the clothing, handles the goods, and makes sure they're ready to go to the vendors. Her name is Juana Herrera. She lives in DC's fifth ward."

"Undocumented?"

"No, not at all. She's a naturalized citizen. Husband was US Army.

He was killed in the middle-east. She was working at the warehouse on the day they unpacked the boxes. She's in Mexico."

"Mexico?"

"When she got home from work on the day the box was delivered, she got a call from her sister, in Mexico. Their father is terminally ill. They don't expect him to live more than a few days. She flew to Juarez the next morning."

Anne opened her briefcase. "I was going to give you this information at our meeting on Monday." She slid her report across the table.

Donovan scanned the paper. "Casas Grande?"

"Juana's village. It's about a hundred miles as the crow flies from Ciudad Juarez."

"Should we contact the Ministry of Health in Mexico?"

"No, not yet. It's the Secretariat of Health, by the way. It would be better if we wait. We need to have a definitive diagnosis. If I contact Mexico City or alert the health provider for Casas Grande, it could start an international panic."

Anne pushed her coffee cup around in circles. "Melanie Lipscomb, the secretary at Fischer and Son, is sure someone from Juana's family will call the office if Juana gets sick."

Donovan rubbed his forehead. "Anything else?"

"Of course."

"What?" Donovan's face turned red. He drummed his finger-tips on the desk.

"Two cartons marked with omegas turned up in New York's Garment District. The merchandise was unpacked and hung on racks, but it hasn't gone to the malls yet."

"Has it all been tested?"

"Yes."

"Did they find biologicals?" Donovan's face was crimson. He glared at Anne.

"Not yet." I better tell him the whole story before he has a stroke. "Calm down, boss. It's been taken care of. The CDC will let us know if they get a positive. Jonas Duckworth is with them."

Connor blew out a breath. His shoulders relaxed. "Duckworth's a good man. How much does he know?"

"I told him there was credible information regarding an attempt to contaminate a shipment. I didn't give him specifics. He'll make sure they test for the whole range of biologicals."

Martha's Vineyard, Massachusetts
The same afternoon

Mary-Katherine tried to stretch the aching muscles in her neck and back. Her throat was irritated. She rubbed her neck and swallowed. Sore throat. Achy Muscles. Tired. Tired. Tired. A week of traipsing around her senatorial district had taken a toll on her.

Today was an uncommonly warm day for mid-March. Even the breeze off the ocean was pleasant. Not at all like the damp cold days typical of early spring in Massachusetts. The beach cottage was isolated and quiet. A place where Mary-Katherine wasn't Senator Fitzgerald. At the cottage, she was Mrs. Todd Fitzgerald and Brittany's mother. As far as possible she removed the problems in DC and all the demands of the senate from her mind.

"Mommy, come outside. I want to go down to the water and look for shells."

Mary-Katherine was usually the first one out the door. But not today.

"Oh, sweetheart. I'm so tired and I've got a scratchy throat. I think I'd better stay indoors."

Todd squeezed Mary-Katherine's hand. "I'll go with you, Brittany. Get your sweater." He turned to his wife. "It's well past time for you to unwind. You've given at least one town hall meeting every day for the past five days. It's no wonder you have a sore throat." Todd patted her belly. "And, I'm sure you and our little one need to rest."

She leaned against him and rested her head on his chest. "I hope it's nothing. I feel terrible. I feel like I'm getting the flu." She tried to stretch out the muscle pain and groaned. "The senate is back in session next week. I don't have time to get sick—I need to be there. I've got some important legislation to vote on."

Todd shook his head and waggled a finger at her. "Get thee to bed. I'll take Brittany to the beach."

Two hours later, Todd cracked open the door to the bedroom. Mary-Katherine was curled up, fast asleep. He closed the door and walked to the family room.

"Okay Missy," he said to Brittany. "I guess it's up to us. What should we eat for dinner?"

"Pizza!"

"Why did I ask?" He smiled. "I don't think Mommy will want pizza. I think she'll want soup." He opened the pantry door and pulled a can of chicken noodle from the shelf. "You want soup, too?"

"Nope." Brittany's lower lip protruded. "Just pizza. With sausage and cheese."

"A good decision," he said. "I don't want chicken soup, either."

Brittany's face brightened. "Can I wear my communion dress tonight?" Her eyes begged for affirmation. "Please?"

"I don't think so. Mommy would be unhappy if we got grease or pizza sauce on your dress. And she'd be mad at both of us if we ruined your First Communion Dress."

"Can I just put my head piece and veil on?"

"Also not a good idea."

Brittany made a face, lowered her shoulders, and bowed her head. "Okay. I'll leave my dress in the closet. I won't even touch it."

Todd patted Brittany's shoulder, ordered the pizza, then walked into the kitchen to warm the soup.

Todd returned to the bedroom. He sat on the bed next to Mary-Katherine and stroked her hair. She felt like she was burning up. "M-K . . . Honey, it's time for dinner."

"I'm awake. I've got a headache, and I don't want to open my eyes," she whispered.

"You have a fever, sweetheart. Let me get you a couple of aspirin."

"Not supposed to take aspirin," she pointed to her tummy. "The baby. I can take Tylenol."

"Wait a minute." Todd went into the bathroom to get the thermometer. He came back and ran the pad across her forehead. "Hundred two. I'm calling Dr. Jones."

She nodded. "I'm thirsty. I need water and a couple of Tylenol."

Todd returned to the bathroom, filled a glass with cool water, grabbed the bottle of Tylenol from the shelf, and returned to the bedroom. Mary-Katherine groaned when she sat up. "I feel terrible. I ache all over." She could barely get the tablets down. "God, it hurts to swallow."

Todd dialed the number for Dr. Jeffrey Jones. The answering service took the message.

Ten minutes later the phone rang. The caller ID said JJONES "Hi, Jeff, thanks for returning my call. Mary-Katherine has a fever and a sore throat. Her temperature is one-o-two. I gave her a couple of Tylenol."

"Any other symptoms? Vomiting? Diarrhea? Cough?"

"No, but she says she has a bad headache and joint pains." Todd perched on the edge of the mahogany telephone table. "She's had a busy week. We've been all over the state. You name it. Talks, town-hall meetings, any opportunity to meet constituents. I think she's exhausted."

"Are you in the city?"

"No, we came to the beach house today for a little family time before she has to go back to DC."

"Sounds like she's got a virus. Bring her into the office tomorrow morning."

The doorbell rang. "Pizza's here!" Brittany sang.

Todd walked to the door, balanced the phone between his shoulder and ear, fished money out of his wallet. "Okay. Sounds good. Ten o'clock? Ten thirty? Since we'll be coming in from the beach we should miss the worst of rush hour."

"Ten o'clock would be fine. Let me give you my cell phone number. If she gets any worse, call me back."

"Hold on a minute, Jeff." He took the cardboard box from the delivery girl and handed it to Brittany. "Take the pizza to the kitchen, honey." He paid the young woman and added a substantial tip.

Brittany balanced the pizza box and skipped into the kitchen.

"Jeff, sorry. Tell me the phone number again. I'm trying to juggle three things at once." Todd scribbled down the number, then went back to the bedroom to check on Mary-Katherine. "How are you doing, sweetheart?"

Mary-Katherine shook her head.

"Do you want to come out to the kitchen to eat or should I bring the soup in here?"

"I'll come out." Her voice was scratchy and her movements slow. She turned toward Todd and winced as she swung her legs over the side of the bed and her feet hit the floor.

Todd knelt and slid her feet into her slippers. "Don't try to stand." He lifted the robe from the hook on the back of the door, held it so she could slip her arms in the sleeves, and gently bundled it around her shoulders.

"I'm honored you accepted my dinner invitation, madam." He stepped back and made an exaggerated bow. "The finest canned chicken soup available in our cupboard awaits you." He swept her into his arms and carried her to the kitchen.

Midtown Manhattan
Same evening

Johnny Emmons rubbed the back of his neck for the fourth time in ten minutes. The pain and stiffness would *not* ease. Tonight the line seemed to creep toward the soup kitchen's steam tables slower than ever. He stepped to one side to see what was in the stainless steel pans. Some kind of chicken casserole, mashed potatoes, and corn. He didn't see any soup. His throat felt like he'd swallowed sandpaper. A sudden chill shook his whole body.

Several uncomfortable minutes later his tray was filled. He turned around and scanned the auditorium filled with people.

Ruthie waved. "Come join us." She pulled two-year-old Alice onto her lap to make room on the bench beside her.

Her son, Ethan broke into a wide grin and jumped from his seat, then snapped to attention and saluted.

Johnny saluted back. "At ease, soldier." He put his tray next to Ruthie's, winked at the boy, and ruffled his hair, "How're you doing?" Johnny eased onto the bench, then lifted Ethan onto the bench beside him.

"Doin' good."

"Ethan, don't say *doin' good*. You're doing *well*." Ruthie's tone was gentle, but firm.

Ethan crossed his eyes and squinched his lips tight.

"She's right, Ethan. You listen to your Ma." Johnny pointed his chin toward Ruthie. "She knows how to speak good English."

"Oh, man." Ethan's hung his head. "I thought you were my friend."

"I *am* your friend. But, you and Alice have to learn how to speak well. You're the big brother. You have to help." Johnny extended his hand to ruffle Ethan's hair again.

"Johnny, your hand is shaking." Ruthie's eyes narrowed. "And your face is flushed. Are you okay?"

"I'm kinda achy and tired. I feel like I could sleep for three days."

He put a small piece of chicken in his mouth, chewed, and choked, trying to swallow. "Man, my throat hurts. I better stick to the mashed potatoes." The fork full of potatoes wasn't any easier to get down. He pushed his tray away. "I must-of caught a bug of some kind."

Ethan wiggled onto Johnny's lap. "Tell me a story, Johnny. A story about being a soldier."

Johnny shook his head. "Not today, champ. In a few days, I'll tell you an extra-long story to make up for it."

Ethan put his hand up to Johnny's cheek. "Your face is hot!"

"I think you better not get so close to me." Johnny slid Ethan off his knee. "I should be going. No sense in exposing you or the kids to whatever I'm getting." He picked up his tray, walked to the rack of dirty dishes, slid the tray into an empty slot, and staggered toward the door.

March 22
Anne's office
Frederick, Maryland
Nine a.m.

Anne's phone rang. She welcomed the interruption. She'd been at work since six a.m. Her eyes and mind were already weary from staring at her computer screen. "Hello?"

"Aunt Anne. I have to cancel our dinner date for this evening. I'm booked on the noon shuttle to Boston."

"Boston? Why are you going to Boston? What's going on?"

"Mary-Katherine's been admitted to Brigham and Women's Hospital. She's got a high fever, sore throat, and muscle aches. Todd asked me to come up and help with Brittany."

"Has Mary-Katherine been spending too much time on the campaign trail?"

"Yes, she has. She spent a whole week giving speeches and shaking hands. I hope that's what this is… Too much talking and too many hours with constituents. Her doctor thinks she has a virus. Her temp was up over one hundred two this morning."

"Sounds like some kind of virus."

"Todd's frantic. He doesn't want to leave her bedside."

"Why would they put her in the hospital? It's unusual to hospitalize a young woman, even a pregnant young woman, for a virus."

"I don't know. I'm guessing they're being super careful—pregnant Junior Senator and all."

"The normal routine is bedrest and plenty of fluids and Tylenol. Does she have nausea? Vomiting?"

"No. Her symptoms are sore throat, fever, and malaise."

"I'm sure she'll be fine." Anne glanced at the computer screen and the maps pinned to the wall. "Don't feel bad about missing dinner. I wouldn't be good company tonight anyway."

"Are you okay?"

"I'm fine. I've been trying to solve a problem."

"What's wrong?"

"I'm trying to find an answer to a question they proposed at work. It's a tough one."

March 24
Brigham and Women's Hospital
Boston, Massachusetts
Two days later

Dr. Jones examined Mary-Katherine's neck and hands. "Looks like you have chickenpox."

Mary-Katherine kept her eyes closed and reached for Todd's hand. He entwined his fingers with hers. "I'm right here, Mary-Katherine."

Todd looked up at Jeff Jones. "How could she have chickenpox? You have a copy of her immunization record. She had the vaccine when she was a child."

Jeff Jones smoothed his hair and gave a dismissive wave. "Vaccines don't guarantee one-hundred percent immunity."

Todd shifted in his chair, annoyed with the physician's attitude. "Is she going to be okay?"

"She'll be fine. Pregnant women infected with chickenpox rarely have complications."

"Rarely? What's rarely? What kind of complications?" Todd squeezed Mary-Katherine's hand. "What should we watch for?"

"Adults sometimes get pneumonia during their convalescent period. But, it seldom occurs."

"What about the baby?" Mary-Katherine's eyes opened wider, worry plainly written in her expression.

"There's a slight chance the infection could affect the baby. If you were in your first trimester, I'd be more concerned. The chance is decreased in the second trimester." He lifted his chin a little while he studied her chart on his laptop screen.

"The chance of fetal abnormalities decreases? So there could be some effect on the baby?" Todd's words became precise, clipped.

"Mary-Katherine is at the end of her sixth month. The baby shouldn't be affected at all."

"When will we know for sure?" Mary-Katherine's weak and tremulous question was ignored by Jeff Jones.

He turned toward Todd. "We need to concentrate on keeping her hydrated and getting her fever down. She won't be allowed—"

Todd cut him off, his anger surfacing with full force. "Mary-Katherine asked you a question, Jeff. She deserves an answer."

Jeff Jones look surprised and took a step back. "We'll do an ultrasound in about a month to make sure the baby is okay." He patted her shoulder. "Let's get you through this first."

Todd felt his face redden and his mouth go dry. "So, what you're saying is we can only hope and pray the baby isn't affected?"

Jeff Jones smoothed his hair again and made another it's-of-no-consequence gesture.

Todd could barely contain his anger. "How come no one's allowed to visit? The entire family wants to see her."

"I've put her in isolation. All of her visitors have to put on gowns, gloves, and the rest of the paraphernalia before they come into the room." Jeff looked at Mary-Katherine's chart, again.

"The infectious disease docs will come by to see her this afternoon. They'll make the final decision on whether or not she has to stay in isolation. For now, you're the only person allowed to visit. She doesn't need Irish a bunch of Irish aunts hovering and weeping—she needs rest."

"Rest? She's not getting any rest. Her family can't visit, but she can have a constant flow of people in and out of the room? The nurses come in pairs just to bring a jug of fresh water. And, it's never the same ones. They're in and out and in and out. She can't sleep more than fifteen minutes at a time. I can't see any reason for most of them being here."

"Well, you know how it is when you're a celebrity." Jeff Jones gave another annoying wave with one hand. "She'll have to put up with it. We get the same complaint from every well-known guest in the hospital. It's the price of fame." Jeff Jones chuckled. "Everyone wants to say they took care of Senator Fitzgerald."

"No." Todd shook his head. "*You* are her doctor, *this* is a hospital, and *Mary-Katherine Fitzgerald* is your patient. Senator or not, I expect my wife to have privacy. She's *not* a side-show attraction."

Safe House
Burke, Virginia
The same evening

Another Donovan arranged pot-luck dinner was at an end.

Yuri and Iveta walked to the line of automobiles with their visitors.

Donovan made arrangements for a small group of Russian ex-patriots to meet with Iveta and Yuri. All of the men and many of their wives had been scientists in Russia. They'd all come to the United States from Russia or other Eastern European countries.

Iveta and Yuri stood on the porch and waved until the taillights winked out. Iveta leaned against the railing and softly whispered a short prayer, "Thank You, for bringing us here. Thank You for sparing Yuri's life. Thank You for the new life stirring inside me."

Clouds obliterated the moon. Showers were predicted, but the brisk wind no longer held a frigid undertone. Winter was over.

"What are you thinking?" Yuri put his arms around her and kissed the nape of her neck.

"I'm thinking about new beginnings." She leaned into Yuri's embrace, not wanting to break the mood.

"Our visitors seemed pleasant." The warmth from Yuri's body surrounded Iveta, and he held her a little tighter. "What do you think?"

"I enjoyed the evening. They were interesting people." Iveta turned inside the circle of his arms, yearning to stay in the warmth of his embrace. "They all seem to like the United States."

Yuri held her a while longer before taking her hand and leading her toward the front door of their home. He laughed. "What they liked was the food you and Olga prepared." He opened the door, followed her inside, and closed the door behind them. From habit, he thumbed the lock on.

"I think they were honest. They miss the family they left in Russia, but they're content to be in the United States. They're happy with their work. They're pleased with the schools their children attend." She picked up the remaining cups and saucers from the dining room table, placed them on a tray, and carried them into the kitchen.

Yuri picked up the platter of leftover grapes, sliced apples, and cheese. "Do you think the United States is a good place for us?" He followed her.

"The United States is better than Russia. Better than Syria." Iveta spoke in a low voice, her tone confident. "We're lucky it turned out this way."

Yuri hunched his shoulders and looked away. "I don't know. All the people who were here tonight decided to come to the United States. I didn't make the decision to come here. *We* didn't make the decision. I wanted you and the children to have a better life—in Great Britain. This is my fault."

"Fault? There's no fault."

The crucifix Yuri had carried from Russia hung on a hook above the back door. Iveta closed her eyes and said a silent prayer for guidance. She pointed to the crucifix. "Do you still believe in God?"

His footsteps faltered. "Of course I believe in God. I called on Him in Jakarta, and He sent someone to help." Yuri placed his hands on the kitchen table and bowed his head.

Iveta walked to the opposite side of the table to face him. She stood, hands on her hips. "I think He sent more than someone to help you. He sent people to help all of us. He intervened. He saved your life. He made sure we would all get to America."

Casas Grande, Mexico
The same day

Juana arrived in time to say a final goodbye to her father. She stayed in Casas Grande for two weeks. Hundreds of friends and relatives came to honor the memory of the well-loved man.

The day before Juana was scheduled to leave Mexico, she complained of generalized achiness and lethargy.

"You're tired," her sister Lena said.

"Of course I'm tired. Mother is tired. You are tired. Half of Mexico has been here the past few weeks. I'll get some rest tonight and I'll feel better in the morning."

But, Juana felt much worse the next day. She was too weak to make the hundred mile trip to the airport in Ciudad Juarez.

Three days later, Juana had a high fever, became extremely dehydrated and was still in Casas Grande.

Lena sponged Juana with cool water. Her fever would not break. Juana couldn't eat solid food. She complained about the pain in her throat. She could barely swallow a sip of water. She moaned with each careful movement.

Juana's mother, Rosa, swathed in black from her mantilla to her shoes, sat in a corner of the room. The old woman rocked back and forth and prayed. Rosary beads slipped through her fingers in an unending circle. The silence in the room was broken by Rosa's murmured prayers, Juana's labored breathing, and the click of the onyx beads.

Lena dipped a cloth in the basin of water and wrung out the excess. She patted Juana's forehead with the cool cloth. Her eyes widened in horror. Pustules appeared on Juana's face and hands.

"Madre mia," Lena gasped. She dropped the rag into the basin of water. Her chair hit the wall when she jumped up and hurried toward the door.

"I must get the curendera." Her feet skimmed the ground in her hurry down the hill toward the medical clinic.

Anne's Office
Ft. Dietrich
Frederick, Maryland

Anne answered on the first ring. "Dr. Damiano."

"Hola, Doctora, this is Margita Gonzales, la Curendera of Casas Grande."

"Yes?" Anne's stomach lurched. Juana's village, she thought. "How can I help you?"

"Juana Herrera, the one who is here from the United States, is ill. Pustules. Face. Hands. Fever. Muy dolor de garganda. Muy enfermo."

Anne translated to make sure she understood what the curandera said. "Juana has a sore throat and is extremely ill."

"Si."

"Have you reported this to your public health people?"

"Si. They will be here tomorrow."

"Why did you call me?"

"I call Senor Fischer. He tell me to call you."

"Gracias. Is Juana at the clinic?"

"No, no, no, Doctora, she's at her mother's house. Her sister takes care of her."

"Good. Keep her isolated. She's not to have any visitors. Who else lives in the house?"

"She has two other sisters but they have returned to their homes near Guadalajara."

"No one but her sister and her mother can be in her room. Do not allow anyone else to visit her."

"Si. Our doctors tell me this, also."

"Thank you, Margita. Call me again after the public health doctors have been there, and let me know what they decide. You can give them my number."

Anne broke the connection and made another call on her secure phone to Dr. Jonas Duckworth at the Center for Disease Control and Prevention.

"Jonas, this is Anne Damiano. We have a problem." She briefed him on the situation.

"My God, Anne. You mean to tell me what we've been looking for is . . . *smallpox?*" He whispered the last word.

"Unfortunately. I'm sure the Mexican Authorities will be calling you soon."

"You know we can't intervene unless Mexico requests our assistance."

"Of course. I'll call Juana's boss and let you know what I find out. I have a feeling the problem is about to explode. Things are going to get worse ... a whole lot worse."

Anne pulled out her notes. Fischer & Sons. Billy Mack, Juana Herrera, Harvey Fischer and Melanie Lipscomb.

Melanie answered the phone with her usual cheery voice.

"Hello, Melanie, this is Doctor Damiano."

"Oh, hello, Doctor."

Anne pulled a yellow pad from the shelf behind her. "I got a call from the curendera in Casas Grande this morning. Juana is seriously ill."

"Yes, Margita Gonzales called us. Mr. Fischer wasn't sure what he should do, so, he gave her your number."

"I'm glad he did. I have a few questions for you, if you have a few minutes. They shouldn't take very long."

"Fire away."

Anne wrote 'Melanie' on the top line. "What childhood diseases and immunizations have you had?"

"I came down with all the diseases my older brothers had. I remember being sick with the mumps, measles, chickenpox, German measles. I remember getting my polio vaccination when I was a little bit older."

"If you don't mind telling me, how old are you now?"

"Sixty-five."

"Did you ever get a smallpox vaccination?"

"My mother told me the funny scar on my left shoulder was from the smallpox vaccination"

"Your mother was right. None of the other vaccinations leave a scar. How about Mr. Fischer?"

"I don't know the details about his health history. But all these questions were on the CDC forms we had to fill out last week when they were here."

"Is Mr. Fischer in?"

"He left about an hour ago. He had a doctor's appointment."

"Doctor's appointment? You said he wasn't sick."

"Oh, no, he isn't sick. He scheduled this appointment weeks ago. His doctor wanted him to have a stress test."

"As I remember, he was in the military."

"Yes, he was in the army. He was in Vietnam. That's all I know. He won't talk about the war."

"Do you know how old he is?"

"His wife had a big birthday party for him about six months ago. He's seventy-five."

"Thank you, Melanie. Please let me know if you get any more information about Juana."

The second phone line into Anne's office was blinking. She pressed the button to access the incoming call.

"Aunt Anne." Maria's words poured out in a flood. "Mary-Katherine has some kind of pustules popping up on her face and hands." Her voice was coarse and strained.

Fear shot through Anne. "Are you having any of the same symptoms as Mary-Katherine?"

"No, I feel fine."

"Have you and Mary-Katherine spent time together in the past few weeks?"

"We had lunch at the Hotel George a little over a month ago, and we went shopping for Brittany's First Communion dress a couple of weeks ago."

"Shopping? Where?"

"Westfield Mall. Why?"

"There's a chance Mary-Katherine picked up a virus at the mall. Where are you now?"

"Mary-Katherine's house. I'm supposed to leave tomorrow. I have to be on duty in a few days."

"Have Todd or Brittany complained of fever or a sore throat?"

"No. Brittany is fine. She's just as active and sweet as ever, no complaints. Todd's exhausted—I haven't seen much of him. He comes home, takes a quick shower, and wolfs down whatever Bella prepares. I'm not sure he even tastes what he's eating. Then he's off to the hospital again."

"Stay in the house. Keep Brittany home from school. Call work and tell them you won't be in for a few days."

"What's going on, Aunt Anne?"

"I'll tell you when I get there. I'm not sure yet. It may be nothing."

Anne called Jonas Duckworth again: "Hi, Jonas. Don't know if this is significant, but it sounds like Senator Fitzgerald may have some kind of orthopox disease. She's at Brigham and Women's Hospital in Boston."

"No one's called us."

"My niece is her best friend. Mary-Katherine has been ill for a few days. Fever, sore throat, joint pain, malaise. She called to tell me pustules appeared on Mary-Katherine's face and hands this morning."

"Are you jumping the gun?"

"Maybe, but my niece and Senator Fitzgerald were shopping at Westfield Mall for children's clothing a few weeks ago. And, the woman I spoke to you about this morning is a Fischer and Son employee. Fischer and Son is the warehouse that supplies the clothing to many of the vendors at Westfield Mall."

As soon as she hung up, Anne called Connor and filled him in on the situation.

"Come out to Andrews. I'll make arrangements for us to fly to Boston."

Anne locked her office and drove toward her house. She called Donovan from her car. "It's started, Chief. Massachusetts, and maybe Mexico."

"Connor's already briefed me on the situation. I'm waiting for the President to return my call. What have you heard from the CDC?"

"Jonas Duckworth's getting a team ready to go to Mexico. They're waiting for the invitation from the Mexican Secretariat of Health. And, he's got people on standby ready to go to Boston. The team can be on their way in the next few hours."

"Can this be contained?"

"Doubt it. Too many people have been exposed. We're two weeks out from initial contamination. We have to assume the disease has been spread over a wide area. It may already be worldwide."

"What else?"

"You better talk to President Julian. He's going to have to decide when to require Health and Human Services to consider drastic measures."

"You think it's going to get so bad we'll have to pull out all the stops?'

"Yes, if it's real, it will to go from bad to horrible. And, that will be just the beginning. The situation will degenerate within minutes of the first press release. It won't take long for someone to leak the info."

Bellevue Hospital
Emergency Room
New York, New York

Ruthie huddled on a bench in the Triage area. The triage area was overfilled and the Emergency Room was packed.

She glanced at the clock. Ten hours since she'd signed in, and still waiting. Ethan had a funny looking rash and a fever. And, three-year-old Alice had been restless and cranky all day.

Ruthie ran her hand across Ethan's forehead. He felt hotter than ever.

A little after ten p.m., the number Ruthie had been assigned blinked onto the sign above the triage desk. She slung her pack onto her back, lifted both children, and carried them in an awkward shuffle to the desk.

"What's your problem?" The nurse's aide who stood next to the triage desk asked. She looked at Ruthie with disdain and wrinkled her nose.

"My boy has a rash and a fever."

"Did you take his temperature?"

"No, ma'am. I don't have a thermometer. But he's burning up."

"From the way you smell, you don't have a bar of soap, either," the nurse's aide muttered.

The triage nurse looked disapprovingly at the aide.

Tears welled in Ruthie's eyes. "No, ma'am. We've had to sleep on the street for the past few days. They wouldn't let us in the shelter because Ethan is sick."

The aide ran the thermometer across Ethan's forehead. "One-o-four point two. He has a rash. Looks like chickenpox to me."

"Chickenpox?" Ruthie's shoulders dropped. Chickenpox would prevent her and the children from staying at the shelter for weeks. The people that ran the shelter wouldn't let anyone who was sick come in. They turned people away even if they had a cold.

"You got no business being here. You should be over in the

pediatric wing. Children can't be seen or treated in this part of the emergency department."

The triage nurse gave her aide a disdainful look.

"But, we've been here all day. Nobody said I should go anywhere else." Ruthie sank into the triage station chair.

"There's no reason to come to the emergency room for the chickenpox."

"That's enough, Shirley." The triage nurse turned to Ruthie. "I'm sorry, but she's right, you have to go to the pediatric emergency room." She pulled a diagram from a pad. "Here's a map."

Ruthie took the proffered paper.

The nurse took a deep breath. Ruthie could see the sympathy in her eyes. "The map gives you directions to the children's clinic." She looked down and shook her head. Her next words cut through Ruthie. "They're busy, too. You'll have another long wait."

The nurse keyed a message into the computer.

"Can you at least give him Tylenol for his fever?"

The nurse shook her head. "I'm sorry, I can't. I'm not allowed to dispense medication without a doctor's order. You can get some Tylenol at any drug store. Be sure to get the one for children. Or, you can go to see one of the doctors in the pediatric ER."

"We can't wait another ten hours." Ruthie felt too weak to move. She didn't think she had enough energy to stand up.

"Ethan needs help." Ruthie whispered.

The nurse nodded. "I'm sorry."

Ruthie caught her breath and gave a quiet sob. She mustered her last shred of energy to stand. Tears ran down her face as she struggled toward the door, carrying both children.

The aide followed her. "What you and your kids need are baths. I should call Child Services and let them deal with you."

The nurse's voice carried to the door. "Shirley, can you please help the next patient?"

Ruthie left the hospital and walked a short way down the avenue. She stopped at a subway entrance.

Johnny. I've got to find Johnny.

She staggered down the steps and tried to remember how to find the way. Months before, Johnny took her along the subway platform and showed her how to get to the door that lead to the tunnels.

Ruthie inched along the walkway beside the tracks until she found the staircase. She opened the door that would take her down to the next level.

When the door closed darkness swallowed her and the children. Ruthie sat on the top step and pulled Ethan and Alice onto her lap. Fear kept her from moving further down the staircase. Rats, drug users, roaches, and other dangers lurked in the tunnels. But, Johnny was there. He would help her. He would know what to do. She gathered her resolve, stood, picked up Alice, and held Ethan's hand. "We have to find Johnny."

Johnny crawled out of bed, poured some water in a bowl and washed his face. He needed to get up to the street. The soup kitchen would be closed soon. He hadn't eaten in two days. He didn't feel a hundred percent, but he felt a whole lot better.

"Hey, Johnny!" a man called from across the tracks.

Johnny peeked around the edge of the door to his shack. "Yeah, Nelson?"

"There's a woman over here with a couple'a kids. Says she's lookin' for you."

Johnny walked toward Nelson's voice. Ruthie, a few steps behind Nelson, carried Ethan and Alice. Her face was blotchy, subway-dust-smeared tears on her cheeks.

"Ruthie?" He pulled Ethan into his arms and felt the heat radiating from the boy's small body. "Ethan has a fever. Are you sick? Is Alice okay?"

"I'm okay, and Alice is just tired. I took Ethan to the hospital today. I waited for hours and hours. They told me Ethan has the chickenpox. They wanted to call Social Services. They told me they'd take my kids."

"You're not ever gonna lose anything again, Ruthie. Nobody's ever going to take anything from you again." Johnny picked up Ethan and turned. "C'mon, follow me." He walked back toward his shack.

Ruthie hurried behind, carrying Alice.

"This is it." He pulled the door open. "Now, tell me what happened."

Johnny laid Ethan near the head of his bed and motioned for Ruthie to put Alice on the other end. "Now, sit down and tell me the whole story."

"I haven't been able to go to the shelter for the past two days. Ethan got sick not long after you left us at the soup kitchen. They wouldn't let us into the shelter because Ethan had a fever. We spent two nights on a bench in the park. I took Ethan to the hospital this morning. We were there all day. They wouldn't help us."

"What do you mean they wouldn't help you?"

Ruthie told him about Bellevue and the long wait and the hateful nurse's aide.

"You're gonna stay right here." Johnny poured clean water on two cloths. He gave one to Ruthie and used the other to stroke Ethan's forehead.

"They said he had chickenpox." Ruthie was close to tears again. Her voice shook, and she swiped at her nose with the back of her hand. "The nurse said he needed Tylenol, but she wasn't allowed to give him any. I don't have any Tylenol."

"I have some Tylenol. The doctors at the VA hospital gave it to me."

"Kids aren't supposed to take the grown-up kind."

Johnny went to one of his shelves and pulled out a bottle. He read the label. "Yeah. That's what this says. I don't know how much he can take."

Ruthie was exhausted. She sniffed and swallowed hard. No matter how she tried, she couldn't stop crying.

"It says adults and children over twelve can take two every four hours, but children under twelve shouldn't take any. Why would the nurse tell you to give him Tylenol?"

"I think it means children can't take the adult Tylenol. I think it's too strong. A long time ago—before we were on the streets"—Ruthie used the sleeve of her sweater to wipe her the tears and took a shuddering breath—"I had liquid Tylenol. It was for children."

"Children's Tylenol. Maybe we can make our own. I have a can of orange soda. We could crush a pill and mix it with some of the soda. If we use the lid from a bottle of water to measure the orange soda, we could figure out how many capfuls are equal to half a pill."

Ruthie nodded. "It might work. We could try. But Alice can't take the same amount that Ethan takes. He could take a whole dropper full, but she should only take half a dropper."

Fifteen minutes later they gave Ethan the Tylenol mixed with orange soda. Ruthie got Ethan and Alice cleaned up as well as she could and put them back on Johnny's bed to sleep.

Johnny stood up. "You stay here with the kids. Let 'em sleep. We'll see how Ethan does with the Tylenol. I've gotta go out for a while—I haven't had any food for a couple of days." He pulled on a jacket. "I'll bring some food for you and Alice." Halfway out the door he stopped. He walked back and turned over a box. "Here, put your feet up. Lean back and try to get some rest."

Boston, Massachusetts

The trip to Boston was uneventful. Hanscom Civilian Air Terminal was small, but efficient. Donovan had made arrangements for a car and driver to take Connor and Anne to the hospital. She called Jonas Duckworth. "I'm in Boston."

"So am I. Senator Fitzgerald's OB doc called me this morning. This doesn't look good."

"I'll be there in forty-five minutes."

Connor grabbed her arm to keep her from crashing into a column. "Take a deep breath and slow down, Anne."

She waved him away and punched in Donovan's number. "Hi, boss. We landed a few minutes ago. We're about to leave Hanscom. I just found out Jonas Duckworth is here, too. Senator Fitzgerald's doctor called him."

"Keep me posted."

Seconds after they walked out of the airport a military vehicle pulled to the curb. The driver got out, introduced himself, and tossed their luggage in the trunk. Anne and Connor climbed into the back seat. The driver slid into his seat and took them on a no-nonsense pedal-to-the-metal ride to the hospital.

Jonas Duckworth waited for them at the front entrance. He signaled a state trooper to unlock the door.

"Anne, it's good to see you."

"Jonas, thank God you're here. Have you two met? Connor Quinlan. Jonas Duckworth."

Anne and Connor turned toward what sounded like a fight in the hospital lobby. Shouts bounced off the marble floors, glass windows and doors.

"What's going on?"

"We're having some difficulty." He gestured toward a far corner of the lobby.

The senior senator from Massachusetts yelled at the hospital security people surrounding him. "How dare you keep me away from Senator Fitzgerald?" he pushed one of the guards. "Do you know who I am?"

Anne and Connor walked across the lobby toward the elevator. "You there!" Senator Tulley shouted at Connor and ran toward him. His narrowed eyes emphasized his bulbous, blue-veined nose. He was an over-stuffed suit with over-coifed hair and an over-bearing attitude.

"I know who you are." Spittle flew from the senator's mouth. "What are you doing here?"

The Boston policemen moved in. "That's enough, Senator."

The senator pointed at one of his staff-members. "Get their names and badge numbers. The mayor is going to hear about this."

Anne stepped between the policemen and the senator. He grabbed Anne's arm. "I want information, and I want it *now*. I have an interview set up with ABC in twenty minutes."

She peeled the senator's fingers from her arm, knowing there would be bruises in the morning. "Sir, I would urge you to call your ABC contact and let them know all official communication will be done by Senator Fitzgerald's physician."

"Who the hell are you to tell me what to do?" He tried to push her aside.

She stood firm. "My name is Dr. Anne Damiano."

The senator blanched. "No two-bit government doc can order me around. I've had enough of this. I'm leaving right now." He stormed toward the front entrance.

A phalanx of Boston police officers blocked his exit.

Anne and Connor donned isolation garb, hair coverings, masks, long-sleeved and high-necked paper gowns, gloves, and paper shoe covers. They walked into a crowded room. Todd sat on the far side of the bed and held Mary-Katherine's hand.

Everyone in the room except Mary-Katherine was in full isolation garb. Two attending physicians stood next to Todd, their backs to the door. Sam Burns, the chairman of the Department of Infectious Diseases and the chief resident, stood on the near side. The remainder of the small isolation room was stuffed with residents and medical students.

Anne took Connors hand and wormed their way through the crowd.

The residents and medical students squeezed together so the newcomers could stand at the foot of the bed. Mary-Katherine looked terrified. "Uncle Connor, Doctor Anne." Tears filled her eyes. "I'm so glad you're here."

Mary-Katherine held tight to Todd's hand and reached with her other hand toward Anne.

Anne excused herself as she slid in front of Dr. Burns and the chief resident. She stroked Mary-Katherine's forehead. Mary-Katherine's skin was hot. Her cheeks were flushed, but a palor encircled her mouth. Her eyes were bright with fever, her eyelids drooped. When she reached for Anne, her hand shook.

"Doctor Anne, what's happening?" Mary-Katherine's voice was hoarse. "Nobody will tell me what's going on. They talk to each other. They won't answer questions. They act like I can't hear them. And, like they can't hear me, or Todd." She fell back on the pillow.

"M-K, we don't know for sure why you're so sick, but we think you've been exposed to a virus. We'll have to do some tests before we know exactly what the problem is."

Anne glared at Sam Burns. She scanned the room filled with attendings, residents, and medical students. "I would like you all to leave. Mary-Katherine needs quiet. She also needs some time to speak to her family." She pointed at one of the residents. "Please ask Dr. Duckworth to join us."

No one moved.

"I'm going to ask once more. I would like all of you to leave the room. Please ask Dr. Duckworth to join us." Anne's voice was firm.

One of the junior residents sidled out of the room. None of the others followed. They glanced back and forth between Anne and Burns, a look of excited expectation written in their expressions.

She faced Sam Burns. "I'm going to politely ask for the last time. Please, clear the room." Her voice was firm. It conveyed no-nonsense and no argument.

"This is my patient." Burns crossed his arms and glared at Anne.

She lowered her voice and straightened her spine. "I know you were called in to consult on Senator Fitzgerald. But she *is not* your patient. Dr. Jones is her physician. We are her family, and I'm asking you to respect our privacy."

Sam Burns huffed, but signaled his team. "We'll be in the doctor's lounge." After they filed out, Anne dampened a clean washcloth to blot Mary-Katherine's forehead.

"Oh, that feels good, Dr. Anne. Thank you for getting those people out of the room. I couldn't breathe. They were all stared at me. I felt like some kind of specimen. They wouldn't talk to me at all, and they ignored Todd's questions."

Anne examined the pustules on Mary-Katherine's face, neck, shoulder, hands, and right arm. They ran in parallel lines. A few of the lines were crosshatched.

Jonas Duckworth joined them. "The vaccine is here."

Todd's head snapped up. "Vaccine? What kind of vaccine? You said you don't know what Mary-Katherine has."

"There's a chance, a very small chance, she has smallpox."

Todd's eyes widened in surprised. "Smallpox?"

Mary-Katherine's eyelids drooped. "Maria . . ." she said. "I wouldn't listen to Maria." The last few words came out a faint whisper.

Anne shook her head. "Don't concern yourself with your disagreement with Maria. Concentrate on getting better."

"What about Brittany, Maria, and Bella?" Todd asked.

"They'll have to be immunized as well." Anne turned toward Jonas.

Jonas nodded in agreement. "I'll need Todd or Mary-Katherine's permission to immunize Brittany before I can send a team to the house."

Todd lowered his head and squeezed Mary-Katherine's hand. "Is the immunization necessary?"

"It's advisable. If Brittany doesn't have egg allergies, or eczema, it isn't contraindicated. It's better to take the precaution. You need to be immunized as well."

Todd looked at Mary-Katherine. She gave a slight nod.

Anne patted Mary-Katherine's hand. "Try to take some sips of water."

"It hurts."

"I know. But, it's important. I'll ask the nurses to bring you chips of ice. Let them melt in your mouth. That will help."

Anne put Mary-Katherine's hand in Connors and stepped back from the bed. "Connor, I have to go to the lounge to speak to the infectious disease docs. Can you stay with Mary-Katherine and Todd? I shouldn't be long."

"No problem," he said and patted Mary-Katherine's right hand. Todd still held tight to her left. When Todd murmured a prayer, Connor joined in.

Anne and Jonas stripped off their isolation garb. On their way down the hall, Jonas made arrangements for one of the public health nurses to go to the house and immunize Brittany, Maria, and Bella Taylor.

Anne stepped into a stairwell, pulled out her cell phone, and hit redial.

"Donovan."

"Hi, boss. We're at the hospital."

"How's the senator?"

"She's got a high fever and she's achy, but she seems to be holding her own."

"Good to hear. I'd like you to stop in and see Sean Welsh. Give me a call from his office."

"Sean? Um, sure."

Sean Welsh was the station chief for the Boston field office. Anne's thoughts were muddled. *Now what's happened?*

"We'll stop by his office as soon as we leave the hospital."

"Good. I'll let him know you're coming."

Anne and Jonas walked into the doctor's lounge. Burns's face flared crimson.

He clenched and unclenched his fists. "What is the CDC doing here? The senator has chickenpox. Why are you all turning this into some big threat? Who called Duckworth?"

"Dr. Jones called Dr. Duckworth. Are you sure of your diagnosis? Chickenpox? What makes you so sure Mary-Katherine has chickenpox?"

"What else could it be?"

"Any one of several other diseases." Anne crossed her arms and stood as tall as her five-foot-two frame allowed, her chin lifted at a stubborn angle. "Chickenpox is pretty high on the differential diagnosis list. But, none of us knows Senator Fitzgerald's diagnosis for certain. And we won't know what she has until we get the PCR results back. The distribution of the lesions does not suggest chickenpox."

"I'm Senator Fitzgerald's physician. I have to tell the press something, and *that* is what I'm going to tell them," Burns shouted. "All of Massachusetts, if not the entire United States, expects a report on her condition. I told the hospital administration to set up a news briefing in the auditorium for seven this evening. Senator Tulley and I are going to address the nation."

"Senator Tulley? What does he know about communicable disease?"

Burns towered over Anne. "Senator Tulley has a direct line to the senate majority leader and the President."

Anne put her hands on her hips and gave him her best "I-wish-I-had-the-power-to-vaporize-you" look. "You are not Mary-Katherine's physician. You are a consultant. Has Senator Fitzgerald given you permission to speak in her behalf? Have you asked the senator if she will allow you to release information? Unless Mary-Katherine Fitzgerald gives you permission, you *cannot* say anything *to anyone*. Not to the state, not to the nation, and certainly not to the press."

Johnny's place
An hour later

Johnny returned to his hideaway and placed a cardboard box on the table. Alice and Ethan were sound asleep on the cot.

"How's Ethan?"

Ruthie still clutched the damp cloth she'd used to cool Ethan's forehead. "The Tylenol you gave him worked—he feels cooler. He drank a small glass of the orange soda before he nodded off."

"Ruthie, I want you to stay here until Ethan gets better. If this is the chickenpox, you can count on Alice getting them in the next two weeks."

"We can't stay here. This is your place."

"Where you gonna go? I don't want you to be sleeping on a park bench. They won't let you back in the shelter with sick kids."

"I don't know. Maybe I should call my mother—"

"Your mother's in Schenectady. How are you gonna get there? Look, I got this all figured out." Johnny grabbed the package from the table and shook out an overused but serviceable sleeping bag.

"I borrowed this from Nelson. There's a lot of unusual people down here. But, we help each other out when we can." He pulled a second sleeping bag out of his make-shift closet. "You can take one and I'll take the other. The kids can sleep on the cot."

He reached in his pocket and pulled out a bottle of Children's Tylenol.

Ruthie wiped her eyes. "I don't want you to catch what Ethan has."

"I had the chickenpox when I was five. I'm pretty sure chickenpox is one of those diseases you can't get twice."

CIA Boston Field Office

Connor held a side door to the hospital open for Anne. Their car and driver waited a few feet away.

Pensive and distracted, Anne couldn't ignore the nagging question in her mind. *I know I'm missing something. Lord, help me. What am I missing?* She could almost touch it, but when she tried the thought vaporized.

She slid across the back seat of the car. Connor sat beside her.

"Anne?" Connor snapped his fingers and waved one hand in front of her face. "What's going on? You look like you left for another planet."

"M-K's diagnosis," she whispered. It's not chickenpox and I'm not sure it's smallpox either. The pieces don't fit for either disease."

Connor gave the driver the address of the Boston office. "Care to share?"

"The time line. I've already told you about all that." She nodded toward the driver. "I don't want to talk about it now."

They remained silent for the remainder of the drive, both deep in thought. The driver pulled into a parking space, jumped out of the car, and opened the door.

"We'll talk later. Let's wait and see what Donovan has to say," she said.

Inside the field office they were greeted by Sean Welsh, the Chief of Station. "Can't say I'm happy to see you guys."

Connor shook Welsh's hand. "You really know how to welcome friends you haven't seen in fifteen years."

Sean's grim smile underlined his memories. "Our last mission together seems like a lifetime ago. We were lucky."

"The odds certainly weren't in our favor." Anne allowed her mind and body to relax. It had been a long time since Sean and Connor were together, sharing stories, bantering.

"Aren't unexpected visitors a pain?" she asked.

"Unexpected viruses are a bigger pain. Plus, you weren't unexpected. I got a call from Donovan thirty minutes ago." Sean picked up papers and pencils. "My apologies, I didn't have time to send out for steak and wine."

Anne faked a frown. "A six-pack of Boston Lager would have been just fine."

Sean pointed down the hall. "The best I can offer is an empty office. I've thrown in a few supplies. And, the room does have a secure phone. And, I'd be glad to get you a couple of cups of coffee."

"Not quite as good as the Boston Lager, but more important for the time being." Anne turned to face Sean. She gave him a brief hug. "It's good to work with an old friend again. We're in a bad situation, but at least we don't have to go through the annoying who's-the-top-cop dance."

Sean ushered them to the small office. "I'm sure Donovan's finished off a carafe of high-octane coffee and eaten at least half a dozen Boston cream donuts while waiting for your call."

Anne dialed.

Donovan picked up on the first ring. "Anne, there's whispers floating through DC. I think someone has leaked information."

"Damn. I was hoping for a few days."

"It's not going to be long before the Post gets wind of this."

"Okay. We'll work with the problems as they occur. We don't have any other choice. No sense in spending time and energy worrying about what can't be changed."

"We've got a few secure locations in Boston. Sean's working on places for you and Connor to stay while you're in Boston."

"You don't have to find hotels for us. Connor and I have a place to stay. We're not undercover and we've both got a good reason for being here. My niece is at the Fitzgerald house helping with their daughter and Connor is Senator Fitzgerald's uncle. There's a spare guest room for Connor. I'll share my niece's room. The Fitzgerald house is plenty big enough for all of us."

Late the same evening
The Fitzgerald home
Boston, Massachusetts

"Auntie Anne," Maria dabbed at her tears. "I'm so glad you're here." The two women hugged.

Bella Taylor's smile was morning-sunshine bright. "It's good to see you Doctor Anne, Mr. Connor. I've been worried. Is Mary-Katherine okay?"

"We have a lot of testing to do. I'm praying this will turn out okay for Mary-Katherine." Anne answered. "Where's Brittany?"

"Here I am, Doctor Anne." Brittany, in her First Communion dress, headband, and veil, stood in the doorway.

"Brittany, you look lovely."

"I think Mommy bought me the prettiest dress." She pirouetted.

"You're right. I've never seen a prettier First Communion dress. Did the nurse come and give you your vaccination?"

"Yes. And it didn't hurt at all. It was kind of scratchy." Brittany showed her the band aid that covered the inoculation site. "I didn't even cry. Auntie Maria and Bella didn't cry either."

"I think you need to take your dress off. You don't want it to get stained. You'll be the loveliest girl in church."

"Do you like my headband and veil? Auntie Maria got them for me. She's my godmother, you know."

"Yes, I know Auntie Maria is your godmother. I think we'd better put your dress back in the closet."

"Okay." Brittany's smile turned to a frown. "Bella says I have to keep it in the plastic bag."

"Show me your room. I understand you picked out new colors for the walls and a new bedspread."

Brittany pulled at Anne's hand. "Okay, c'mon, Dr. Anne. I love my room. It's pretty. The walls are pink and purple. And my new comforter and pillow . . ."

"I've got soup and sandwiches ready in the kitchen, Mr. Connor. I knew you'd be hungry," Bella said as Brittany's voice faded down the hall. She wiped her hands on her apron. "No telling when those two will come down."

"Thank you, Bella. It's been a long day, and we never got to eat lunch or dinner with all the commotion. Soup and a sandwich sound wonderful."

Bella laughed. "I had them send over cannoli, Mr. Connor. So, leave room for dessert."

"You always remember how much I love those pastries."

Maria sat at the kitchen table. She stared at her spoon and aimlessly stirred the cold soup that remained in her bowl.

Connor held out his hand. "Hello, Maria. I know we've met before, but we've never gotten to know one another. I'm Connor Quinlan, Mary-Katherine's uncle. Your Aunt Anne has kept me up on your career."

Bella bustled over to the table. "S'cuze me for a second. Here you go, Mr. Connor. Chicken soup and a turkey sandwich."

"Thank you, Bella. The soup smells delicious." He took another deep breath, savoring the rich aroma. "Maria, your aunt said you enjoyed your days with US AMRIID."

Maria sat a little straighter and brightened. "I did. Thank you so much for the recommendation—the course was fabulous." She paused while Connor scooped a spoonful of soup. "*Really* fabulous. I learned so much."

Connor put down his spoon and stood when Anne entered the room. "Maria was just about to tell me about her experiences at Fort Dietrich and Aberdeen Proving Grounds."

Anne hugged Maria. "Oh, sweetheart, I'm sorry you have to put your training to a test this quickly."

March 28
Brigham and Women's Hospital

"Good morning, Mary-Katherine," Anne whispered with a glance toward Todd, who was asleep in a recliner next to Mary-Katherine's bed. At the sound of Anne's voice, he stirred, scrubbed his face with his hands, and blinked.

Mary-Katherine opened her eyes a slit. "Doctor Anne."

"Do you feel any better?" Anne felt Mary-Katherine's forehead. "Your temperature is still pretty high."

Mary-Katherine sighed and shook her head. "No, I feel terrible. I hurt everywhere," she mumbled.

Todd glanced at the wall clock. "Good morning, Dr. Anne. It's six a.m. What brings you to the hospital so early?" He stood and reached for Mary-Katherine's water pitcher.

"Jonas and I have a busy day ahead of us. I wanted to check on Mary-Katherine before the rush starts."

"She's had a restless night. She complained of a headache and joint pain at about two this morning."

Mary-Katherine moved her head less than an inch to underline Todd's words.

Anne took careful note of the lines of pustules on Mary-Katherine's face and hand. Mary-Katherine shifted and winced. "Light hurts my eyes."

Todd pulled the curtain closed. "Can't she have a stronger medication for her discomfort? They're only giving her Tylenol liquid."

"I'm sure it's because they don't want to give her drugs that might injure the baby." Anne pulled out her stethoscope and listened to Mary-Katherine's lungs. "They sound clear." Anne checked Mary-Katherine's back, abdomen and legs. "You don't have pustules anywhere but on your arms and face."

Todd watched Anne examine Mary-Katherine. "Is that a good sign or a bad sign?"

"I think it's good." Anne smiled. "Do you want to go downstairs to get some breakfast, Todd? I can stay here with Mary-Katherine."

"No, they'll bring me a tray. I'd just as soon stay here."

Anne lifted a paper grocery bag. "Bella sent this, Todd. It's clean clothes for you, and I think she wrapped up one of her red velvet cupcakes as well."

At seven a.m. Connor carried a tray to the table and sat next to Anne in the hospital cafeteria. "I got a call from Donovan this morning. The rumors that started last night have taken on a life of their own. Senator Fitzgerald's illness has been the go-to topic on all the morning shows. The press is reporting that Senator Fitzgerald has smallpox."

Anne's chin dropped to her chest. She sighed, and pushed her plate away, her appetite gone. "Here we go."

Anne's cell phone rang. It was the Surgeon General. State Health Departments in Maryland, New York, Massachusetts, and New Jersey were begging for information. Had she been in touch with Jonas Duckworth? Were the rumors true?

As soon as she ended the call, her phone rang again. It was Donovan.

"Washington, DC, is in a state of panic. The President, First Lady, and the Vice-President and his wife, as well as White House personnel and the congress, their families, and their staff have been sequestered in secure areas. Some are close to Camp David, others are in the bunkers and underground tunnels in West Virginia. Military leaders have been moved to secure bunkers. Rumors of smallpox are all we hear from radio, TV and, the internet. Government offices are closed except for emergency personnel. Many of the emergency personnel are not showing up for work." Donovan paused and took an audible, deep breath. "How is Boston holding up?"

"I haven't been near a TV or a radio station so far this morning. Mary-Katherine is still extremely ill."

The Fitzgerald house
Boston, Massachusetts
Early afternoon

Anne sat at the table with Connor and Maria and stared out the window. The sky was overcast. Rain was predicted. The cheerful yellow and white decor didn't elevate the mood inside the kitchen.

"Any news from the surgeon general, Aunt Anne?" Maria stirred her already cold cup of coffee.

"Yes, I have. None of the news is good. They're considering implementing Emergency Disaster Function Number Eight." She tapped her finger tips on the table top.

"I have a general idea of Function Number Eight," Connor said, "but I don't know the specifics."

Anne rubbed her forehead. "Function Number Eight is overwhelming and extremely complex. It essentially gives Health and Human Services total control over populations whose members may have medical and other functional needs before, during, and after an incident that may lead to a public health, medical, behavioral, or human service emergency, including those that have international implications."

"That comes close to Martial Law."

"Martial Law implemented by the Director of Health and Human Services."

Connor's brow furrowed. "What are we doing now?"

"Not much. State health departments are using the Emergency Broadcast System to warn the public to remain at home if they have a fever and a rash. The CDC has established a specific phone number people can call for further instructions. Everyone has ignored the warning; they all want to be seen immediately. And, *everyone* wants to be admitted."

Connor took a deep breath and blew it out through pursed lips. "Seems like that's what you've been saying all along. What measures has the government taken so far?"

"The existing emergency disaster plan calls for hospitals to go on lockdown when one suspected case of smallpox comes in. The problem is that the hospitals don't have the facilities to handle the volume of patients that want to be evaluated at the emergency departments. The patients complain of the prodromal symptoms of smallpox. Some claim to have pox-like lesions. Our current program doesn't work well. But at least the CDC and President make the decisions."

"I guess it's no consolation to know this is exactly what you predicted," he said.

"No, it doesn't make me feel vindicated. I'm betting that right now every agency in DC is jockeying for power. No one knows who's doing what, when, or why."

Anne's phone had rung more times than she could count. Constant calls from the media. NBC and CNN wanted statements from her. Fox News invited her to do a segment debating Jeffrey Delaney.

"I don't want to talk to Delaney. Just the thought of him gives me indigestion." She covered her face and shook her head.

Anne didn't mention that ABC and CBS called as well. They wanted her to do exclusive interviews with their talking heads. She refused. According to her office, MSNBC had tried to reach her. Her secretary didn't return the call. She watched Connor and Maria push food around on their plates with their forks.

Anne looked down at the food in front of her. She'd taken two bites from her sandwich and choked down a few spoonsful of soup. Their collective anxiety ratcheted into high gear, eliminating hunger.

At two o'clock, Donovan called. "The twenty-four hour news stations are having a field day. The mayors of Baltimore, Washington, New York City, and Philadelphia have established cordons sanitare. No one in, no one out. National Guard Units have been called into service. Interstate commerce is at a standstill. Bridges are shut down. The Ben Franklin, Betsy Ross, and Walt Whitman from New Jersey to Pennsylvania are closed. The George Washington, Verrazano Narrows, and Goethals Bridges are closed. The Lincoln and Hudson Tunnels are closed as well."

The gravel in Donovan's voice echoed his exhaustion and frustration. "Thousands of people—no, tens of thousands—have no way to get home, have no way to contact their families. They have no way to protect their loved ones. Roads are jammed. And the President has ordered a halt to all air traffic."

"Is there any good news?"

"No." He took a deep breath. "We have reports of mobs in Chicago and Los Angeles setting fires, looting grocery stores, and emptying the shelves." A short pause. "Damn it."

"Has the President declared a national state of emergency?"

"His staff is putting the language together right now. They've also contacted all the news outlets to stand by for a Presidential address at one p.m. Is Connor there?"

"Yes, he's right here. My niece, Dr. Maria De Costa, is here as well."

"Put the phone on speaker."

Anne complied. "Speaker's on," she said.

"The entire East Coast is in total chaos," he continued. "Plus, all traffic between the US and Canada, as well as between the US and Mexico, has stopped. National Guard personnel have been stationed on the border with shoot-to-kill orders if anyone attempts to cross into the US. The Mexicans have a similar contingent on their side of the line. All commercial air traffic has been stopped. The only planes flying are military. To top it off, I just got word that some CDC people are sequestered at the airport in Juarez."

Anne shuddered. "Oh my God... That's the team Jonas Duckworth sent to Casas Grande."

Connor leaned toward the phone. "Can we get any of our people to the airport in Juarez?"

"Funny you should ask." Donovan gave a grunt. "Bill Samuelson is in Juarez, at the airport. He was already in Mexico to take care of a problem related to border security. His presence at the airport was coincidental. His son is getting married in a few days. Bill was supposed to fly to Minnesota this morning. As soon as he got to the airport, the President of Mexico stopped all international flights."

Connor spoke up again. "Is there a way to get word to him? Maybe he can join up with the CDC folks. Doesn't look like he'll get to Minneapolis any time soon. Have him talk to the CDC team. Maybe he can convince them to keep a low profile. Any show of force or arrogance could get them killed."

"This is just the beginning. It's going to get beyond ugly, real soon." Anne reached across the table to squeeze Connor's hand. "Donovan," she said, "Jonas is getting his team ready to start immunizing the staff and patients at Women's Hospital. And they're trying to find any visitors who have been at the hospital since Mary-Katherine was admitted."

Maria stacked the plates and picked up the silverware. "How about Mary-Katherine's staff in DC and the press corps who traveled with her? What about all the places she's been for the past four days?"

"I better call Jonas. He's probably made arrangements for immunizing her staff," Anne said. "He needs more information to follow up every detail."

Brigham and Women's Hospital
Later the same day

"Anne turned to Mary-Katherine. Hang in there M-K." She glanced across the bed to Todd. "You, too. We'll be back in the morning."

When Anne, Connor, and Jonas stepped into the anteroom, they pulled off the isolation garments and stuffed them into the red plastic contaminated-linen bag.

"How are you coming with the immunizations?" Connor asked.

Jonas stopped before they walked into the lounge. "We've vaccinated all the hospital personnel who've had direct contact with Mary-Katherine. We'll start on the monumental task of immunizing the patients, medical, and nursing staffs, as well as all the employees and all the visitors."

"You've got one heck of a job in front of you."

Jonas gave her a tired smile and nodded. "Right now a chicken-pox epidemic is sweeping the East Coast. That's making our job fifty times harder."

Anne paused at the door to the doctor's lounge. "Have you heard from the Mexican authorities?"

"I got a call from their Secretary of Health today. Juana is still quite ill, but they don't have a definitive diagnosis."

The lounge was filled with physicians and medical students. Some struggled to stay awake, the rest stared at the TV

Anne, Connor, and Jonas joined them. The news anchor smiled at the camera. "We're fortunate to have Dr. Jeffery Delaney with us today. He's got some interesting information for us."

She grabbed the remote control and snapped the TV off.

"Turn the television back on." Dr. Burns walked to Anne and reached for the remote control. "Jeffrey Delaney is about to speak. *He's* the expert on smallpox."

"He's the expert at denial and the *self-appointed* expert on small-pox. He's spent his entire career denying there would ever be a bio-terror attack. Now his efforts have unleashed uncontrollable fear of tremendous proportion. His denials stopped the smallpox immunization program proposed in 2002. That immunization program would have prevented the panic we're witnessing today. What makes you think he has any good answers now?"

Burns again tried to grab the remote.

Anne's stance changed to one of defense. Her feet were shoulder width apart, arms away from her body, knees slightly bent. Her actions were subtle, but definitely sent the message.

Burns backed off.

"You don't need Jeffery Delaney. You need facts, cold hard facts. You need the test results. You need to formulate a plan."

"Smallpox was eradicated decades ago," Burns shook his head and tried to match her defiance. "Delaney said the New York Times report about Senator Fitzgerald was the work of some nutcase conspiracy theorist."

"Sounds like Delaney."

"Well," Burns huffed. "The information was leaked to the New York Times by an unidentified source. I'm with Delaney—I don't believe it for a minute."

"I don't know Mary-Katherine's diagnosis. And, I don't know who decided to spread false rumors to the Times. But what I do know is that our nation is in chaos because of rumor, inaccurate information, and speculation."

She handed Burns the remote control and walked out of the lounge into a hallway jammed with hospital personnel. Anne hopscotched her way through the crowd until she reached the nurse's station. "Is there a way to clear this hallway? The noise is at thought-numbing levels."

"The guards won't let anyone leave the floor." The head nurse's voice dropped to a whisper. "The elevators are closed. They have guards at each landing, staircase, and door. No one's going up or down without permission."

"Are there any empty rooms? Can you divide the people into smaller groups? That would make things easier for Dr. Duckworth's team to get the immunizations done."

"What if someone doesn't want a shot?" the head nurse squeaked. "Most of these people haven't had any direct contact with Senator Fitzgerald."

"They'll have to have a darn good reason for not getting an immunization. Smallpox is airborne. There are a few reasons to not get immunized. So unless these people want to carry the virus out of the hospital and expose their families, they should get the immunization."

The nurse nodded.

"And," Anne added, "it's just a scratch—it's not a shot."

March 29
Brigham and Women's Hospital
Laboratory

"What kind of numbers are we getting?" Jonas Duckworth stood with one hand in his pocket. His nervous habit prevailed as he jiggled the change in his pocket.

The technician looked up and back at the PCR readout, then shook her head.

"How long is this going to take?"

"Might be a couple more days, Doctor."

"Damn. We need those results."

The Fitzgerald house
Kitchen nook
Later that evening

Anne, Connor, and Maria sat at the kitchen table. They'd just finished dinner. Bella was an excellent cook, but tonight none of them appreciated or even acknowledged the food.

A flash of gray and white ran through the kitchen and darted under the table. Brittany skidded to a stop, flopped onto the blue and yellow braided carpet, and elbow-crawled under the table.

"What on earth?" Maria leaned down and caught the hem of Brittany's school uniform. "What are you doing? Why do you have your school clothes on?"

Brittany turned over and peeked at Maria from under the tablecloth. "I'm story acting and I need the kitty to play with me." Brittany scooted backwards. She was able to close the distance to the cat by another foot. "He's my audience."

"Come out from under there right now, missy." Bella's voice demanded instant obedience.

Brittany bumped her head in her hurry to do Bella's bidding. She faced the grownups, mouth downturned, eyes shiny with tears. "I don't have anybody to play with. It's no fun being home from school. And, and, I miss Mommy and Daddy." Tears rolled down her face. "Trisha told me Mommy has a terrible 'fection. Is Mommy going to die?"

Maria reached for her napkin. "Come here." She patted her lap and helped Brittany up and wiped the child's tears. "I miss your mommy and daddy, too. And, no, your mommy is not going to die."

Maria looked at Bella. "Who's Trisha?"

Bella closed her eyes, her mouth turned down. She shook her head. "She's in Brittany's class. A troublemaker. I'll tell you all about *her* later."

Maria nodded her understanding to Bella and gave Brittany a hug. "I know you're bored. I am too. What do you want to play?"

"I want to play First Holy Communion. It's important. Sister Mary-Joseph made us practice before catechism class every day."

Anne's smile reflected her instant understanding. "Now I know why you're wearing your school clothes."

"Bella won't let me wear my First Communion Dress. It has to stay in the plastic bag."

Bella stopped washing the dishes and turned toward the kitchen nook again. "I spent enough time on cleaning that Communion dress. It took me an hour to brush off the cat hair."

Anne perked up immediately. "How did cat hair get on your First Communion dress?"

"Mommy left the dress on her bed. The cat slept on it." Brittany jumped off Maria's lap, knelt down, and looked under the table.

"Cats aren't supposed to sleep on pretty dresses."

"I know." Brittany started to crawl toward the cat again. It yowled, shot out from behind Connor's chair, and dashed out of the kitchen.

"Mommy must have been mad at your cat."

"Not my cat. Alley Cat." Brittany backed out from under the table.

"An alley cat slept on your dress?" Anne was confused. "How did an alley cat get in the bedroom?"

"Alley is the name of Mommy's Washington cat." Brittany stood up and brushed off her uniform. "She's nasty."

Brigham and Women's Hospital
Two hours later

Anne tiptoed into Mary-Katherine's room. Todd raised a finger and tapped his face mask covering his lips to let her know Mary-Katherine was asleep. Anne examined the pustules on Mary-Katherine's face and neck. The pustules on her arm had progressed to the same stage as the others. All were pearlescent white, rimmed with red.

She gestured for Todd to come out of the room. "Brittany told me Mary-Katherine has a cat in DC."

"Oh my gosh, I forgot all about the cat. One of her staffers usually takes care of it when Mary-Katherine is away. I better check. With the blockade in place and the government shut down, maybe she can't get in and out of the city."

"Brittany said M-K's Washington cat is a meanie."

"She's the meanest cat I've ever seeen. M-K comes home with scratches all the time."

"Has she considered getting it declawed?"

"She's been hesitant to have the cat declawed, but she was having second thoughts after her last encounter."

"Oh?"

"The cat was sick. Mary-Katherine had to give her some pills. Alley wasn't having any of it. That damn cat scratches at any provocation."

The missing piece slid into place.

Fischer and Sons
Washington, DC

Melanie tucked a stray strand of hair behind her ear. The warehouse was filled with unopened boxes. There was no place to send the merchandise. The malls were closed. The roads were closed. The busses weren't running and the Metro was shut down until further notice. Thank God they weren't getting any more merchandise. DC was closed for business.

All the media could talk about was smallpox. Pediatricians were on the television and the radio. They denied the rumors of smallpox and emphasized that the children had chickenpox. The doctors were urging calm. The US was experiencing the worst chickenpox outbreak since the 1950s.

A dome of fear covered Washington.

Mr. Fischer closed the warehouse and told Melanie to stay at home.

Still, Melanie continued to go to the office on a daily basis. No television. No radio. A silent phone. No Billy. No Juana. No Mr. Fischer. Just the piles of unopened cartons.

Gangs roamed the streets. Going to the warehouse was dangerous. A trip to the grocery store could be deadly.

But she couldn't stay home—that would be admitting defeat.

March 30
Brigham and Women's Hospital
Boston, Massachusetts
Midmorning

An armed guard opened the lobby door for Anne. Jonas stood a few feet behind the guard. "What's happened?" she asked. "I got here as fast as I could."

Jonas ushered Anne into the hall. "Let's go to the coffee shop. It's quieter in there."

Coffee and bagels in hand, Anne and Jonas moved away from the counter. Jonas whispered in her ear. "I've got news I couldn't tell you over the phone. The Mexican Public Health Secretariat called me this morning. Juana has developed pneumonia, and her pustules have spread to cover her face and trunk."

"Is she still in Casas Grande?"

He shook his head. "They're moving her to a hospital in Juarez. She needs intravenous fluids, antibiotics, and isolation."

"She's a healthy woman. The secretary at the warehouse told me Juana's only complaint was allergies."

"Exactly, and therein lies the problem. The damp weather in DC aggravated her allergies. I'm guessing Juana lives in a building that's old enough and damp enough to have mold. She got a prescription for steroids from her doctor in Maryland about a week before she left for Mexico."

Anne closed her eyes and pinched the bridge of her nose. "So, she was not only exposed to the virus, she was taking a medicine that made it more difficult for her body to fight any infection."

"Yes, and her sister crushed up the pills and put them in applesauce so Juana could swallow them after she got sick. The Public Health Secretariat docs found the bottle when they visited Casas Grande."

"How bad is Juana?"

"Extremely bad. The Mexican doctors said they'd let me know if her condition changes."

Anne leaned back in her chair, covered her face with her hands, and rubbed her forehead. "I don't want any more bad news, but I have to ask. Do we have the PCR results from Mary-Katherine yet?"

"I haven't had time to check today. I'm sure the lab would have called if they had any information. It wasn't available yesterday."

"I don't think Senator Fitzgerald has smallpox—and I don't think she has chickenpox either." Jonas finished off the last of his coffee and pushed his chair back. "Her symptoms aren't indicative of either disease. The strange distribution of the pustules tops the list."

Anne grabbed his sleeve and indicated he should lean closer. "I'm sure she doesn't have chickenpox or smallpox," she whispered. "I think I've figured out why the distribution of Mary-Katherine's pustules is so strange."

"Oh?" Jonas crushed his Styrofoam coffee cup and scooted his chair back to the table.

"First, the timeline isn't right. The Syrian's haven't had the virus long enough to turn it into a reliable weapon."

"That's been my thinking, too."

"Mary-Katherine's pustules are along parallel lines. And some of the lines are actually hatch marked."

"I've wondered about that."

"About two weeks ago Mary-Katherine was trying to give her cat some medication. He scratched her face, neck and arm. We need to get an electron-microscopic study done on the fluid from one of Mary-Katherine's pustules."

Jonas puzzlement was still apparent. "Her cat scratched her?" Jonas pursed his lips and rubbed the back of his neck. "But, what . . ."

Anne related the story beginning with the First Communion Dress covered with cat hair to the cat's resistance to taking the medication.

"Let's see if there are mulberry or capsular forms floating around in the fluid from the pustules. We might not have to wait for the PCR results."

CIA Boston Field Office
The same day

An hour later Anne arrived at the Boston office. The weather reports had predicted rain for the past two days, and when the rain arrived it was torrential. Flooding was reported all along the Eastern Seaboard.

Anne stepped into the foyer, closed her umbrella and shook the raindrops off her trench coat. Sean Welsh greeted her.

"Hi, Sean. Do you mind if I use the phone?"

"Sure, let me get you a cup'a coffee. Looks like you need to warm up."

"You're right. And I need to dry off. I'm sure Donovan doesn't want to hear my teeth chatter."

"Go ahead into the office, its open. I'll bring your coffee in. You still take it black?"

"Sure do." She hung up her coat and walked into the office. A few minutes later she dialed Donovan's office from the secure line. "Hey, boss, is the weather as bad in DC as it is here?"

"We've had lots of rain, but I'm willing to bet we're a good fifteen degrees warmer than Boston."

Anne filled him in on the news from Casas Grande. "We're still not sure what kind of infection Mary-Katherine has, but we're pretty sure it's not smallpox."

"Really? What do you think she has?"

"We're waiting on a few more test results. I'm hoping we'll have the answer in a few hours. And, I'm still uncomfortable with the timeline on all this. What's the chance of my getting to see our friend from Burke?"

Burke, Virginia
The same afternoon

Yuri and Iveta stared at the television screen. The sound was muted, but the banner flowing across the bottom of the screen described violence in cities across the United States. Pictures flashed on the screen of soldiers, weapons at the ready, standing guard at the on and off ramps of highways. There were pictures of churches overflowing with parishioners, photos of mobs storming city halls, clinics and hospitals. There seemed to be no end to the images of trains at a standstill. There was even footage of truck drivers complaining about produce from California and Texas rotting in their trucks. The TV cut to footage of miles of trucks abandoned on interstate highways.

Yuri and Iveta glanced at each other, then lowered their eyes to the carpet. Ondrek and Josef played on the floor in the next room. Maruska toddled from coffee table to chair and back again.

"Where will they take you?" Iveta whispered

"I don't know."

"How long will you be gone?"

"I don't know. All Mr. Donovan said was to bring a bag with enough clothes to last a few days."

"Does it have to do with . . . ?"

Yuri nodded.

"When will they come for you?"

"Soon."

"Will they arrest you?"

"I don't know." Yuri stood, walked to the kitchen, and plugged in the electric kettle to boil water for tea. He didn't want Iveta to sense his fear, but he worried over silent questions. Should I tell her the truth? Is it better if she doesn't know?

Iveta followed Yuri to the kitchen, walked to the cupboard, pulled two glass mugs from the bottom shelf, and scooped leaves into a tea ball. She waited by the kettle, and her fingernails drummed the Formica counter.

Yuri straightened his spine, his lips rigid with determination. His decision had been made. He turned off the kettle and whispered, "Walk out to the garden with me."

Iveta scooped up the toddler, slipped her hand into Yuri's, and walked with him to the front porch. The garden promised a beautiful spring. Trees were enveloped in a light green mist of budding leaves, a few tentative tulips and daffodil shoots sprouted along the garden path. Crocus lined the walk.

Yuri hugged his wife. "Iveta…," he whispered in her ear.

Donovan's car pulled in the driveway. He rolled down the window. "Ready?"

Yuri nodded and returned to the house and picked up his suitcase. He gave Iveta another quick hug and whispered, "It's not what it seems."

Fox News

"Breaking news out of Seattle. Two people are in critical condition at the University of Washington Hospital. They are a ten-year-old child with a diagnosis of leukemia, who was awaiting transfer to St. Jude's Medical Center in Nashville, and a twenty-four-year-old AIDS patient who had never been immunized against chickenpox. Doctors say their prognosis is grim. There are unconfirmed reports that another patient was transferred to Seattle's Northwest Hospital in critical condition from an outlying hospital with a poxlike illness."

Safe House
Cambridge, Massachusetts

"Hello, Yuri." Anne held out her hand. He took it and looked over her shoulder. Her car and driver sat in the front of the house. They were alone.

"Relax, Yuri."

"I've been watching the television. I've seen the violence. They are saying smallpox. Smallpox. Smallpox. I know what you think. But . . ." Yuri sighed.

"No, I don't think you do. Please tell me what was in the vials you took from the lab in Russia. I don't think it was smallpox."

Yuri nodded. "I gave the Syrians Variola minor."

"Why did the Russian authorities tell us you brought RAHIMA?"

"I filled two vials with whey and put the RAHIMA labels on them."

"What happened to the original vials of RAHIMA?"

Anne watched Yuri's eyes, his body movements, his hand gestures. He was telling the truth.

"They are still in the freezer at Vektor. I changed their labels. They now say 243V and 244V. I made them appear to be vials from a failed genomic integration series." He paused to wipe sweat from his forehead. "The failed series originally ended with 242V."

"Why wouldn't they have noticed the Variola minor was missing?"

"I knew the technicians would look at the most deadly viruses first. So I put vials of whey labeled as RAHIMA in the place of the original RAHIMA vials."

"You said you gave vials of Variola minor to the Syrians."

"Yes. But the virus in those vials couldn't have caused an epidemic."

Anne blinked several times. "I don't understand."

"I brought vials from another of the failed gene experiments. We attempted to insert part of the Lassa fever genome into Variola minor.

The virus multiplied in cell culture but mutated. It did not produce either disease. In fact, it didn't produce any discernable disease."

"You must have known the Syrian's would . . ."

"Yes," he said, cutting her off. "I knew they would find out that I tricked them. I hoped I could convince them it wasn't my fault." Yuri hung his head. "I was going to blame it on the poor conditions at Vektor." He stared at his hands.

"I knew there was a chance they would kill me. But, I hoped they would not harm my family."

Yuri sprang from his chair and paced the length of the room.

"Their offer was the answer to my prayers. I had to send my family to the West. We had to get out of Russia. Iveta and the children were starving." He swiped at his eyes. "Have you ever seen someone die of starvation? It's horrible."

Yuri dropped back into the chair, and rolled his hands into tight fists. "I knew my family would be well away from Russia and would have adequate money to live without me." He winced and flexed his fingers to relieve a muscle cramp.

"I prayed. I trusted God to guide them and guard them." He looked down at his hands again. His fingers burned. "It was stupid, but I couldn't find another solution."

"Trusting in God isn't stupid."

April 1
The Fitzgerald House
Early the next morning

Anne swung her legs over the side of the bed. Time to face another day of questions. The anxiety and exasperation of not being able to control the panic or come up with a workable solution made her feel like she was climbing the wall of a bottomless pit toward an unreachable level ground.

Her cell phone rang. The display read: JDUCKW. She sucked in a breath. Fear ran through her gut, wrenched her heart, and prickled her skin. "Hello, Jonas. Good morning . . . I hope." Anne walked to the window.

"I got the PCR report a few minutes ago."

"Finally." Anne hiccupped, and wondered if the hint of joy in Jonas' voice might be good news.

"It confirms our suspicions. Vaccinia."

"Cowpox." She walked back to the edge of the bed and picked up a pencil.

"Okay. Has the electron microscopy report come in?"

"Yup. Same thing."

Anne sank down to the edge of the bed. "At least we know what we're facing."

"Yes." The note of optimism was gone.

"What now?"

"All three of the patients in Seattle died last night."

"Oh, no." Anne rested her left elbow on her knee and bowed her head. She pinched the bridge of her nose with her thumb and forefinger.

"There's more bad news." Anne heard Jonas take a deep breath. "We're beginning to get reports of compromised patients: seniors, AIDS patients, children with histories of eczema and asthma, and leukemia. They are being admitted to hospitals from Virginia to Connecticut with generalized rash, necrotizing cellulitis, and necrotizing lymphadenitis."

April 20
Anne's home
Fredrick, Maryland
Three weeks later

Anne and Maria sat on identical deep-blue recliners in Anne's den. A tray with two cups of cappuccino and a dish heaped with pizzelles sat on the table between them. "I talked to Todd today, Aunt Anne. Mary-Katherine's doing well. It looks like she's going to have one little scar on her arm but everything else is healed. The sonograms of the baby look good. There's no evidence of complications."

"Thank God. I hope we never have a repeat of the past two months."

"You know they're going to try again, Aunt Anne. Somewhere. Somehow." Maria reached for her cappuccino.

"I think I'll let the next generation pick up the reins on that one." Anne turned to Maria. "Feel up to the task?"

Maria took a deep breath. "I'm working on it. Can't imagine trying to fill your shoes."

"Once you finish your training with the Company . . ."

"We can talk about that later." She studied the troubled look on her aunt's face. "Have you spoken to Dr. Duckworth?"

"Yes, he called a few days ago, said he was finally able to get a full night's sleep. The largest outbreak of chickenpox in sixty years hit the US almost simultaneously with the smallpox scare."

"From what I hear the entire public health community was overwhelmed."

"Has he heard from the doctors in Mexico?"

Anne's face brightened. "Yes. Juana has been improving steadily. Looks like she's going to recover completely."

"You said PCR confirmed both Mary-Katherine and Juana were infected with cowpox?"

"Yes. I knew the timeline wasn't appropriate for the production of weaponized smallpox. Our best guess is Al Halbi sent the vaccinia to see if it would get through the ports to infect anyone." She sipped her coffee. "I think Al Halbi sent out the cowpox as a trial balloon. He wanted to test our port monitoring systems, our response time, what we would do to overcome the chaos."

The two women sat in silence for a minute. Anne reached for a pizzelle.

"We were lucky this time. Weren't we, Aunt Anne?"

"Yes," she nodded. "Yes, it's amazing how few deaths occurred. Two from chickenpox and five from cowpox. We were unbelievably lucky."

Silence filled the room for several long minutes. Maria collected her thoughts.

"I need to talk to you . . ." Maria bit her lip and tried again. "I wonder if you could—" Maria shook her head and felt the blood drain out of her limbs leaving them cold. "I've got a problem."

"Oh? Is this the 'we'll talk about it later'?"

"Sort of. I've met someone. And I really, really like him. I think I'm in love."

"Sounds like a good problem to me."

"He's in Texas."

"Tell me more. How did you meet your 'Texas problem'?" Anne's voice lilted.

Maria shook her head. "Don't act like this is nothing. He was my field buddy from US AMRIID. He's an army doc at Fort Hood. We were a good team."

"Does your army doc at Fort Hood have a name?"

"Antonio Ulibari."

"Why is Antonio a problem?"

"He's in Texas and I'm in Maryland."

"And? C'mon, Maria. I still don't see a problem. He won't be at Fort Hood forever. And, you don't have to stay in Maryland."

"But, I'm from New Jersey. He's from New Mexico."

"Last I heard New Mexico was a part of the United States. A beautiful part, by the way."

"But, if I'm with the . . ."

Anne's focus drifted from Maria's face to a framed five-by-seven black-and-white photograph on her desk. The picture was a grainy snapshot of a young, unsmiling soldier in a dusty compound, rifle in hand, combat ready.

Maria didn't finish her sentence. Her gaze drifted to the image as well. "You've had that picture on your desk for as long as I can remember. Who is it?"

"The man I didn't marry because we let imagined problems keep us apart."

"Mr. Quinlan."

"Yes, a *very* young and a very brave Lieutenant Quinlan."

'It is the strong in body who are both the strong and free in mind.'
Peter Jefferson, Thomas Jefferson's father.

June 9
Cathedral of the Holy Cross
Boston, Massachusetts

A radiant Brittany Fitzgerald marched down the aisle with her class to receive First Communion. She wore the beautiful dress, headpiece, and veil purchased at Westfield Mall. Her class filed into the two rows closest to the altar. The girls sat in the first row, boys in the second.

Sister Mary Joseph and the remainder of the faculty stood in the third row, fully prepared to stop any misbehavior.

Mary-Katherine, Todd, Maria, Antonio Ulibari, Anne, and Connor stood smiling and proud in the fourth pew. Connor Fitzgerald, now three days old, rested in the arms of his godmother, Todd's sister Julia.

Connor Fitzgerald was to be baptized after the First Communion Mass.

Monsignor Aloysius Quinlan officiated.

Proud parents, grandparents, and family friends of the Communicants were packed into the church pews.

Washington, DC

Juana knelt in a side pew at St. Francis De Sales Church.

The church was simple. White walls, small depictions of the Stations of the Cross, and a garden devoted to the Blessed Virgin. Mass was over. She knew the rector would come in soon to lock the church. But she also knew he would wait until she completed her meditation and prayers. Still, her rosary beads circled in her hands. She had so many people to pray for. So much to be thankful for.

"Lead all souls to heaven, especially those most in need of your mercy." She made the sign of the cross and kissed the beads in her hands. "Bring my father to heaven with you. Have mercy on the soul of my friend, Billy Mack."

Juana stood and slid out of the pew, genuflected, and made the sign of the cross again.

Bryant Park
New York, New York

Ruth and Johnny sat on a bench and watched Ethan and Alice play. Ethan was "it." The trees were safety zones. Alice dashed from tree to tree until Ethan caught her.

"Tag, tag! You're it, Alice."

Alice flopped on the grass. "I don't want to play tag anymore."

"Oh, you never want to be 'it'."

"I can't run as fast as you." Alice stuck out her lower lip.

Ethan stamped his foot and ran to the bench. "Tell me a story, Johnny."

"Please tell me a story?" his mother corrected.

"*Please* tell me a story." He wrinkled his nose at his mother. "Johnny hasn't told me a story in a long time."

"Okay, chief. Let me think. I must know at least one more story." Johnny picked up the boy and sat him on his lap.

"Once upon a time . . ."

Author Comments

This book is fiction.

However, I believe absolute evil does exist in our world. The possibility of a biological weapon being used against the United States is real.

We are, as a people, trusting and in many way naïve to the dangers we face. Those who wish to destroy Americans take advantage of our trusting nature and gullibility.

My thanks to the many people who have assisted me with this manuscript: Hugh Welsh and Richard Favella for their expertise; Joseph Badal and Jodi Thomas for their encouragement, patience and suggestions; Margie Lawson for her outstanding courses; Jeanie Horn for her excellent editing; and my husband Harold, who encouraged my writing and never complained when I was lost in my story.

Historical Note

Sir Jeffrey Amherst, the commander of the British forces in North America, suggested the deliberate use of smallpox to diminish the native Indian population hostile to the British. An outbreak of smallpox in Fort Pitt led to a significant generation of fomites and provided Amherst with the means to execute his plan. On June 24, 1763, Captain Ecuyer, one of Amherst's subordinate officers, provided the Native Americans with smallpox-laden blankets from the smallpox hospital. He recorded in his journal: "I hope it will have the desired effect." As a result, an outbreak of smallpox occurred among the Indian tribes in the Ohio River Valley.

Contacts between European colonists and Native Americans contributed to several epidemics. Smallpox was not the only disease introduced by the movement of people from Europe to the Americas.

Churchill spoke of the extremists that Mohammad's ideology could engender in 1877.

Thomas Jefferson went to war to rescue American merchant sailors from the Barbary pirates. Jefferson was warned about the extremist beliefs in 1784.

De Costa Italian Wedding Cookies

PREP: 45 mins
BAKE: 15 mins
Preheat oven to 325 degrees F (165 degrees C)

Ingredients
1 1/2 cups unsalted butter
3/4 cup confectioners' sugar
3/4 teaspoon salt
1 1/2 cups finely ground almonds
3 teaspoons vanilla extract
1/2 teaspoon lemon extract
1 teaspoon rum
3 cups sifted all-purpose flour
1/3 cup confectioners' sugar for rolling

Directions
Cream butter or margarine in a bowl, and gradually add confectioners' sugar and salt. Beat until light and fluffy. Add almonds, vanilla, lemon extract, and rum. Blend in flour gradually and mix well.

Shape into balls using about 1 teaspoon for each cookie. Place on ungreased cookie sheets, and bake for 15-20 min. Do not brown. Cool slightly, then roll in the remaining confectioners' sugar.

About the Author

Gloria Casale grew up in a small blue collar town in New Jersey. She earned her medical degree at the University of Kentucky and completed advanced training in anesthesiology as well as preventive medicine and public health.

She received training in bioterrorism and bioterrorism response at the United States Army Medical Research Institute of Infectious Diseases and is a recognized expert in the international transport of disease.

Dr. Casale was a consultant to the Division of Transnational Threats at Sandia Laboratory.

She has been an invited speaker to members of the United States military, as well as members of various ports associations on the topics of bio-weaponry and the international transport of pathogens.

She lives in New Mexico with her husband, Harold Traurig, and their tuxedo cats, Hugo and Thumbs.

Made in the USA
San Bernardino, CA
30 May 2016